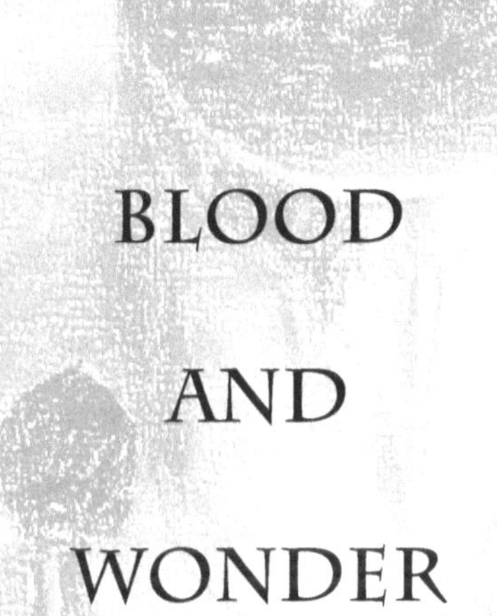

BLOOD

AND

WONDER

A MEDICUS CORPUS NOVEL

KAMI KING LARSEN

ISBN:978-1-7377973-8-8
Lily Fern Books

Cover Design: Brian Larsen
Cover photo and art: Kami Larsen

This is a work of fiction. Names, characters, places, and incidents are the products of the author's imagination or are used fictitiously and any resemblance to persons living or dead are coincidence. In addition, medical treatments are used fictitiously and should not be taken as medical advice.

For Brian. Thanks for crossing the desert with me.

Extreme remedies are very
appropriate for extreme diseases.
                    -Hippocrates

1

HALE

Match Night. The time to learn my fate had come. For what it was worth, I couldn't really bring myself to actually give a damn about the tiny slip of paper in the thick envelope with my name on it. A location was written there—the name of a small settlement or, if the practitioner was lucky, a larger hub. That was all. North. West. Coast or mountains. It was all the same to me. No matter the location, I'd finally be performing my services within a span of a few weeks.

I hadn't always longed to be a Medicus Corpus practitioner. Some even said I lacked the passion of my colleagues. *But* . . . I had gifted hands. They would finally be put to use. It didn't matter where.

No. The envelope reading Hale Belstrohm barely piqued my interest. The thick cream-colored sleeve labeled *Roe* Belstrohm was the one I cared about. Where would Roe be sent? And more importantly, who would my kid brother be sent off with? Or worse, would he be sent off alone?

Time crept by, as first the dean gave a talk touting duty and the privilege of caring for our fellow man. Then the oaths. And finally, one by one, each of the members of our class was called to the front. The dean handed each recent graduate an assignment, and a hush fell over the small space until it was read aloud. Then the silence would shatter as clapping and shouting erupted to fill the tightly packed room.

When my turn came, I slid the scrap of paper from the opening and read aloud, my voice steady, strong, and indifferent. "Devil's Meadows."

Applause. Some polite, some quite boisterous.

To the desert then. I could handle the desert.

My ass had barely hit the seat as a hushed quiet returned and Roe tore into his envelope. His hands were shaking. Just a touch, but I noticed. His eyes caught on the words and opened wider, a smile spreading across his face. He raised his arms in triumph and clearly read, "Devil's Meadows!"

No polite clapping this time. It was a roaring torrent of whoops and shouts.

I just chuckled and shook my head. I could have done worse. The desert hub hosted three openings. The only remaining unknown was who would be the third member of our team. I had my suspicions and wasn't sure how I felt about them.

In the end, it really didn't matter how I felt about anything though. We got assigned where to go and with whom, and that was it. No amount of crying or threats or idiot behavior would change our fate once it was penned on that thick parchment and put into the envelope. If you were going to plead your case, you better have done it weeks ago.

I didn't have long to wait for my suspicions to be confirmed. Several more grads proceeded to the front. Each opened their individual futures with the rip of the paper. Many read the hopes and dreams with smiles. Some like me read them with indifference. A few greeted their future with barely contained—or in one case, not contained at all—tears.

Then a pretty, petite girl with warm terra-cotta skin and thick tortoise-shell glasses shuffled to the front. Aurelia Morris took her assignment, glanced at Roe and crossed her fingers before ripping it open.

Her curls bounced as she moved up onto her toes before yelling—literally yelling—"Devil's Meadows!"
I closed my eyes and ran my hands through my hair—a long breath escaping through my nose. Maybe I should have cared a little more about my assignment. I was now facing the rest of my life with these two, and knowing my luck, I was going to live to a very old age.

2

ROE

The school was a manic hive of activity. The teams had been packing up and leaving for destinations both near and distant for the past forty-eight hours.

Now it was our turn. Time to start the long trek from Renfield—a large settlement hub, nestled serenely in a mountain valley, and the home of our Medicus Corpus campus—to the distant location we would soon call home. For those of us making the journey, it would take roughly four weeks—maybe a little longer depending on the travel conditions and the medical care needed along the way. All of the arrangements had been made in advance. We would stop in several settlements, but the plan was to get to Devil's Meadows before the scorching temperatures became overwhelming. The desert was an unforgiving place, and as it now stood, the daytime highs would be pushing the century mark— enough to draw water from our bodies quickly and leave any exposed flesh a lovely mahogany for some and cruel scarlet for others.

Thirteen of us in all were traveling. Six new practitioners, four escorts, and the tram masters who were responsible for the horses, trams, food, and most importantly, the water. The escorts would help the masters a bit, but in reality they were half advisor, half Medicus administrator, and all armed guard. We were told the road ahead was riddled with marauders and desert animals—either of which would be happy to make a meal of a wayward traveler.

My mother used to tell me you could win more flies with honey than vinegar, and that lesson has served me well. It didn't suit me to sit idly by and let others do all the work, so I made myself as busy and useful as the team loading our tram. Crates of tools, cartons of supplies, books, medications, and perishables needed to be neatly organized and hauled into place. Sacks of horse feed sat in the dew-coated grass opposite heavy five-gallon drums of clean drinking water. All of this needed to be loaded at the direction of the tram masters—Luc, Hera, and Minton—to ensure weight was evenly distributed among the available space. Within minutes, a steady trickle of sweat was dripping down my neck. As I heaved a drum of water—marked with the same snake and staff logo painted on the trams—up to the waiting arms of the leathery master, I felt a light elbow in my side.

"Careful flaunting those guns, Roe. You seem to be causing a stir." Aurelia flashed me her brightest smile and shifted her eyes and eyebrows to the side, indicating I should check over my shoulder. Looking back at me were the timid eyes of Phoebe, one of our fellow graduate practitioners. She was far enough away to miss Aurelia's words but not my glance.

"So funny, Goldie-Locks. You know my heart belongs only to you," I crooned.

She said she despised the nickname, but I had a hundred different endearments for her. It was nothing new. Goldie-Locks—not because of the color of her hair but because Aurelia was a mouthful and I'd learned, once upon a time, it meant gold. I also favored Shrimpboat, Little-bit, Specs, or Tiny Goddess. She protested them all, but I think she secretly loved it when I used them. She didn't mind Auri, and I could generally get away with using the shorter version. There just wasn't any fun in it when I wasn't the only one who called her that.

Using a towel I'd swiped from one of the nearby cartons, I wiped the sweat from my face. Despite the early hour, it was already unseasonably warm. I'd have dark stains blossoming down my sides and back soon enough, and the swampy feeling reminded me I would be bathing out of a bucket for the next few weeks. I was homesick for my small shower and we hadn't even left yet.

"Oh, I don't know, Roe. I'm pretty sure Phoebe has me beat by a landslide. Brains, boobs, and butt. Plus she's sweeter than agave nectar and isn't aware of any of it." Aurelia Morris could only see the best aspects of people. It was genetically woven into the tapestry of who she was. My problem was I rarely agreed with her. I knew how to act the part, but deep inside I was a cynic, born and bred.

I shrugged and grabbed another water container, heading for the second of three supply trams. The travel cartons had been color labeled to let us know which items went on which tram. The trams themselves were fairly amazing to behold. Great rubber tread tires were arranged in a way to allow not only smooth road travel but off-road desert crossing as well. Retractable steps led up to the fiberglass hull, which was reinforced to hold the weight of the cargo while simultaneously keeping it light enough—even with the solar panels attached to the sides—for the horses to pull.

After helping with a few more supplies, I gathered my belongings and placed them in a designated area marked for the graduate practitioners. The last thing I needed was to find my stethoscope squashed between livestock feed and toilet paper.

My folks had instilled in me many characteristics—some good, others much more questionable. Among these was a love of spicy foods, a decent work ethic, and a knack for packing light. The latter meant I was going to need a few laundry stops in the coming weeks or I would smell rather gamey by the time we arrived. It also meant Aurelia would have a little extra space, which she was likely to need. I wanted to make the trek as painless for her as I could. Leaving my home behind was tough, but at least I had my brother coming along.

Aurelia was leaving her home and family, with only the two of us to compensate. Not much of a fair trade.

She was still lingering by the first tram when I turned back.

"Hey, Shrimpboat. Are you just going to stand there and watch me slave away all morning?" I asked.

"Thinking about it. Especially if you call me Shrimpboat again. Besides, watching you labor away brings me a certain enjoyment, and I have to keep myself entertained somehow, don't I?" She gave me her most innocent look. I didn't buy it for a second.

She pulled her long heavy hair up into a ponytail and fastened it with a ribbon of the same deep green as her shirt, both of which brought out flecks of color in her multihued eyes. She said they were hazel, but they certainly weren't the typical muddy hazel I'd seen in other faces.

Most folks on first meeting Aurelia would comment on one of three notable physical attributes—the diminutive stature, the hair, or the eyes. It drove her crazy. She complained ceaselessly about her unruly hair and by necessity kept her eyes partially hidden behind the thick lenses of her glasses. Her height she didn't mind so much, but it bothered her that others found it worth mentioning. I of course was excluded from this.

"You know, if left to my own devices, I'll go insane," she continued. "I am trying to keep it together and dangerously close to failing. You don't want that on your conscience."

The worry was plain on her face.

Aurelia was smart, period. In this particular moment, however, she was really on the money. The weeks and months ahead weren't going to be easy on any of us. Honestly, I wasn't sure if life would ever be easy on us again. We were heading to a hub settlement in the middle of a ruined city, smack in the center of an inhospitable desert. Our purpose was to join the team of practitioners who had been serving the community of residents settled there. How those folks survived, eking out a life amid the ruins was a mystery to me.

The trams would stop in Devil's Meadows, and when they headed out beyond—into the desert south of the settlement—Auri, Hale, and I, along with our two escorts Asher and Geneva, would not be moving on with them. Jave would be the final stop for the rest, off-loading the other group of practitioners, their escorts, and the remaining supplies, before the trams headed back north again. The masters and their rigs would stay at the home base here and prep for wherever Medicus sent them next.

Contemplating the journey and the years to come had me thinking of Hale. Where had he gotten off to?

"Any idea where that slacker brother of mine is? He could probably keep you entertained for a bit."

"Not sure. Probably drowning his sorrows somewhere," she replied. "Besides, I don't get the impression he wants anything to do with me. I'm fairly certain he's more worried about the relocation than I am."

Hale had seemed more than a little off for the past couple of weeks to be sure. He wasn't excited about the terms of our relocation, but I didn't think any match would thrill him. He hadn't really bonded with anyone during our training, so it wasn't as if there was someone he would want to be working with more than Auri and me.

I put on my most reassuring face, which was not reassuring at all. "He'll survive. Help me pack up some of our gear then."

She stopped—serious. So serious.

"I want Hale to be happy, you know. I want you both to be happy. You . . . well. Whatever . . . or whoever makes you happy. I want that. This match, I know it might not be right for you. I know he hates it. Hates me for matching with you both."

The match. What a ridiculous archaic term for what Medicus did. It supposedly harkened back to when "doctors" had a partial say in where they went to practice after their training. Now no matching was involved, just an assignment meant to last a very long time. Perhaps our entire career. In some cases an entire lifetime. Goldie was saying we didn't want her. I was thrilled we were together, but Hale could be such a complete ass sometimes. He'd made her feel unwanted when in truth she was likely to be the strongest among us.

I tried to cool the heat rising in my cheeks. I had a lot to sort out myself, but Aurelia in no way made this worse. "Come on, Auri. Right now, you are exactly who I need to make me happy."

She offered me a weak smile and climbed the steps, carrying a heavy box of dried fruit, nuts, and canned vegetables.

"And DM?"

My confusion must have been clear on my face.

"Devil's Meadows."

I nodded and lifted my eyebrows.

"I don't even know what to expect. I mean it's in the middle of the never-ending desert. It might not exactly be the most fun. For the rest of our lives."

I kept my voice as light and easy as I could. "It will be amazing, Goldie Girl. I've been doing a little reading while you've been toiling away in the pharm lab. We—all three of us—are going to love it."

Her next carton was overloaded with packets and jars of her own special medicinal herb blends. It weighed a ton. She grunted as she handed it to me. Aurelia didn't mind a bit of hard work, but she preferred mental labor over physical. It was one of the things I adored most about her.

"Ah-hmm."

I jumped at the gravelly voice that could only be Asher, one of the two escorts assigned to the DM crew.

"Either get moving or get outta my way, Doc."

"I've asked you to call me Roe."

He nodded. "Yeah. You did. I call everyone Doc. Don't have a great memory for names."

Asher pushed past me. I wasn't convinced his statement was entirely true, but I got a kick out of his use of the antique endearment for a medical practitioner—as if he were old enough to have been alive when the title meant something. It brought a grin to my face, stretching from ear to ear.

"All right . . . I'll just move along then." Glancing over my shoulder, I caught Aurelia silently giggling at me.

"Grab the medical supplies before you finish loading your personal gear. I want those med cartons buried deep in case we run into trouble on the road. I'm told some of it's worth more than you six combined." His voice boomed from within the tram.

"What a gem!" Auri was pulling boxes of sterile saline pouches over to the steps. She handed them up to me after I climbed back up the steps.

"Well, I don't think they really get paid to be friendly." I took the containers and strapped them into place. "If you give me the med boxes next, I can put them under the lighter packs of bandages and gauze. Did the surgical tools get packed in the other tram?"

"How the hell should I know, Roe? This isn't our job, remember?" It was unlike her to snap. Particularly at me. She was letting the stress get to her. The silence that followed was broken by a barely audible "sorry" a heartbeat later.

I stepped down and placed my hand on her shoulder. I had touched the petite girl I called my best friend hundreds of times but had rarely felt so much tension in her small frame. With our recent assignment news, it was hard to tell what was anxiety about the journey ahead and what was anxiety about other things.

From the first time Aurelia and I had met—way back in secondary school—we knew we made a good team. Intellectually we were a match even if socially we were not. I tended to hang with the more outgoing testosterone-driven types, always trying to increase my physical training, pushing my levels of stamina and agility. The world was cruel, and I was determined to survive it. At the time, my adolescent brain thought that meant I had to be the strongest and the fastest.

Auri, on the other hand, was more concerned with saving whatever could be salvaged of this miserable planet. She wanted to right wrongs and lift up her fellow inhabitants. Or die trying.

Despite our differences in perspective, we had been placed together in most of our classes and often were matched as study partners. We clicked into friendship the way children's blocks fastened together—easily and with amazing stability for such small pieces. We remained bonded all through secondary school, advanced vocational testing, and finally training at Medicus Corpus. And now, well, now we were embarking on the next leg of our journey together.

Together. Me and Auri . . . and Hale.

Hale wasn't exactly charming. Hale was clever and brooding. Like me, he was a natural cynic, but unlike me, he had no desire to hide it. And I suppose he was handsome (being that he was my older brother, I don't imagine I was a very good judge of this). If he would just act like he cared for a few minutes, Auri would relax. I was sure of it.

"Take a deep breath and find your inner peace. It will all work out." I didn't honestly know if I was trying to convince her or me. Both of us I suppose. "As for Hale? He doesn't dislike you. He can just be a bit of an overprotective SOB sometimes."

"Since when do you need protection, especially from me?"

I chuckled. "Maybe I meant it the other way around. You never know." I lifted my eyebrows and stuck my tongue between my teeth at her.

"I'm sure you're right." She sighed dramatically. "As always. Let's finish up so I can shower and wash my hair for the last time in the foreseeable future."

I inhaled the smell of grass and wet leaves. The rain had cleared earlier in the day and now it left the air heavy and clinging. Folks told me I'd miss the smell of moisture in the air, the feel of it on my skin. Standing in the humid hot afternoon, however, I could not for the life of me fathom how that could possibly be true.

The sweat was dripping down my neck at flash flood rates. Aurelia too had small streams from her brow down the gentle slope of her nose. Reaching up to wipe beneath her glasses, she missed a step and fell from the upper stair of the tram. Her knee connected with the steel grating, creating a gong similar to a wooden mallet striking a bell. She cried out with a sharp yelp and rolled after hitting the grassy turf. She lay there for a moment rocking gently, cradling her knee in both hands.

Now the moisture on her face was equal parts tears and perspiration.

I was down the flight in moments to assess the damage. Thankfully, it was not quite as bad as I feared. The shallow gash could be cleaned and glued shut fairly easily, but the bruise was going to be a real beauty.

A small audience gathered, and I could see Auri—never wanting to be the center of attention—was not happy about it. I murmured a few assurances that she would be shipshape in no time, no amputation necessary, and helped her hobble out of the way to a spot where I could bandage her up.

As expected, it didn't take much to clean the wound. I finished the skin adhesive and applied the necessary antibiotic salves with only a few curses flowing from Aurelia's lips up to my ears.

"Sorry, Roe." She winced as I pulled the last gauze dressing tight. "You really lucked out. Getting stuck with an uber-klutz for the rest of your natural life."

"If I am going to be with a klutz, at least I get a cute, smart, uber-klutz."

"I'm serious. In fact, I should have just waddled away and cleaned this out myself. You don't need to coddle me. I need to pull my weight. With the decision for us. . ." A faint flush rose under her bronze complexion. "You know."

"Uhh, yes. I know. And I'm not worried in the least." I ducked my head down, trying to get her to look me in the eye. "I realize this relocation isn't ideal for you, Aurelia. I know it's not what you wanted either."

"Roe, it's not that. I am happy to be . . . together. The thought of going off alone makes me want to vomit. I just don't want to see you get tied to something neither of us can control. You should get a clean slate. Why don't you or I get a say in what happens? You deserve to choose."

"I knew what I was signing up for, remember? We all did."

None of us had a choice. Not now and likely not ever. That just wasn't how Medicus worked. But if I had been given a choice, I would have picked Aurelia. Maybe not for the reasons most people assumed, but I would have chosen to go to the end of the earth with Auri.

I ran a hand through my hair and started to speak only to be interrupted by the sound of my dear brother's voice. "Hello, love birds. Better pick up the pace or we'll never get settled into our happy little home."

3

AURELIA

We were three days into the journey when the river began to dwindle and the lush pines and waist-high greenery thinned from the sides of the road. This was meant to be farmland, but it was as if the sand were eating the foliage bit by bit, swallowing the wildflowers and grasses and leaving stunted desert scrub in their place. It made me strangely sad to see the landscape shift from kelly to khaki. We were due to be in a small farming settlement tomorrow where we would spend a couple of days before we moved on, aiming for the really harsh terrain of the desert and Devil's Meadows at its heart.

My parents had come to the campus the night before we left, and as my father crushed me to his chest, he'd made me vow to work hard and stay safe. My mother, who was generally less practical, surprised me by offering some bits of advice. "Wear your sun salve and keep your glasses safe," she murmured through a face full of tears.

I had no siblings, and while I'd lived on campus for the past few years, they made it a point to get me over for dinners at least twice per week. Now neither they nor I knew when we'd embrace again.

Recalling my mother's wise words, I stared out toward the scraggly vegetation. My skin, my hair, my eyes and lips—all of it seemed to protest the change in the air. As the moisture evaporated from our surroundings, it drew the hydration straight out through my pores. I was beginning to think the only water in my body could be found in the myriad blisters now inhabiting my feet and toes. I had been assured my boots were good. Maybe it was the socks that were bad.

The golden sun took harsh swipes at the tip of my nose and the exposed skin on the back of my neck. We were still in the relative comfort of the not-yet desert. I'd be a desiccated husk by the time we finally arrived at our destination.

Other than the change in scenery, nothing much had happened in that first few days after leaving the valley bowl of Renfield. As we climbed the low foothills to the east of the valley, the road was clear, the horses, tires, and our feet fresh. We made good time—about thirty miles each day. The first evening, I'd looked out from camp and seen wild mustangs running over the hills, their shadows elongated in the setting sun. I hadn't seen any since.

As always, I enjoyed the easy company of Roe. Hale, moody as ever, kept mostly to himself. I made small talk with the tram masters, when they would let me, joked with the other practitioners, and chatted with both Asher and Geneva. I was sure to like our escorts just fine. They were both capable, and while not exactly friendly, they weren't malicious or condescending. Jake and Jude, the escorts continuing on to Jave, were a complete joy to talk with. They were easygoing and quick to smile, but I could tell the congeniality was covering their inner capability and deadly skill.

My earlier anxiety about the trip hadn't resolved exactly, but during the first few days on the road, it had dulled significantly. Whether this was from the monotony of the walk or because I had more time to process our futures, I still couldn't say. Despite this, I woke on the fourth morning to a new feeling of disquiet. It wasn't the same jittery nervousness I had previously experienced but more a sense that something was about to change. A crackle of it hung in the air—a hum of unspent energy in the stillness of the scenery around me. My mother would have called it unused thaumaturgy. My father would have laughed at her and rolled his eyes behind her back. Me . . . well I would have agreed with my father.

Still something was there. I could feel it. Maybe it was just nerves, but I had never really been the type to have stress affect me in a physical way. I could be snappish sometimes, but that was generally the biggest sign I was under pressure.

We had left camp in the grey light of morning, the sun not yet peeking above the low hills to the east. We'd made the turn south sometime the day before, and for a short while we'd traveled through what looked like it might once also have been relatively fertile farmland. Now it was just flat scrubby-looking parcels. Miles of callous dirt and shrunken plants stretched out in front of the wagons.

After a couple of hours traveling in the tram, I decided to walk for a bit. I caught up with Geneva near the front of the supply train.

She was a very striking woman, all sharp planes and sun-bleached hair. She stood over a head taller than me—not as tall as Roe, but close—and carried herself with a combination of grace and power. The skin around her eyes was folded with the beginnings of crow's feet, but her eyes were the crystal blue of clear water in the afternoon sun. Those eyes were currently the only signs of movement in her beautifully still face.

"It's lovely now, but I bet it gets pretty hot today," I greeted her.

She spared me a quick glance and resumed her constant scanning of the terrain on either side of the ancient asphalt.

"Yes, ma'am, it will be a warm one."

"Can I ask you something, Geneva?"

"I suppose." Not too wordy was our female escort.

I hesitated, not really wanting to sound timid or jumpy. Then slowly, "Do you sense anything in the air today?"

"Other than dust and the smell of horse?" She kept scanning the desert. Eyes left, right, quick left again, center.

"Well, yes. Different from that. Kind of like a crackle . . . or something?" I realized I sounded like an idiot. "I don't know. It's similar to the smell of ozone before a lightning strike. I know it sounds silly, but I can't shake it. I feel like something is slightly off."

I swiped my hand along the back of my neck, shifting my twin braids over one shoulder. "I tried mentioning it this morning to Roe."

"And what did Roe tell you?" She flicked her eyes toward me briefly and went back to scanning the ever-expanding tan landscape.

"He thinks I'm just nervous about our future. I get the sense he thinks I can't handle the coming responsibilities we have."

"Is he right?" she asked, matter-of-fact. "Are you nervous?"

How could I explain this to her? I was nervous about some things but not my responsibility as a practitioner. I had been waiting for this my entire life.

"Not like he thinks I am. I'm ready for this. I worry about messing up, I guess, but this feeling I have today is nothing to do with that. I'm sure it's something else."

She finally turned her head to look me straight in the eye. "Good. That is what I wanted to hear. I am fairly certain you are going to handle this new transition better than either Roe or Hale."

Her expression didn't change, but I think mine did. I think the corners of my mouth might have ticked up just a smidge.

"Thanks. But what about the feeling in the air? What is it?"

"Not sure I know. I don't feel anything, but I'm not one to dismiss what I'm not privy to. It could be you're on to something." She'd gone back to looking straight ahead, eyes left, right, left, center. "You've never experienced something similar before?"

I shook my head before realizing she couldn't see me while also focusing on our surroundings. "Nope," I said, and she nodded.

"Head on back and ask Asher if he can spare me a minute, would you?"

I turned to go and had just made it to the front of the first tram when a high-pitched whine filled my ears, vibrating through my teeth and to the base of my skull. Half a second later, the morning sun flashed noontime bright. My ears popped with a wave of pressure and then came the deafening boom. I was knocked off my feet, banging my partially healed knee hard into the cracked and worn pavement. I didn't immediately feel pain, but I was sure it would come later. Blood blossomed up through the material of my cargo pants and welled in new scrapes on my hands. All around me the calm erupted in sound. Men were yelling orders and horses were stomping and whinnying in fear.

I had only a moment to register the scene before Geneva was hauling me back to my feet.

"Into the back of the tram, now!" She was ushering me back, all the while keeping her body, and her rifle, between me and the surrounding terrain.

"Once you are in the tram, keep the med supplies buried. Don't get anything out unless Asher or I tell you to." With that, she ducked down and headed to the other side of the train of carts and horses.

I nodded my understanding, but she was already gone.

I was trying to clear the ringing in my ears as I rounded the corner to the back of the first rig. I glanced up and saw a lone figure darting from the roadside ditch. He was sprinting directly toward me.

He was a slight wiry thing—covered in dust and grime. My immediate thought was that a strong wind would blow him over. His clothes hung on his frame, and his face was partially obscured by a long graying beard and a tattered piece of red and white plaid cloth. It was tied to keep the sun off his head. Some sort of plum wine stain covered one half of the exposed skin of his face—a birthmark perhaps. He looked nervous as he raced toward me but didn't strike me as particularly dangerous given the slight build and his haphazard movements. Then he lifted his arm and I noted the small handheld explosive in his grip. That six-inch cylinder caught my attention. Clearly having decided I was an easy target, he barreled straight toward me.

Not wanting to let him near our precious medical supplies, I stood my ground, unsure of what else to do.

"Move!" Hale tore around the corner from the other side of the wagon, Roe close on his heels.

Hale's shoulder connected with the man's midsection, all six foot four inches and two hundred pounds, driving him off his feet and toward the roadside ravine.

"He has an explosive!" The words tore from my lips.

Roe's face took on a frantic expression as he raced to help his brother, apparently not mindless of the danger, but heading toward it nonetheless. He dove into the fray, trying to simultaneously kick the plastic tube away from the attacker while helping to pin him down. The brothers fought to free the deadly object. For being so slight, the grubby little man was viciously aggressive, thrashing and biting at both Roe and Hale.

The commotion soon had several of the others heading in our direction. The sound of horses dancing with anxiety and shouts from our traveling companions returned as the ringing in my ears dulled.

Jude, the youngest of the escorts, arrived first and was able to wriggle the explosive from its owner's hand. He pulled his arm back and pitched it far off the road into the surrounding scrub. This action brought on a new frenzy from the attacker. He bucked and twisted, snarling and snapping—more rabid animal than man. With one forceful lunge, he sank his teeth into the meat of Hale's arm.

Hale yelped, swore, and then in one powerful move, he brought his forehead swiftly down and connected with the assailant's face. The sound was similar to wood hitting stone. The ragged head of the smaller man cracked back hard against the pavement, and he lay still.

"Son of a bitch! He f'ing bit me!" Hale held his left forearm with the opposite hand, blood dripping between his fingers to speckle the ground below. "I can't believe the crazy bastard bit me."

Roe was up from the road and panting hard. He stepped out of the way to allow Jude to see to the restraint of the attacker.

"Let's have a look at it, Hale." Forgetting my own battered knee, I walked over and gently pulled his arm into my scraped and bloody hands. A clearly defined set of incisor marks were depressed deep into the torn and swollen flesh. Blood continued to drip from the site, and as horrid as it was, it could have been so much worse. The maniac could have removed that hunk of flesh rather than just marred it.

"It needs to be cleaned and bandaged. I'll grab my gear." I moved toward the cart where my supplies were stowed.

"I told you to keep those supplies hidden, and I meant it." Geneva was stalking toward us, rifle still up to her shoulder as she scanned the area.

"Hale is hurt, and he"—I pointed at the prone figure on the pavement—"is unconscious."

"What makes you think he was alone?" she asked.

I opened my mouth to reply, but Hale cut me off. "Aurelia, she's right. Just give it a minute. I'll survive."

"But—"

"No buts. Just chill a sec, okay?" His tone was biting.

I didn't want to relent, partly because the bite looked bad and partly because my shaking hands needed something to do, but I figured if he could wait, so could I.

Wiping my stinging palms on the canvas of my pants, I glanced around at my traveling companions. Or the ones I could see anyway. The three members of the other med group, Phoebe, Helena, and Wade, were peeking from the back of the tram they had been riding in, the masters flanking both sides, weapons raised. They were interesting things, these firearms. Despite the desperate conditions and lack of resources many people struggled with daily, there seemed to be no lack of gunpowder for the aged guns. They were easy to obtain, and with a little elbow grease and a bit of knowledge, they could be cleaned up and set to working order. It was too bad not all man's inventions stood the test of time so sturdily.

Jake swept in a steady path from the back of the caravan to the front, eyes following where the barrel of his long rifle led. After several moments, he met up with Asher approaching from the opposite side. A nod from the older man seemed to indicate the caravan's safety.

"Looks like he was alone. I don't see traces of anyone else," Jake said.

"I'm guessing he was waiting for someone to pass by and decided we looked like a good target. Trying to get a quick smash and grab." Asher surveyed the damage.

Geneva had joined them by the roadside and added, "The explosive hit too far away to do any real damage. Flying debris took some tread out of the back tires on tram one, but I think that's all."

"Wish his teeth were as harmless," Hale groused.

Roe raised his eyebrow quizzically. "Maybe you just taste good?"

"I am the perfect combination of sweet and salty, it's true." Hale's voice was so dry, I honestly couldn't tell if he was being serious.

Asher was all business. "If you two are done, we need to figure out what to do with this lovely specimen, patch you up, and get moving before any of his friends do decide to show up."

He motioned to Jude and Jake, who immediately rolled the limp body to the edge of the road. They searched him for any other weapons and bound his hands behind his back.

"You can't just leave him there. He'll die if it gets much warmer." I was mortified by the idea of leaving him like road kill.

"Goldie-Locks, he tried to steal our supplies," Roe pointed out. "You could have been killed."

"Still, Roe, we're trained to heal not to murder."

"No one's talking about murder. We aren't killing him." He sounded exasperated with me.

"We aren't making sure he lives either," I hissed. "Is than any better?"

I was met with only silence.

"For the love of the heavens, I can't believe you." I turned and stomped away to retrieve my med supplies whether Geneva liked it or not. Thankfully I met no resistance when I climbed into the tram and selected one of several crates I had meticulously packed several days earlier in Renfield. It was a simple container full of first-aid treatments I thought might be handy and useful for the trip. The remainder of my other supplies were better packed and buried beneath heaps of supplies.

Sorting through the crate, I ran my hands and eyes over various vials and packets, containers of salves and crushed herbs, ointments, and elixirs, and of course a tiny portion of the rare and expensive collection of high-grade pharmaceuticals I had collected. I chose two different jars, the contents of which I had crushed, mixed, and sterilized myself. I also grabbed a small dark bottle of alcohol, distilled in the basement of our school, and a clean metal needle with a sterile packet of silk—hoping desperately not to have to use it. Stitching human bites closed was always risky business. The human mouth is akin to a cesspool, and the risk of infection would increase substantially if the wounds were sutured shut.

As I walked back, knee singing with each step, I thought of my first days of training and how scared

I was just thinking about using the tools and medicines in the school's stock room. Then gradually over long days and longer nights of studying, I became familiar with the intricacies of the human body and the basics of illness. I, along with Roe, Hale, and dozens of our other classmates, learned how the body worked and how any one of thousands of small alterations could make the body fail. One missed step in a chemical pathway could lead to pain and suffering, sickness and death. We learned how the basic DNA structure created cells, cells created tissues, tissues created organs, and organs combined to make the most miraculous of all things—the human body. We studied diseases and the causes of those diseases. Slowly after mastering those things, we learned about the myriad of ways the body could be cured and healed. We learned about medications and surgeries, supplements and therapies. We learned how once pharmaceuticals were created by the tons in marvelous factories and were shipped all over the world, curing things with a few pills or injections.

And then we learned how it had all fallen apart—how many steps backward we had stumbled in the past century. Back to hand mixing basic ingredients and solutions, hoping for one tenth the results our great-grandparents and their great-grandparents had been able to achieve, simply by scribbling a few words on a prescription pad and sending a patient to pick up a handful of capsules or tablets. What a waste of knowledge the world had experienced.

There was no sense in crying over it now.

With every lesson and day of study, the fear melted away, and gradually a new confidence and eagerness bloomed in its place. I wanted to get started for real—to use this new knowledge. These skills. Before we left Renfield, I had spent the better part of two months in our pharmacology lab making my own supplies and stocking up on all of the standard premade preparations I could get my hands on. I packed a multitude of cartons with basics but had a few containers of my more precious antidotes and medicines. While Medicus assured us we would be well supplied, I wanted a good stock, not knowing how much time I would have to prepare fresh tinctures and ointments when we finally arrived.

By the time I got back to Hale, his attacker was coming to. Groaning, he looked slowly back and forth between the hulking masses that were Jude and Jake. Despite the fact that Jude stood at least six inches taller than Jake, there was no question of who was in charge. Unlike Asher and Geneva, who were partners in both work and life, Jake and Jude were a father and son team. They shared the same coloring, dark mahogany skin, kind but serious eyes the color of melted caramel, and warm welcoming smiles. Neither man was smiling now.

"You are going to want to move real slow, my friend," Jake drawled.

The shaken captive sat up slowly and blinked. Blood flowed freely from his nose and split upper lip, staining his facial hair a bright crimson. What I had initially taken as a birthmark must have been some sort of paint or stain—the perspiration running under the cloth on his forehead left trails through the pigment.

Jake continued, "This is precisely what we are going to do. Me and Jude here, we are going to get you on your feet, and then the three of us are going to go for a little stroll. We're going to walk a few hundred yards back the way we came, and then we'll part ways. You behave yourself and you get to keep on strolling. You don't and well"—he tapped the barrel of his long gun against the man's cheek—"you get the picture."

The scruffy head nodded, drops of blood and snot flying with the movement.

"Jude, help the man to his feet please." Jake's voice remained lazy, nonchalant. His posture and the gun in his hands weren't relaxed at all.

"Yes sir." Jude hauled the man up and then half pushed, half carried him down the road.

As soon as the shuffling sounds of the ungainly trio faded, I turned to Hale. "Let's get sewing then."

"I can do it, Auri." Roe moved to take my kit.

"I don't think so." I might have sounded petulant or I might have sounded angry, but either way he must have heard the warning in my voice. He looked at me, clear green eyes squinting against the brightening sun, and stepped back, hands raised in surrender.

Hale made himself comfortable, leaning his back up against the heavy tread on the rear tram tire. Perching on a overturned bucket, I grabbed the cleanest cloth I could find and spread it out over his knee and thigh, then had him rest his arm atop it. I opened the small flask of sterile water from my kit and used it first to clean my hands and then to flush the edges of the bite mark as best I could— registering and ignoring the sharp intake of breath and subsequent hiss of pain escaping Hale's pursed lips. When it came to cleaning the area with alcohol, there was no ignoring the flood of verbal warfare issuing forth and aimed not only at me, but anyone else who happened to be in the vicinity. Knowing it was best just to get through it, I applied a small bit of ointment from one of my jars. It contained a topical antibiotic mixed with ground yucca and phenol which would help reduce the bleeding until I was done tending the wound. In a perfect world, I would have liked to leave the bites open, but clearly, we were living in anything but a perfect world. A deep set of puncture wounds ran along the top of the bite and needed to be stitched. I threaded a length of silk through my needle and placed small delicate stitches. Hale wouldn't be thrilled if I did sloppy work, and I had no intention of leaving him with worse scars. He grunted a few times when the needle drove in but was otherwise blessedly quiet during the closure.

"Had to be done. Sorry." I rinsed the area one more time and slathered it with a thick goopy layer of antibiotic salve. My fingers were tingling. I must have been in an awkward position while suturing. Hale eyed me warily. "Keep a close eye on it. If it starts to look infected, you need to open it back up."

He knew all of this as well as I did, but I said it anyway.

He nodded as I applied the dressing. I took the second jar of salve and handed it to him—all the while silently hoping this healed quickly and well. "It's just a mix of prickly ash and neomycin. I didn't grab you any oral antibiotics. Mine are buried. Do you have some?"

"Yes, Aurelia." He looked at the dressing and then added begrudgingly, "Thanks."

Hale wandered off while I cleaned up my supplies. At times like this, I couldn't help but compare him to Roe. In some ways they were so similar—smart, athletic, and ready to fight at the drop of a hat, particularly for those they cared about. The differences were more interesting, however. The physical variations weren't incredibly striking—Hale was only a couple of inches taller and slightly broader across the chest and shoulders. Those added inches meant I barely came up to his chest and had to crane my neck back anytime I spoke to him. And while they both had gorgeous green eyes and sandy hair, Roe wore his good looks with a certain confidence. Hale though. Hale wore them like a collar—something he was burdened with and would rather not have.

Hale was quiet and moody, often self-deprecating and always tense around other people. Roe was outgoing and funny. Charming when he needed to be—and for Roe, that need was almost always. I thought Hale would have been just as happy to live the life of a hermit—alone in a secluded cabin—rather than in a cramped hub providing surgical services to those in need. Roe, on the other hand, wanted to be in the middle of a community. He needed to surround himself with his neighbors and, by virtue of this, his patients. He wanted to know them, not just treat them.

"Thanks for fixing him up." Roe emerged from around the side of the tram.

I didn't need his thanks. After all, we were supposed to be a team.

"Gets my mind off everything else."

"I mean it. We're lucky to have you." He looked over at his brother. "I know he feels the same."

"Maybe." I wasn't nearly as convinced as Roe.

4

HALE

My arm was throbbing.

It kept me from sleep. The desert was simultaneously too quiet and not quiet enough. I couldn't identify the strange animal noises, and the wind made an eerie whistling sound. The temperature had dropped significantly as soon as the sun was behind the hills. I was going to need to adjust to the temperature swings. Sweltering and wretched during the day, cold and wretched at night.

This whole venture was off to a miserable start.

The threat of real damage to my arm worried me. If the antibiotics . . . shit. I never took the first dose of antibiotic. I made a mental note to pull some out of my pack and down one at first light. If it didn't kick in and my arm got infected. . . I couldn't let myself think of the possibility. Without my arms—my hands—I was useless.

That line of thought would do me no good. I drew in a ragged breath. The air had lost its grass and moisture scent. It was dry. Bone dry as the saying went. But that saying was false. Bones aren't dry at all. They aren't brittle or arid, but moist and supple. At least while inside the living.

Some sort of dog howled in the distance. I rolled over again, drawing the thick bedroll above my shoulder and tried to sleep. Next to me, Roe snored contentedly. Beside him, Aurelia stirred. She sat up and looked in my direction. Without her glasses, she had to squint in the darkness.

I didn't let her ask about my arm. "Go back to sleep, Aurelia."

And she did.

5

AURELIA

The bells drew my attention from the elderly gentleman before me. We had been mired in a discussion regarding his inability to easily urinate. Not my favorite subject, but a common one and simple enough to start treatment. With the right tablets, he might be able to enjoy a good night's sleep again. His urinary malady had been preceded by his numerous other complaints—everything from sore joints to a painful rash on his back. I'd already compiled a mental list of all the ointments and powders he'd be relieving my bags of. I added a specific pouch of tablets to the list.

As expected, we had stopped in small settlements along the way. Most, like this one, might have been called something once but now were too meager to even warrant names. We traded our services in exchange for a few glasses of cool well water and shelter from the unrelenting sun. At one spot, soft beds had been provided, giving us a reprieve from the thick mats and sleep rolls we used on the road. Our services gave the assigned practitioners in these spots a day or two of respite, or in several cases, we would be the only medical services some of these people would receive until the next Medicus trams, or one of the traveling groups of practitioners, traveled through.

The tinkling sound coming from down the road seemed so out of place I wondered if the heat was getting to me. It wasn't the gong of a church bell but rather the melodic high-pitched ringing of the winter bells I associated with snow in the mountains outside Renfield. When I twisted to see what could be causing the noise, the diaphragm of my stethoscope thumbed against my chest. I swear, I could the thing as a weapon if need be, it was so heavy.

A cloud of dust had been kicked up several buildings down, and emerging from it I could just make out a wagon. It was large and cumbersome, pulled by four horses—three roan and one deepest black, all covered in dust and road grime. The body of the wagon towered above the team in a way that looked not only ridiculous but unstable as well. Apparently built from thick lumber and weighing heaven's knew how much, it was painted a deep maroon red with faded yellow letters proclaiming *Miracles and Wonders Await You.* Lining the top, strings of tarnished brass bells swayed with each movement of the horses. The cords holding them were frayed and brittle.

I sighed inwardly and rolled my eyes—mere grifters trying to separate good people from the money they did not have. We might have snakes emblazoning all of our cartons and trams, but these folks were the real reptiles.

The garish thing pulled to a stop in the middle of the main road, and the driver used a ladder to make his way from his perch to the ground. He stepped inside the nearest building, a small sundry shop and didn't emerge for several minutes.

I turned away from the sight to go over the basic instructions of the ointments, elixir, and tablets for my elderly patient and sent him on his way. I set off to find either Asher or Geneva, to get their take on the newcomers. As it happened, I interrupted what appeared to be a rare moment of quiet for the pair, sitting in the shade under a tattered cloth tent, enjoying some canned fruit and quiet conversation. Neither looked pleased at the interruption, but Geneva agreed to come with me to see what the arrival of the new wagon would bring.

A small crowd had gathered along the dusty benches lining the road. A child tugged on his mother's hand trying to pull her closer to the rig. He wore pants a couple of sizes too large, the cuffs frayed from dragging through the gravel. His small hoarse voice was imploring the skeptical woman. "Mom, I heard Gentry say they're gonna be giving out sweets to the kids." She allowed herself to be pulled closer to the crowd.

A dazzling woman—all curves and tight bodice—stepped down from the back of the wagon. She was so at odds with the scene surrounding her, I almost didn't believe she was traveling in the dilapidated thing. Her midnight hair was piled high on her head and shimmered with a glittery powder. The burnished bronze hue of her skin reflected the sparkles as they trailed down both sides of her face, along her clavicles, and dropped between her cleavage. She moved with quiet confidence—the sort which springs from the knowledge that every man within a mile would be thinking of her as they drifted off to sleep that night and hoping she would appear in their dreams.

Behind her, a tall, broad-shouldered man appeared. On first glance, he looked as though he belonged anywhere but in the middle of the desert. A handful of years older than me, his copper red hair and neatly trimmed auburn beard revealed skin better suited to lush green pastures and overcast skies. The sun should have turned his pale skin to cracked leather, but interestingly enough it appeared smooth and unmarred by the environment. He was no match for his female companion, but he was clean and not unattractive. His clothes were tidy and well cared for.

The ginger muttered something to the woman, and she smiled before turning and sizing up the crowd.

Geneva looked at me and sighed through her nose. "I hope we get out of here before these folks get run out of town. I have no time for being stuck behind that death trap"—she nodded toward the wagon—"when we round the dry lake. Road there is terrible enough as is."

"I imagine we can leave here tomorrow, don't you?" I asked.

"By sunrise, God willing and the creek don't rise." My face must have looked baffled. "Not literally. Just something Asher's old gran used to say. It always tickled me. What?"

"Nothing." I smiled back at her. I'd never taken Geneva for the sentimental type. It was endearing.

We watched a little while longer as the driver—having returned from the shop—rubbed down the horses. He alone matched their transport. His hair was sparse on top but long and stringy in the back, a nondescript shade somewhere between dirty blond and brown, his clothing worn and tattered with a large yellow smear across the front. He barely reached the shoulders of the animals he was tending, and his gut kept bouncing off their legs.

All the while, the broad-shouldered redhead shook hands and smiled at children. His companion didn't speak with anyone in the crowd. Rather she seemed content to let them watch her as she unfurled a lovely rug and attached a matching canopy to the side of the wagon. She occasionally smiled at a passerby, nearly always a man—some young, some old. She disappeared for a time into the back of the wagon and emerged with a small lacquered table which she set atop the tapestry rug. The table was furnished with a lace drape and a small bowl which she filled with an assortment of jewel-colored hard candies.

At one point, a child ran up to the door to the wagon trying to see though the sliver of opening where the door remained slightly ajar. The woman tutted and wagged her finger at the boy and stepped up to the entrance, firmly pulling it shut. I was watching her fan the sweat from her brow when a man next to me cleared his throat. I hadn't even noticed his approach.

"Nanette does have quite an effect on folks, doesn't she?" His voice was full and smooth. The elocution perfect.

I nodded curtly. "She's quite beautiful."

"Ah yes, but not the only beautiful woman here today." He smiled at me and winked. "You *do* positively *radiate,* don't you?"

I pulled back slightly, and a frown formed on my face.

"Forgive me." He bowed his head in a sham of an apology. "I didn't intend to be forward. My name is Hollis." He grimaced as he gave his name, and I noticed the muscle in his jaw tick a little. "We'll be in town for a spell. If you ladies, or anyone you know, are in need of some healing, I'm sure we've got just the thing for you."

Geneva snickered, and he glanced at her, the smile slipping for a blink. He dipped his head again and moved on to a group of older ladies standing nearby.

I let myself laugh as Geneva motioned for us to go and find the others.

Many of the houses in the area weren't habitable, so the hundreds of people who called this settlement their home occupied ramshackle buildings up and down the main thoroughfare.

Our group had taken up a small area between a battered old school and the main road. We were camped in what might have been a field or a park, or possibly a sports venue, at one time ages ago. Faded metal slats crumpled at one end of the area. Asher had placed us far enough away to be unobtrusive but still accessible.

We had passed other small groups of travelers on the desolate roads, occasionally even shared the hospitality of a settlement with weary groups. However, nothing compared with the spectacle of the wagon and its inhabitants. With the arrival of the miracle man Hollis and the buxom beauty Nanette, it was unlikely the settlers would immediately miss us when we left.

I spied Hale across the field, piling up his surgical kit and cleaning his tools before he placed them in the solar battery-powered autoclave to sterilize them. By my count, during the short two days we'd been there, he'd managed to remove three infected toenails, perform an emergent appendectomy, lance and drain a nasty-looking abscess from an unfortunate man's back side, and most notably, amputate the foot of a severely overweight woman. Why the settlement's own practitioners had let her ulcerations go for so long was anyone's guess. Most of these souls would be just fine in the coming days, but I worried about her. As a new amputee, without proper care, she might not do so well.

I was profoundly happy Hale had elected to study surgical processes and had been chosen for that position on our team. My hands were capable of minor operations, but my stomach found them hard to bear. Plus, Medicus Corpus never would have placed the three of us together if two of us were strong surgeons. They wanted teams which balanced each other out. No settlement needed multiple surgeons but no one good with pharmacology or women's issues. Roe and Hale would have been sent off together most likely, and I would have been separated from my closest friend. Thankfully, the three of us complemented each other and presumably the other practitioners we were to join.

Thankfully the wound on his arm was healing nicely. It was still a puffy pink and the sutures were taut across the opening, but no angry red color surrounded it and no purulence leaked from it. I couldn't imagine the dark turn we would have taken if anything affected his ability to use his talented hands this early in his life.

I waved as I walked by, and Hale gave me a curt nod. One day maybe I'd get on his good side. Today wasn't that day.

Geneva and I found Roe and Asher gathering fresh water and relayed the events of the afternoon as best we could. I wasn't able to convey the total and absolute slime factor emanating from Hollis, but Geneva looked steadily at her husband and said simply, "They're trouble."

This was all it took to have him calling Jude, Jake, and the tram masters over for instructions.

"We're out at first light. I agree with Gen. Best to get ahead of any trouble before we hit the lake."

This was met with a few grumbles, but all in all, most of us would be happy to be moving again.

As the sun sank and the desert blessed us with a breeze, I dropped slowly into my cot. Roe sat beside me. A tingle raced up my back, and the wonderful breeze carried a trace of that ozone scent to my nostrils. I wrinkled my nose briefly but dismissed it.

"I don't know what these people eat, but I've seen more gout today than I care to recall." Roe was stretching his back and shoulders. It had been a long day for all of us.

"Perils of the job, I'm afraid."

"Indeed." He leaned back, hands behind his head, lids closing over the green of his irises. "So the snake oil crew was actually bad enough to send Geneva running, huh?"

I snorted a laugh. "You know the type. Probably selling jars of bovine urine and touting it as a cure-all."

He made a noncommittal noise of understanding.

"They were obnoxious. But after what happened on the road the other day, I really think Asher and Geneva just don't want to be traveling close to anyone. Especially not someone looking to make a quick buck and definitely not around the lake."

The lake. We'd heard bits and pieces about the ominous place over the past few days. We would stop in another small settlement tomorrow night, stay for the day there, and then in three days' time we would encounter it. Apparently what had once been a thriving oasis was now just a desolate, dry expanse of land, the road around which was treacherously perched along the side of the adjacent mountain. The tram masters went so far as to call sections of it murderous—passable only in the best of conditions and only if no travelers were coming from the other direction. It sounded less than spectacular.

I was still thinking about the road ahead when Phoebe jogged up. She was breathless as she wiped sweat from her brow.

"Roe. Do you mind coming with me to help Helena with a sick kid? His mom is having a fit about him needing attention before we leave." Out of breath, she paused and added hopefully, "I thought we could tag team."

"Absolutely. I've got nothing better to do other than you know, sleep." His words were biting, but he said it with that classic Roe charm that let him get away with it. "But if I'm coming"—he stood and extended his hand to me—"so is she. She's the best with kids."

I groaned and tried to ignore the look on Phoebe's face.

6

ROE

We entered a small building from the street side, the noise of the wagons and horses dying down as the night began to claim the inhabitants' activity along with the light. This was still technically a farming settlement, but only in the loosest sense of the word. Most folks had small plots they could get a few crops to grow in. The livestock could feed off the scrubby brush hardy enough to withstand the dryer months, but the animals lacked the robust muscle grain would provide.

Phoebe didn't have many details about the child. She only offered that Helena and Wade had been approached earlier by a tired-looking woman who had asked them to see if they could help her son. Wade had been busy tending to a young man with debilitating headaches and had sent Helena on alone. In general, we tried not to make house calls but rather to see patients in our tents or at a settlement's meeting house. Helena, feeling discomfort in going alone, found Phoebe along the way. After seeing the child, Helena had urged Phoebe to get another practitioner for a third opinion.

Despite the rickety appearance of the small building, the inside of the home was spotless and meticulously cared for. Murmuring voices drifted from one of the back rooms, and we entered to find Helena bent over a boy of about five years lying on a narrow a cot. He was covered with a thick quilt, pieced together in hues of brown and green. It was frayed at the edge but, in keeping with the rest of the home, clean. A small woman—presumably the boy's mother—sat on a wooden stool to one side of the bed. She brushed her hands over his forehead, lovingly smoothing the hair from his face. They shared the same chestnut hair color, thick dark lashes, and full eyebrows. But where the mother's skin was a rich olive, the boy's was sallow and waxy—the color of milk left out too long.

The child moaned quietly and tried to roll to his side. So much discomfort in such a small body.

Aurelia stepped past Phoebe and me, squatting next to Helena at the boy's side.

"May I?" she asked, gesturing toward the slim frame tucked beneath the thick quilt. The mother nodded, and Auri pulled the cover back from his small body.

She ran her hands lightly over him, feeling first his neck and collarbones, then under his arms and along his legs. She murmured soothingly to him as she placed her hands on his chest and gently, ever so gently, felt along his abdomen, a slight frown creasing her face. As she placed her stethoscope on his chest, she closed her eyes, listening intently. When she asked him to sit up so she could listen to his back, he cried and shook his head.

"He complains of terrible pain in his back," the boy's mother explained.

Helena turned to Aurelia. "This is Lita and her son, Jonaten. Lita states he was fine two weeks ago but began to get tired while playing. He started complaining of pain in his legs and back around the same time. Apparently she mentioned it to the regular practitioner here, but he thought it was a passing illness, and she didn't ask him to see Jonaten again. Today he seemed worse, so she grabbed us."

Aurelia wasn't Helena's supervising practitioner. She had no seniority and no special training for this type of case. We were all taught to help patients from birth to the grave, but Auri was just better with children than the rest of us. She often joked it was because she was the same size as them. Maybe at first that was true—the kids tended to relax and smile when she played with them. But over time, her medical knowledge of childhood illness expanded more than ours did. We all had our strengths. Hale was a gifted surgeon—the scalpels, retractors, and forceps an extension of his elegant hands. Phoebe was great with pregnancies and women's health. Wade a master of the microscope and other technical tools. The elderly seemed to think I was a gift from the heavens. Aurelia—children and pharmacology were her strengths. Not that she suffered in any area of healing really. At times, particularly with extraordinarily ill patients, I thought her shear force of will forced them to improve. I hoped this was one of those times.

"I thought it was growing pains at first," his mother explained. "But then he stopped getting out of bed altogether. He won't eat and he sleeps all the time, but so fitfully."

"Has there been anything else?" Aurelia asked. "Funny rashes or fevers? Any unusual bleeding or bruising?"

"Well, he's always been an active boy, so bruises are nothing new. But yes, I'd say he's had more of them lately. He gets hot at night."

Phoebe and I stood near the door, not wanting to interrupt. My mind was whirling through the possibilities. Each diagnosis I came up with was worse than the last.

Helena looked concerned as she asked, "Has anyone else been ill? Other family members with the same type of thing?"

"It's only just the two of us. His father died a few years back."

"I don't mean to be overly blunt, but do you mind telling me what he died from?" Auri asked.

"It was an accident. Nothing like this."

Aurelia nodded, the frown deepening on her face. She sighed and pushed her glasses up on the bridge of her nose.

"Do you mind if I take a few drops of blood, ma'am? I'd like to get a look at it under our microscope."

"I'll go get the scope and some slides," I said from the doorway. "Anything else you need?"

"Maybe a bag or two of fluids."

I was out the door before I realized Phoebe was coming with me.

"Well, this isn't good," she said.

"No," I replied. "No, it's not."

When we made it back to the camp, the sun had fully set. I grabbed Hale and asked him to let Asher and the others know we likely wouldn't be back anytime soon and to ask if the escorts could spare an extra body at the small house on the edge of the settlement. If this was heading the direction I feared, we might need help.

I was gathering items which had just been tucked away, much to the chagrin of the tram masters.

"Aurelia's there by herself?" my brother asked, an edge in his voice.

"No. Helena's there." I looked at him over my shoulder. "I thought I mentioned that."

"You probably did. You don't need me, do you? I might try to catch some sleep."

He turned from the tram. Phoebe looked after him and shook her head.

"My brother is. . ." I couldn't think of the right words.

"You don't need to apologize for him. We all have our roles. His is to operate, not to worry about a dying child."

I should defend him, but what was there to say? She was right of course.

We hustled back to the small wooden house and the slow moving calamity inside. Aurelia needed the microscope. I feared what it would show her. Feared her having to tell that poor woman what I thought I already knew. Feared what it would do to Aurelia when she told her we could do nothing to help.

7

AURELIA

No light trickled through the cracks in the curtains and the lamps inside the home were all lit. They cast strange and terrible shadows across the walls. Using a sterilized syringe, I removed a few milliliters of blood from Jonaten's arm. I let a drop fall onto the glass rectangle I held and used another slide to spread the blood into a thin coating on its surface. I set it on a table to dry while I retrieved a small brown bottle from our supplies. The dropper was stained a deep damson plum when I withdrew it from the bottle. Once the blood had a dull matte finish, I applied a bit of the violet dye on top and repeated the process of smearing and drying, then finished off by placing a thinner sliver of glass on top and positioning it under the cylindrical lens of the microscope.

The room itself seemed to hold its breath as I gazed through the eyepiece of the microscope. Red and fuchsia blobs materialized on the slide as I brought it into focus. The buzzing of the night-loving insects in the tree outside was a cacophony in the stillness of the small crowded room.

If I had been born an artist, I might have called what I saw beautiful. Bright magenta blooms, speckled with indigo and violet, interspersed with dusky red disks, swam over the glass surface. The colors offset each other in a sea of pinks, purples, and rusty reds. Unfortunately, I was not an artist and the vision in the eyepiece brought me horror rather than joy. The slide showed too few red disks, and those which *were* present were far too pale and much too small. Some were fractured and misshapen. In contrast, the speckled magenta and violet shapes flooded the available space.

I switched the slide out for another I had made from the same sample. Readjusting the focus, I prayed it would show me a different view. A different future for this child and his sweet mother.

I took one look and straightened, placing my hands on my lower back and gave the faintest shake of the head to Helena. She looked through the eyepiece, her short brown hair falling around her face, and blew out a long breath. She wiped at her eyes before turning to face Lita.

Helena grew progressively paler the longer we sat with Lita and her sweet little boy. I couldn't gauge how much Jonaten understood. What he grasped of our conversation as he drifted in and out of sleep— occasionally moaning as he shifted position in the sweat-damp sheets—only the heavens knew. I desperately hoped he didn't understand any of it. Lita however? She understood everything all too well. She asked appropriate questions and processed what we discussed— including the prognosis—a bit at a time. I watched as she shifted from initial denial to a resigned understanding mixed with stark and obvious grief.

Leukemia is a horrid monster. White blood cells multiplying exponentially until they choke off all normal functions of the bone marrow and overwhelming the patient's—too often a child's—ability to stay alive.

We answered the questions we could. We told her honestly when we didn't have the answer she wanted or when we didn't have an answer at all. I held her hands in mine for a period. Helena held them when I set out for her what I believed would be an excruciating few weeks to come.

She sobbed for what felt like hours, my own tears, as well as Helena's, flowing freely in sympathy. Occasionally a sniffle came from the doorway where Phoebe and Roe waited. When Lita was able to collect herself, she told us three other children in the past six months had suffered a similar illness. The practitioners stationed here had tried all the meager remedies they could—each time hoping for a happier outcome than was possible. One child, after receiving some concoction of medicines, had gone into an apparent remission, only to relapse and succumb to his illness a few months later.

It nagged at me, this cluster of blood cancer. It wasn't unheard of. We had been told in our classes clusters could occur, but it certainly wasn't common. Perhaps some long-buried toxin was responsible. However, it was just as likely to be triggered by an unknown virus or simple, terrible, atrocious luck.

I was torn from my thoughts and Lita's overwhelming sadness by the sound of tinkling bells from outside. They seemed to have stopped just beyond the weathered windows. Roe motioned to Phoebe, and the pair disappeared out the door together—presumably to head off any unwanted visitors. As soon as the door shut, however, the creak of wagon wheels could be heard moving on.

"We'll leave a document for your regular Medicus practitioners detailing what we've discussed. It'll be ready before we go." My voice sounded foreign in my ears. Was I really just going to up and leave this desperate child and his equally desperate mother? The answer was one I knew but hated. I had no choice. My future belonged elsewhere and to other ill people.

I sat there for a few minutes more, the tiny pale hand in my own. I was hesitant to leave, despite knowing I had nothing more to offer them. It must have been the position of my stool, but soon my arms and hands were full of pins and needles. I'd had this feeling in passing before, generally when I'd sat in an awkward position, healing or soothing a patient. I squeezed his hand and stood, rotating my shoulders to restart the circulation to my upper extremities.

Helena had been jotting things on a fresh pad of paper.

"We'll leave more of the medicine we gave him for the pain as well. I don't want them wasting time mixing more up if they happen not to have any on hand. I'm sorry. . ." My voice broke and I wiped under the frame of my glasses at the salty moisture escaping my eyes. "I am so, *so* sorry we can't do more."

Helena looked as if she couldn't even speak.

Lita nodded her understanding and turned back to her sleeping child, running her hands over his hair and face. I looked back as we left. Whether from the medication we'd given him or simply from pure exhaustion, the little boy finally seemed to have found a measure of peace and was sleeping comfortably. Lita had placed her head on the bed next to him. Her back and shoulders heaved as the sobs racked her, but she muffled the sounds in the mattress, trying not to wake him.

Jake was sitting on the steps outside. He didn't pry, just walked ahead of us as we left. I felt drained to my very marrow. I knew stars were twinkling overhead, but I did not see them. Knew the scent of dirt and hay hung in the air, but I did not smell it. Knew my friends and colleagues walked with me, but I did not feel them there. The night was empty. As empty as I was.

What was the point in learning medicine if when it was really needed—when it really counted—it was inadequate? We were inadequate. *I was inadequate.*

Lita and Jonaten needed a cure. Not some bits of this and that to stave off the pain, the nausea. They needed him to be fixed, and that was something we could not offer them.

As we trudged back toward our camp, the sound of bells broke through my hollowness.

"You all look terrible," a firm smooth voice called. "Looks like what you need is a miracle."

I spun around. All the rage and grief and feelings of ineptness flowed up from my gut into a voice I barely registered as my own. "Shut your disgusting mouth. This isn't a game. Not some ignorant fool who wants to throw their money away on whatever piece of trickery you want to sell them. That boy is dying." My voice cracked. I sobbed a breath. "He is *dying*. So no. We do not need your brand of miracle."

I felt a strong arm around my shoulder and Roe's calm clear voice in my ear. "Don't waste your time or energy on him, Auri. Let's go."

We started to walk away. The breeze picked up and carried the sound of bells and Hollis's voice to us. "I never said *my* miracle. That boy and his mother need *your* brand of miracle, Aurelia Morris."

I stopped dead in my tracks. I'd never told Hollis—or his companions for that matter—my name. I wanted to ask how he knew it. Who had he been speaking to about me? I wanted to rage at him. I wanted to call him a liar and cheat and a charlatan. Roe held me to his side, and by the time we finished crossing the road, the wagon and its despicable occupants were already gone.

True to his word, Asher had us up a bare few hours later and heading out of town. I hadn't really slept, just tumbled from one exhausted night terror to the next. I would feel myself slipping toward the edge of sleep only to jolt awake as if I had stepped over the edge of a cliff. Just before I opened my eyes, I would see Lita, her face a mask of fury and sorrow. She'd said she didn't blame us, but still I could feel the reproach. Feel the disgust at our shortcomings. I flung the same unspoken admonishment at myself.

Now the combination of emotional and physical exhaustion had me walking like the undead behind the last tram. We were climbing and descending a steady string of gentle rolling hills, flanked on both sides by vast expanses of straw-colored weeds and desert plants. The road here was better than in other spots, and we had been making good time through the morning.

Feeling like I would fall on my face if I continued to try to keep up with the teams of horses, I climbed up the rear ladder, slipped inside the tram, and closed my eyes. Someone had been smart enough to set up and start the autoclave, wanting to get our equipment sterilized and ready to go before we needed it. Being fed by the solar panels, it hummed noisily from deeper inside the tram. Water sloshed in one of the barrels. Adding in the sound and sway of the road, I was hypnotized within minutes. I lingered, not fully awake but not asleep either. Residing in a place on the edge of my consciousness were a woman's hushed broken sobs. My mind drifted, and soon the sobs were joined by a pair of too large eyes floating in a small frightened face.

8

HALE

I found Aurelia sitting alone on a rock in the midst of a cottonwood grove. It was a small stream oasis in the middle of what was becoming a more desolate place by the day. The air there was thicker, full of the smells of growth and decay, but it was a peaceful heaviness. I didn't want to break the silence. Still. . .

"You should come get something to eat."

She didn't look at me, just pushed those damned glasses back from where they'd slipped to the tip of her nose. "I'm not really hungry, but thanks." Her voice lacked the perkiness I associated with her. It was dull. Lifeless.

"If you want to faint on the road, that's on you." I turned to walk back to the camp.

"Good of you to care." No longer dull, her voice dripped sarcasm.

"I thought not wanting you to pass out was caring."

"You know, we can't all be stone-cold assholes."

"It's too bad. Sometimes being a stone-cold asshole is all that gets a person through the day." I was striding away but stopped. "Look. I know it sucks. I know you are tearing yourself up over that poor kid."

She looked so cold as she said, "You don't know shit, Hale. You weren't there. You didn't see how small he was. How frail . . . like he'd blow away in a slight breeze." She paused and drew a deep breath, seeming to muster something deep inside. "You didn't see how much his mother loved him. She was dying right along with him."

My chest burned. Before it could kindle into something bigger, I tamped it down quickly.

"Did it ever occur to you why?" I stared at her, but the expression on her face didn't change. I shook my head. "Never mind."

She was right of course. I hadn't been there. I was the stone-cold asshole who didn't want to be there. She'd had Roe at her side, and I knew he would help her through it. I couldn't really tell her I had stayed away because I knew she didn't want an audience, so I just kept my mouth shut on the subject. She took off her glasses, giving me a glimpse of the beautiful irises amidst the red and puffy lids. Waves of fatigue rolled off her.

I walked back to where she sat and knelt down next to my kid brother's best friend. I didn't touch her—we didn't have that kind of relationship. I waited a beat until I knew she was listening and said the only thing I could think of that was both true and not condescending.

"Sometimes our medicine works and sometimes the universe has other plans. I can't say for sure, but I imagine you'll carry that boy and his mother with you, if not always, then at least for a very long time. That doesn't mean you shouldn't feel what you're feeling or bury it down deep. That's not who you are. It just means you are doing the very best you can with what you've got."

She didn't look at me, didn't say a word. She just slipped her glasses back on and stood.

We walked back to camp together in silence.

9

ROE

"Is it true?" I asked Jake that night as we ate our tinned stew. "Is the lake haunted?"

"Now, who went and told you such a tale?" He smiled and took a swig from the bottle of beer he'd gotten in the last settlement. He allotted himself one only every couple of days and only when he was off watch.

Jake's bulk was intimidating, accentuated by the slight figure with the blonde ponytail next to him. Phoebe looked up—light in her eyes—at the unexpected conversation.

"I don't know," I said. My gaze drifted from his face back to the bottle in his hand. I was supremely envious of that beer. "People talk."

"You're a man of science. You mean to tell me you heard some foolishness about ghosts and whatnot and you believed it?" He shook his head, grinning like a fiend, and took another long swallow. "I've made this trip a few times, and I haven't seen any sign of ghosts at the lake."

Wade sat next to me, also eyeing the brown bottle. Why had none of us thought to buy a few for ourselves? "Then why do we need to take this supposedly dangerous road around the lake bed? Why not just trek right over it? Ground there is flat enough, isn't it?"

"I can't really answer as to why we go around rather than over or through or whatever." Jake waved a massive hand next to his head. "It's just the way the trams are taken. Medicus pays us to do what *we* are told. *You* are told to heal. *I* am told to guard you and the *tram masters* are told to take the long way round that dry bit of earth. So. We take the road around it."

"Okay, so maybe there aren't ghosts," Phoebe's light high voice chimed in. "But what about the fairy fish? Those are real. I'd love to get some to look at."

"Fairy fish?" Wade looked disgusted by the notion.

"Well, they aren't real fairies obviously. They're these teeny, tiny freshwater crustaceans—shrimps or something—I can't remember. They mate and lay eggs when the ground is wet, and the eggs go dormant when the water dries up. When the next year's rains come, they hatch and the cycle starts over again."

Wade still didn't look convinced.

"They, you know, look like little fairies when they swim." Elbows bent, she flapped her hands at her sides in the portrayal of tiny wings.

I smiled and raised my eyebrows. "Wow. That's cool. I've never heard of them."

Phoebe blushed and said quietly, "I was hoping to get some soil from the lake bed and see if I could hatch them once we get settled."

"So do they have a purpose?" Wade asked.

Phoebe's hair swung violently from the back of her head as she whipped it around to look at him. "The purpose is just to be."

"Just to be? Like a pet?"

"Do you have a problem with that, Wade?" This was the most animated I had seen her.

He held his hands up in surrender. "Nope. No problem at all."

Jake's laugh was warm even as he gently crushed Phoebe's hope. "No, ma'am. I don't believe you are gonna be able to collect your dirt. Fairy fish or no. We stay on the road. No crossing out into that place, even for someone sweet as you are." The smile faded from his eyes as he said the words again. "We stay on the road."

"While we are on the subject of dark things," Wade interjected, "any word on the missing supplies?"

"What missing supplies?" I hadn't heard anything about that.

Any thought of Jake's booming laugh or infectious grin returning vanished. "At some point, while we were packing things up in the little farm town, two cartons of meds went missing. Mostly antibiotics and some saline bags. I think some chokeberry and belladonna pills might have been in there too. Asher didn't give me the whole list. Anyway, likely you'll never see any of it again."

"But why take those things?" A frown creased Phoebe's forehead. "We can get most of that from the supply chain when we get to Devil's Meadows or farther down the line in Jave."

"Likely didn't know what was in the cartons, just someone looking to get lucky with a quick grab. Like the guy with the pipe grenade, but instead of open warfare, this time they opted for stealth. Whoever it was, probably thought we had stronger painkillers. Morphine is good, but even antibiotics can be valuable."

None of us said much to that. We still had a long way to go before we were off the road. How much more would we lose?

We must have been quite the sad sight. Looking around at us, Jake smiled again. "Here," he said, passing us each a dark brown bottle from the box behind him. "Next time use those big brains of yours, and get your own."

When the dawn had us up and moving the next day, a queer sort of calm had fallen over the group. The plan was to spend the early part of that day on the road and then hole up when we reached a small stopover that afternoon. We would rest there for the evening and head out super early the next day, traveling for much longer, perhaps eighteen to twenty hours, in a push to make it around the massive lake in one move.

Aurelia had slept fitfully again the previous night, curled up next to me. She was nervous and agitated again this morning. She muttered to me as she passed about something feeling off but never elaborated. Hadn't she said something similar the day Hale had a chunk of his arm nearly bitten off? I couldn't remember.

We hadn't taken any med supplies out since we'd left the little farming town, but still Asher made me check the medical cargo to ensure it was all stored up nice and tight. I'd asked if he thought another surprise was coming, but he reassured me he believed the incident which had left Hale's arm banged up was likely an isolated event, made out of desperation. The missing supplies had been taken when our backs were turned. I was in the back of a tram carriage, staring at all those snake and staff emblems, when I heard the tinkling of bells and horse hooves.

Asher's rough voice rose in the dry morning air. "Just hold on up there."

"We don't want trouble. Just a word," a smooth male voice responded.

"You keep your setup where it's at, and we'll talk." Asher was in no mood.

"With respect, sir, it's not with you I wish to speak. Where's your girl with the miracles? The petite one. Where is the girl with the magic and starlight, sunshine and saving? It is with her I'd have a word."

I climbed out and noted the tall broad-shouldered man and his dark-haired companion. A third short, unhealthy-looking specimen sat at the reins of the wagon. I'd seen them only briefly before, and even then it had been dark, casting them all in shadow. In the muted grey of dawn, I saw what Aurelia had meant. The woman had a sort of magnetism to her I couldn't quite explain. She was pretty, I suppose, but it wasn't really that. She seemed to pull the focus to her, a magnifying glass collecting the sunshine and turning it into a blazing beam. I wanted to know what kind of innocent creatures she was planning on burning with that beam.

The "ginger," as Auri had called him when she told me his name, took no notice of his companion. His eyes were searching our camp. Presumably searching for Aurelia, given his little speech. My gut told me letting him find her would do none of us any good. Unfortunately, there weren't many places to stay unobserved, and my friend seemed to know it.

"Say whatever it is you want to say and then let us be on our way." She stood next to Geneva, scowling in the newcomers' direction.

The leader tilted his head. I could feel the cogs spinning before he spoke. "Why the rush to leave the adorable little farm community?"

Asher answered. "We'd been there for a few days already. It was time to move on."

Hollis tilted his head and looked over at our escort, his eyes icy and intense. He held the stare for a beat and turned to look once more at Aurelia.

"You had unfinished business there, and you let them take you from it."

Aurelia's posture changed then—her chin lifting and her hands fisting at her sides—but she remained silent.

Asher filled the silence for her. "As I said. It was time to move on. We have a schedule to keep. Lots of folks expecting us. More needs down the road."

This time Hollis didn't even deign to look in Asher's direction before he asked, "I simply want to know how it felt to walk away. Knowing the child will be dead by the end of the month?"

"You filthy asshole." I was storming across the camp before I could stop my feet. Jude and Jake met me just feet from the wagon and gripped my arms as if physically restraining me would restrain my anger as well.

"Now," he continued, taking absolutely zero notice of my intention to wipe the calm from his smug face. "It is not my intention to cause discontent. I simply would like to know why the young lady did not save the child."

I was going to do more than wipe the calm from his face. I was going to make sure the next time he smiled, there would be holes where his teeth should be. Aurelia was devastated by the entire encounter with Lita and Jonaten, and this bastard was throwing it in her face.

"And what is it you think I was meant to do? Four of us were in Lita's home. Four of us who know our limitations." Aurelia's voice was firm and strong. I glanced at her, and a wave of pride rushed through me. "Jonaten has leukemia—a malignancy of the blood. We have no medicines for that. Not anymore."

"Are you sure?" he crooned at her.

Whether it was the question itself or the tone he used, something burrowed further under Auri's skin. "Of course I'm sure," she snapped. "I wasn't the only one to look at his slides."

"I didn't mean were you sure of the nature of his illness. Are you sure you couldn't have helped him? Healed him?"

Helena chimed in. "As Aurelia said, there are no medicines for those types of things. Not since the Grand Divagation. A long time ago, yes, we would have poisoned him to have a chance to heal him, but those chemicals can't be made or manufactured without certain technology. We left his mother with enough things to make him comfortable until. . ."

She couldn't continue.

"That's *also* not what I meant. I'm quite aware of the nature of his illness." Despite his genteel mannerisms and well-spoken words, I agreed with Auri's assessment. He oozed unpleasantness.

"Well, then, what the hell *do* you mean?" I spat at him.

"She knows what I mean, don't you, my petite? You hold the keys within you. The thaumaturgy. The wonder-working. The *miracles*." I could have sworn a look of ecstasy flashed across his face and was then gone—replaced by that calm smugness.

"Don't be ridiculous," Aurelia answered. "I am a Medicus Corpus trained practitioner of medicine. Not some delusional hack trying to separate desperate people from their money. I prefer to leave the quackery business to you all. Take your hocus-pocus somewhere else and leave us alone."

The dark-haired beauty cast a speculative look at Aurelia. The single arched eyebrow came across as practiced rather than genuine. I expected her to speak, but she remained aloof. Removed. I looked to the driver who said nothing but appeared to be struggling to contain his mirth.

Jude and Jake seemed to sense the fight was leaving me and released my arms.

I had the vague impression the woman—was her name Nanette—was trying to draw my attention again. I wasn't in the mood for more games. I needed to check on Auri. Hale, appearing from wherever he'd been, stood just behind her looking exactly how I felt.

"Well, then. I think we're done here." Asher clapped his hands and looked around at the outraged faces on most in our party. "Load up. We are out in ten."

10

HALE

None of it was what I'd expected. A long, tiresome, boring trek from Renfield to Devil's Meadows—yes. Tedious hours of walking and riding, broken only by slightly fewer tedious days of medicine in the dumpy little settlements along the way—yes. Feeling a sense of unending sameness and spending time with the needles and lengths of old silk I'd packed so I could practice sutures and knots—keeping my hands busy during the hours I rode in the tram—yes. What I hadn't anticipated was so much *drama*.

I was taking a few moments for some much-needed privacy before setting out for another, albeit shorter, day of walking and was just exiting the small copse of cottonwoods when a voice I knew as well as my own rose above the noise of camp. Interesting. It was not unlike Roe to use such strong and colorful language. He had a passionate personality at times. It was, however, unlike him to be physically aggressive. That was generally more my style, but as I rounded the trees, I saw Jake and Jude bodily restraining him.

My eyes caught on the cause of his ire, and I couldn't blame him. I wouldn't mind having a go at that bastard Hollis myself. Checking my temper, I held my tongue and walked over to stand near Aurelia. It was beyond obvious she was taking things hard, but I also had a feeling she would deal with it better if we weren't always jumping to her aid. She was tougher than she looked and needed to be treated like an adult, not the child her height suggested. This probably made me a world-class hypocrite because Roe was just as tough—if not tougher—than he looked and still I couldn't stop trying to protect him.

Things were finally simmering down when I noticed the woman. She was enchanting in some intangible way—curvy and elegant at the same time. Beautiful but *more* than that.

I shook my head to clear it and watched as she focused on my kid brother. She never called to him, not with her voice, but in every other way possible. The look in her eyes, the posture of her body, the very essence of her soul seemed to croon in his direction. This was a woman who knew how to use her assets and use them well. The fact he didn't even flick his eyes in her direction? Oh, that was more than shock on her face. Outrage hardened her resplendent features.

"She's wasting her time," I muttered. I hadn't intended to say the words aloud. Aurelia looked at me with understanding in her eyes.

I couldn't stop the frown from creasing my face. Aurelia understood nothing.

11

AURELIA

Fiberglass and rubber groaned and squeaked along the narrow strip of land. To my right, the rocky mountain walls crowded overhead. To my left, a steep drop led to the dry lakebed. The white glistening surface came in and out of view as an eerie fog parted and converged over and over again, like lace sliding over a sheet of ice. I tried to envision what it must have looked like once—a vast expanse of water in this arid stretch of the world. Now, it was simply a drier stretch in an already desiccated environment.

Despite the fog, it wasn't humid. The clouds were more like airborne dust or powder particles. It felt unpleasant on my skin and tasted vaguely of minerals. At least it kept the sun from glaring in my eyes. I pushed my glasses up on my nose again, sure I would find a fine layer of silt coating the lenses and was surprised when my fingers came away clean.

From this distance, the ground at the bottom of the incline could have been marble or an unmarred blanket of snow—smooth, with a faint shimmer. Up close, it probably wouldn't be nearly as intriguing. Probably just like any other dry lake, full of snakeskin cracks and scaly fissures.

I hauled my attention back to the road. We were moving at a slug's pace. Slow and methodical.

Before the stars had gone to bed and the sun had even considered rising, Minton and Luc had collected us together and made a few things abundantly clear. First, the only souls in the trams that day would be the three drivers, ready to jump from their perches should the horses or trailers slip over the edge. The rest of us would walk. The entire distance. Second, while we were hoofing it, we were to stay either in front of or behind the carriages. Under no circumstances were we to find ourselves between the loads and the mountain wall. Luc went so far as to regale us with a gruesome tale from a few years back in which the horses had spooked, resulting in two travelers becoming "meat pies" on the rocky outcrops. Lastly, we were to stay together. No wandering off or lingering behind. We would start the traverse as a group and end it as a group. Anyone who didn't mind this rule would be forfeit due to his or her own stupidity, and Medicus didn't need stupid people in their service. No rescue missions would occur that day, the next day, or *ever* for souls lost to the walls or drops.

After their wonderfully cheery speech, Hera lit the fuse on some sort of firework rocket. It shot from her hand into the still dark sky, and a shower of brilliant blue sparks filled the air high above us. She, Minton, and Luc stood in hushed silence for several minutes, staring out across the landscape. Finally, far off and barely visible, an answering green flash appeared. Satisfied with what they saw, Luc yelled it was time to go.

Geneva explained if red sparks had been seen, it meant someone else was on the road headed north toward our location. As the road wasn't wide enough to pass in several areas, we would have had to wait and try again the next day. The settlements on either end had watchmen on duty for the first few hours each morning to ensure the signals were sent and followed.

Now, many hours later, the sun should have been well into its assaulting march across the sky. Instead, the unusual fog muted everything. The normal taupe and brown mountains were an off shade of grey. Even sound fell victim to the peculiar atmosphere—the groaning and rocking of the tires on the hard pack lacked their normal high tenor. The desert heat wasn't nearly as intense as it should have been, but it was still a far cry from cold. Despite this, a chill ran down my spine and fed the goose bumps cropping up on my arms.

The shiver didn't help the fact that I needed to urinate. Badly. Although at first it was awkward, I had quickly gotten used to stepping off the road by myself to relieve the pressure in my bladder. Thanks to Luc's instructions this morning, however, I couldn't very well sneak off alone that day. We still had a way to go before our next planned stop.

All thoughts of my bladder vanished when I smelled it. The same faint odor of wrongness—a whiff of ozone before a lightning strike—in the air.

I checked my spot in the line and made sure Roe was still next to me. He was comfortably quiet, keeping pace with me between the second and third trams. We were a safe distance from the drop but not too close to the rock face.

Roe knew me better than anyone, I suppose, and he must have sensed my nervousness. He looked at me sideways, golden eyebrows raised upward in question. *You good?* I struggled to project a calm and confidence I didn't have. He knew it for the fraud it was.

Voice barely above a whisper, despite the fact there was no reason to be quiet, he asked, "What is it?"

"Not sure," I breathed back.

"The last time you were spooked, I didn't pay it any attention and my brother almost lost a finger or two."

Technically it hadn't been the last time, but he didn't know that.

"I'm not spooked," I said as another involuntary shiver ran through my body, "and don't be so dramatic. His fingers were never really in danger. It was his arm."

"I don't like it either, but I have been somewhat assured the lake bed isn't actually haunted."

"Haunted? Who said anything about it being haunted? Not helpful."

As if to prove him wrong, a low undulating moan rose out of the fog to our left. It hung in the air around us, wavering up and down but never dissipating. The horses behind us stepped their hooves up and down. Only Luc's firm hand on the reins kept them in check.

It went on for several long minutes, during which I gradually drifted closer to Roe.

The first of the trams ahead of us turned with the road, momentarily disappearing behind a wall of mountain and dust or fog or whatever this unnatural cloud cover was. Irrational though I knew it to be, I had a moment of certainty we would never see that tram—or Hera who was driving it—again. It had vanished into another world entirely. My breath quickened, and I opened my mouth to voice my fear when the road straightened and we could see them again through the gloom.

Luc called from behind us, "Pick up the pace a bit if you will. I don't want a gap forming."

Roe didn't turn but raised his arm in affirmation and grabbed my hand in reassurance. We walked faster, but still not quickly. The noise persisted from our left. If wraiths and demons did exist, they would sound just like that. I decided it would drive me mad by the time we made it to our next camp.

"Tell me a story," I begged my friend. "Something I don't already know about you."

"Aurelia Morris, you know everything there is to know about me. Everything that's worth knowing at least." He chuckled.

"Please, Roe? Just talk."

He ran a hand through his sandy hair. It had grown more and more unkempt each day we spent on the road.

"Okay . . . let's see." His voice was still pitched low. Luc had just yelled and nothing catastrophic had happened, but still we shared a sense that quieter was better.

"I could tell you about the time I stole a basket of strawberries from our neighbor and ate the entire thing in one go."

"You were greedy and paid for it by being sick for three days. Couldn't leave the toilet? I've heard that one." I didn't mean to be argumentative, and he knew it, so he squeezed my hand and tried again.

"How about the time Hale saved me from Margaret Theodore? I was nine and she was ten but a good head taller than me. She wanted me to walk home with her, and when I said no she decided my nose would look better with her fist in it. Hale arrived just in time for me to avoid a pretty bad walloping. I think she had anger issues."

"Heard it."

"The banana in the woodpile?"

I nodded.

"The day we got accepted to Medicus?"

"I was there," I hissed indignantly.

"Oh yeah. You were."

He was quiet but smiling devilishly as he tried to dredge up some ridiculous story or adventure I had not yet heard in all of our years of friendship. I adored that grin and the way it lit up his face, transforming him from merely handsome to near glorious. I desperately wanted him to find a life which would ensure that smile never left him.

In the quiet, the sounds of the horse hooves and the crunch of the gravel beneath the carriage wheels were louder but still tamped down. Growing impatient for him to decide, I glanced at his face and stilled. In the gloom, no sign of the wicked good humor remained.

"What about the day my dad left us?" His voice was barely more than a breath in the wind.

My brow furrowed. Roe and Hale's dad hadn't left. I'd seen him almost as much as my own father in the past few years. We'd had dinner together dozens of times, gone on outings to the river, and he'd even embraced me fiercely in goodbye before we'd left the Medicus campus. Roe seemed to read my thoughts.

"You've never met my real father." He stared ahead for a moment and amended, "I mean, you've never met my biological father. Marten Belstrohm, my dad, *my real dad*, you've met loads of times. The man I am biologically related to is named Wendell Watt. Cringe, I know. Well, Wendell left us when I was seven. Hale eight."

Somewhere ahead and to the left of us, the horrid moaning intensified and faded back. I must have tensed up again because Roe flicked a look my way and said, "I think it's just the wind," before he continued.

"I really don't remember a ton about him other than he was always angry. Angry at me. Angry at Mom and Hale. Angry at the world. He was full of seething. Always. He never smiled. Never laughed. Unless it was in that cynical 'you got what was coming to you' way. Mom never talked about him either before or after he left. I think he must have been different at some point, or she never would have loved him or stayed with him as long as she did. Not if he was an ass from the beginning."

I imagine he was right. Bonnie Belstrohm exuded light and love. I felt it every time I was near her.

"Hale remembers more than me." His body slumped a little. "Everyone who knew the man says Hale reminds them of Wendell. He hates it. People see his size and how he can sometimes get distant, and they just make this stupid connection. Hale isn't anything like that asshole."

I was momentarily ashamed to think maybe I would have agreed with the assumption.

I didn't say anything. Just kept walking, trying not to trip over my feet and listening to the sound of the horses behind us. Trying not to listen to the sound of the haunting wind all around us.

"The day he left. . . It was a bad day and a great day at the same time. Do you know what I mean?"

I nodded.

"We'd gotten home from school, and Hale told me to go play while he gathered us a snack. Wendell was supposed to be at work. Our mom was at the market or something. Anyway, I was playing with some toy on the floor in the room Hale and I shared. I could feel this shadowy presence behind me. A looming storm about to break. I turned and as I realized who it was, his hand connected with my face. I was dazed and didn't cry right away, but the tears flowed as soon as the blood ran out of my nose. Blood and snot and tears just running down my chin. The worst part was, I didn't even know why he'd hit me. I figured it out later, but right then, he was just raving about how no son of his would act the way I did. Play the way I did. *Be* the way I was."

My heart ached for little Roe. I hadn't known him at that age, but I hated this man on his behalf.

Roe let go of my hand and shoved both of his fists into his pockets. His face had gone sort of distant, his lips in a tight straight line.

"Hale came into the room as I was wiping the blood from my chin. He looked so small next to Wendell. Our father. He was small but *so* angry. The same rage I'd seen on my father's face dozens, if not hundreds, of times was on Hale's small young face. His eyes simmered with it. But Hale's anger was a righteous rage born of love for me and hate for Wendell. He had an apple in one hand, a slice of it missing, and a small paring knife in the other. He dropped the apple, and I can *so clearly* remember the thunk it made as it hit the floor." Roe's voice was soft but full of emotion—pride and love for his older brother.

The tram in front of us swayed too close to the mountain, the rear panels hitting stone and brush. A small rockslide trailed into the road at our feet— mostly pebbles but some chunks as large as my fist bounced into the road as well. That couldn't be good for the solar panels.

"Easy now," Luc called over our heads to Minton.

I was captivated by the story. So much so, the crying and moaning from the lake bed were just background noise.

"He held the knife in both hands, pointing it straight out in front of him. Straight at our father. His hands were shaking, but still he held it there." Roe cleared his throat and waved a hand in front of his face, swatting the memory away like a bothersome fly. "Mom came home just then, and thank the heavens she did. Hale might have tried to kill him and probably would have ended up dead himself. She took one look at me with my bloody face, at Hale with his tiny knife, and at the waste of a man she had married. And that was that. She told him to get out and never come back. For a wonder, he did. We never saw him again. I have no idea if he is dead or alive. I don't really care. Despite Hale being only a year older than me, he has taken it upon himself to act as my protector every day since." He flashed his lovely smile and added, "Mom met Marten a year later, and he's been our 'dad' ever since."

"That's . . . wow. How did I not know any of this until now?"

It wasn't Roe who answered. I'd been so engrossed in the story, I hadn't noticed Hale float back from the front of the tram to where we were walking. He must have gone between the trams and the cliff drop because even Hale wouldn't have chanced being "meat pied" by the mountain wall.

"You never knew because it isn't something we talk about." He wasn't angry or condescending, just matter-of-fact. "Some bodies are best left buried."

I couldn't disagree. We all had bits of our lives—stories or embarrassing moments—we didn't want out there in the ether. If we could keep them tucked in tight to ourselves, they were less apt to grow fangs and bite us.

"Well, at least now I know why you have such an affinity for scalpels and knives," I said sweetly to Hale, trying to lighten the mood. He snorted in reply.

Again, I felt that flush of shame. I hadn't thought the worst of Hale, but I hadn't thought the best of him either. He was prickly and harsh more often than not. Maybe he had reason to be.

My terror momentarily abated, I decided it would be a great time to change the subject. "I really need to pee."

Roe and Hale exchanged a look over the top of my head and simultaneously broke into laughter. Hale was able to contain himself to a few chuckles, but Roe's laugh turned into full-bodied shaking guffaws—the emotion of his story being replaced with a kind of manic hysteria. He stopped and placed his hands on his knees, trying to catch his breath.

Luc was unsympathetic. "Keep moving."

Roe straightened and swiped the tears streaming down his dusty cheeks with his sleeve, leaving swatches of mud in their wake.

We walked on in silence for what felt like days or weeks. The light shifted from the warm golden ash of afternoon into a more cool grey suffused with violet and indigo. Although the sun was still hidden by the shroud of powdery fog, my head told me we were moving toward late afternoon or evening.

We never stopped moving but ate mixed nuts and dried fruit from a small pack in the open end of the tram ahead. Our steps went on and on and on. The eerie noises from the drop would rise and fall at intermittent periods, but I'd grown somewhat accustomed to them.

We were approaching another bend, causing the train of wagons to slow. Asher and Geneva called back down the line. Up ahead, Wade, Helena, and Phoebe were presumably slowing as well. Muffled footsteps came from around the outside of the middle carriage. Jude appeared and informed us the road was in bad shape. It would be a slow process to get the horses past as the ancient asphalt was crumbling over the side. Not unlike the wind to our left, I groaned audibly, the pressure in my bladder protesting the news of even further delay. Despite my dearest hope of holding out, I was going to need to relieve myself sooner rather than later.

The road was a bit wider where we were, so I made an executive decision.

Trying to keep attention from myself, I whispered to Roe, "I'm going to the side of the road. Keep a lookout, okay?"

He nodded, and I hurried to the roadside, searching for a small crevice or rock jutting out. When I found one a few minutes later, I squatted as quickly as I could, silently praying to whoever would listen not to be seen. Because we were moving slowly as a group, I was able to keep myself from being separated, and I pulled up my pants, thanking the universe I hadn't urinated on my shoes. Jude gave me a disappointed shake of the head as I rejoined Roe and Hale. I ignored him.

Fortune smiled on my choice. As I rejoined my friends, a blood-curdling scream rent the air around us. It would likely have led to me soiling myself if I hadn't just gone.

The wail rose from somewhere ahead of us, not sounding the least bit human. My mind immediately conjured visions of ghastly spirits rising from the lake bed below. My heart raced as my bones shivered in a visceral reaction to the sound.

"It's got to be a horse," Roe said as I stepped closer to his side.

Hale looked at him and raised his eyebrows. "I don't know. That doesn't sound like any horse I've ever heard."

Thinking I wouldn't notice, Roe looked pointedly at me and gave his head an almost imperceptible shake.

"You know I can see you, right?" I snapped.

At least he had the grace to look embarrassed. One corner of Hale's mouth ticked up in response.

"If it's not a horse, what is it?" I directed my words to Hale, seeing as he seemed to be more likely to answer me honestly.

Both of my companions offered only silence in response. Thankfully whatever was making the insanely awful noise also chose to remain silent.

We came to the section of road which had slowed our progress so drastically. The hull of the tram barely fit between the mountainous wall of boulders on our right and the gaping hole where asphalt and concrete had once been on the left. The fiberglass carriage rocked back and forth as the rubber wheels gingerly negotiated the ruined ground. Rocks slid again, this time not only from the wall on the right but also tumbling down the slope to the lake bed below.

From what I could see peeking around the bend ahead, this bad patch ran for about a hundred yards. Hale and Roe flanked me on either side, Jude close on our heels. Unspoken instructions had us inching closer to the rock wall. As much as the idea of being smooshed along the rocks was unappealing, a fall from here over the edge would not end well. Minton must be delicately coaxing the horses to keep on the narrow passable portions. Luc was making similar adjustments behind us.

The incessant moaning of the wind intensified, and the air was pushed around us with a force I could not comprehend. The cloud thickened and ran like a wave over us. Shrieking the likes of which I'd never heard accompanied the physical push of air. Instinct had me throwing my palms against my ears, sure my tympanic membranes would rupture at the assault. The world was the screaming. All else ceased to exist. Hands covered my own, and I looked up to find Roe's frantic eyes searching all around us. Hale stood quiet and alert, scanning the surrounding area, poised to fight off our unseen assailant. Only a look of slight discomfort marred his face. The pressure lifted, and once again the afternoon was deathly silent. The silence was perhaps even more unnerving than the howling. I couldn't take this much longer, and a small sob escaped from my throat.

From behind, in what might have been answer to the push of sound, I heard firecrackers. Why would there be firecrackers? Hale grabbed my wrist, and Roe came up close as well, forming a Belstrohm brothers wall around me. I couldn't see past their shoulders. The protective stance made me realize it wasn't firecrackers I'd heard but muffled explosions. Another louder and closer than the last echoed off the rock around us. Someone must have been behind us on the road. My mind flashed back to the ragged man—his teeth buried deep in Hale's arm. Then Jude was there, pushing us forward and speaking urgently to all three of us.

"Now listen carefully." His deep calm voice filled the void. "By my measure, this last stretch should take about an hour, maybe two, at our current pace. We *don't* want to be out here for another hour and certainly not two. Any moment now, Asher is going to give the signal, and we are going to step it up. It is going to be quick. I expect you three to stay together. Luc will keep those horses behind us, but he's also going to want to be moving at a good clip."

My stomach twisted, threatening to bring my meager lunch up. He was telling us we would need to run. It wouldn't be a problem for either Roe or Hale. They were both athletic and strong. Long legged and sure footed. For me though? Oh, this was not going to be pleasant.

"Can't I just hop into one of the trams?" I was not beyond pleading. "I'm not made for running."

"Afraid not. It's still too risky." I could tell he didn't want to waste time with this conversation, but he sighed and added, "The road isn't any better up ahead, and the masters will need to make some quick decisions. Can't have our most valuable commodities falling out of the back."

Hale had a look of disgust on his face as he stared at Jude. Clearly my lack of physical ability was another thing he found unpleasant about me. Well, screw him then.

Roe nodded and tried to look reassuring. It didn't help.

"You've got this, Auri-Girl," Jude said. "I'll be right behind you trying to keep an eye on things."

He'd barely closed his mouth when a sharp whistle sounded up ahead. It was answered by the groaning wind from the shrouded wasteland below us. It took only a moment for Minton's tram to pick up the pace. Hale, Roe, and I followed suit, attempting to keep the gap between us to a bare minimum. The road really was no better, and the boxes, crates, and instruments in the rig's hull shifted and jostled as the tires bounced over the degrading asphalt. Before long, I was jumping between rocks and potholes, trying and failing to keep my tempo at a brisk jog while also attempting to keep my heart from beating out of my chest.

"Quicker now," Jude called from over my shoulder. How was he not even out of breath?

I turned to look and caught sight of Luc struggling with his reins. Clearly the horses wanted to move at a pace which exceeded the capacity my short human legs could provide. The glance cost me; I tripped and nearly went sprawling but managed—barely—to stay upright. My glasses slipped down the slope of my nose and bounced there until I could shove them back in place.

"Don't look around, just keep moving," Hale chided me.

I didn't have enough oxygen in my lungs to form a reply, and still they wanted me to go faster. I thought I had been getting stronger, the days of endless walking conditioning my muscles. I was wrong. Walking was not running. I was tired, sore, and sleep deprived and had been on my feet for ages. I had blisters on top of blisters, and *still* they wanted me to go faster.

I didn't think it was possible, but the dust fog grew thicker, obscuring the visibility to nearly nothing. I could only just make out the wheels ten yards in front of my face.

The sighing groan surrounded us and grew in swells. Worse, the screaming started again in earnest. I was going to die out here. Whatever demons or wraiths or ghosts inhabited this ghastly place did not welcome our presence. They were going to rise up and snatch us from the road.

I was terrified my legs would give out and I would freeze up right there on the ruined asphalt. The terror, however, drove my body—adrenaline flooding my system. Somehow my arms were able to pump faster, urging my legs to sprint as well. I held the pace for what felt like hours, scalpel blades tearing through my burning lungs with every breath I heaved in. I wouldn't be able to keep it up much longer. I was slowing when a firm hand touched my lower back, urging me, pushing me to keep moving.

Hale had clipped his long, graceful strides to keep time with my much shorter legs. "Just a little farther, Aurelia."

It became my mantra. *Just a little farther. Just a little farther. Just a little farther.*

I could feel the horses behind us, wanting to break loose and run faster. Could sense Luc struggling to keep them in check. Could hear the clanking and jangling of jars and instruments bouncing around the carriage hull and the footfalls and even breathing of Jude just behind me. The screaming rose in crescendo, and then, when I couldn't push forward one more step . . . when my tattered lungs couldn't drag in one more breath . . . couldn't imagine this ever ending . . . the cloud around us dissipated. It was like a curtain had been drawn back, and suddenly I could see the road ahead, along with the small settlement in the near distance.

The entire train of carriages drew slowly to a stop, Medicus practitioners, escorts, and horses slowly forming a clump. I struggled to stay upright and drew great gasping breaths of clear air into my chest. I bent over, planting my hands on my knees, and vomited in the powdery remains of the road.

Roe clapped a hand on my shoulder in reassurance or sympathy. I wasn't sure which. When I finally stood, hands on the back of my head to expand my chest further, I looked for Hale to thank him. He'd stayed with me and helped push me forward. When my eyes finally found him, all I saw was his back as he walked away.

12

ROE

Clearly the weird little settlement had once been some sort of military installment. Uniform lumps of earth stretched in every direction, a series of building blocks toppled on their sides, creating an interesting geometric pattern in the otherwise flat desert landscape. I didn't know or care what had once been housed in those bunkers, just as I didn't know or care why anyone would choose to still eek out an existence in the shabby little settlement—situated as it was just a stone's throw from the horrid dry lake bed.

I'd collapsed into my bedroll as soon as we'd camped, pausing only long enough to make sure everyone—Aurelia most particularly—was unharmed after our little sprint through hell.

Jake had insisted the moaning and screeching we'd heard were merely the wind and the calls of desert condors. The muffled sound of explosions he wasn't as clear about, but he suggested it was nothing to be overly concerned over. This certainly didn't jibe with Asher's urgent call to essentially have us run for our lives. Nor did it explain the haunted look Geneva still had on her grave face.

"I suppose I might never know what resides on that dry expanse of land, but if I ever travel back to Renfield, I'll find another route. Even if it takes me six months out of my way." I'd overheard Wade talking to Helena as she snuggled into her bedroll. I didn't disagree with him at all.

Over breakfast, Hale and I were comparing notes on our stiff and sore muscles. Wade, Phoebe, and Helena also didn't look so hot, but Aurelia seemed worst off. I winced as I took her in, lowering herself to the ground. Every bit of her petite frame shouted an expression of pain. Her lovely hazel eyes glossed over with tears as she gingerly stretched her legs out in front of her.

"You get *any* sleep last night, Shrimpboat?" I asked.

"More than I expected. The trick is to not move." She didn't take the bait; instead, she smiled weakly at me and then asked no one in particular, "Do we know the plan for today?"

Phoebe answered for all of us. "Asher asked us to go through the med supplies and take a quick inventory. I think he really wants to know about the glass vials and jars to see if there was much damage to the stores yesterday. We should also look at the equipment—our microscopes and stuff—to see if anything needs to be repaired."

"We should look at everything we can. I want to inspect the autoclave, and if any supplies have been taken, we might get a better idea of what needs to be replaced." Count on Wade to be both pragmatic and pessimistic at the same time.

Phoebe nodded. "At least one or two of us will need to set up the tent for med checks on the settlers. See if anyone needs anything. I don't know when they last had a team come through."

Helena cocked her head. "They don't have their own practitioner here?"

"Nope. Not enough people to make it worth Medicus's time or money, I guess."

"Thank all that is good and holy. Can you imagine being matched to this place? I think I'd rather gnaw off my own arm."

"I'll do it," Hale said.

"Gnaw off Helena's arm?" I asked.

"Take the tent, smartass. I can't stand poring through Asher's manifests."

I looked at Auri. "You want to go with him? You don't look like you're in the mood for repeated squats while we look in the cartons."

She closed her eyes, tilted her head back, and groaned.

"I'll take that as a yes."

"Fine. Fine. I'll help Hale with the locals. But if any of them are possessed by the spirits of the lake, I will never forgive you."

"Just keep any comments about their hygiene to yourself," Hale added. His tone was so flat, even I wasn't sure whether it was meant as a joke.

13

AURELIA

It wasn't just the building next to our tent which was in shambles, it was the entire settlement. Many of the places we'd stopped had been run down. But this? This was something else entirely. Old hunks of metal rusted on the roads. Many of the dilapidated buildings were crumbling. Dirt and dust were layered on the surfaces, obscuring any paint which might have once been present. And it smelled. Like musty wool and tired dreams.

Just like the settlement, the woman before me might once have been pretty. It was hard to say. Either way, what remained was a malnourished, unkempt shell of a person. The left side of her face held a conglomeration of bruises—one overlapping another in a vivid kaleidoscope of green and black and plum. Her hair was lank and dirty, matted together in spots.

She cast her eyes downward, not wanting to meet my gaze as I asked her about the most obvious concern.

Her right shoulder sat noticeably lower than its counterpart. Any movement of her right arm, or even her hand, brought a grimace of pain to her face—the only sign of emotion I'd seen from her.

I'd run my hands over her clavicles to make sure they weren't broken, and I couldn't palpate any other clear fractures of the long bones. I was certain from both her posture and my exam that her shoulder had been dislocated.

"Well," the thick meaty voice said. "You gonna fix it?"

The woman—Tif she was called—flinched just a bit.

"Yes. We can fix it, but it would help to know how long it's been this way and how the injury occurred."

They had both been less than forthcoming with the details.

"Don't much make a dif'rence what happened." His voice was as greasy as his balding scalp and the stains on his shirt.

I looked at him steadily, assessing how best to proceed.

"I fell," Tif whispered. "I just fell."

So we would play it this way. I knew better than to argue with her. "I see. Well, it's dislocated for sure. It can be popped back in, but it's going to hurt when we do it. I'll give you some tablets for the pain afterward. They won't do much good beforehand."

She finally raised her face to look at me. Her eyes were so sad and so tired, it was tough to tell if she was also scared of the pain to come.

"And then you're going to need to take it easy for a few days." I looked pointedly at the human filth standing behind her and called through the opening of the tent, "Hale? Can you assist us please?"

Tif's husband? Boyfriend? Owner? took one look at Hale and shook his head. "Nope. He's not touching her."

"I'm sorry? What do you mean?" I asked.

"He's not touching her. You can do it." He crossed his arms and jutted his chin in my direction.

Hale stood at the entrance, legs slightly apart and arms also crossed—an answer to the other man's posture. He didn't say a word. Of course this would be the guy. In general, if someone was unhappy with the practitioner, it was the other way around. They wanted Roe or Hale or Wade to tend to them, not someone who looked like she could be their adolescent daughter.

"I assure you, Practitioner Belstrohm is a complete professional, and for a procedure of this nature, his strength will mean the difference between a quick fix or a longer more uncomfortable one. Although I *could,* I *will not* do it on my own."

He opened his mouth to argue, but I didn't give him the opportunity.

"I'm afraid"—my voice rising—"you have no say in this. I'm sure that's difficult for you to grasp, but I suggest you keep quiet or you can leave."

If it was possible to slam a tent flap, he did as he grunted and stormed outside.

I placed my hands soothingly on Tif's shoulder again. She shuddered at my touch, finally worried about what was to come.

"It's going to be all right. It'll be over before you know it."

I had no need to explain to Hale what had happened. He might have heard our discussion from his place outside the tent, but even if he hadn't, the injury was obvious enough. I stepped out of his way as he took a place at Tif's side.

"Hi there. My name's Hale. We're going to get you all fixed up." His voice was tranquil, reassuring. Brimming with confidence and warmth. So unlike the person I interacted with every day. "It's best if you try to relax. I know that sounds ridiculous, but it will help the muscles loosen. They want to go back where they belong. They just need to be coaxed a little into doing it."

Tif's haggard face remained tight and pinched, and her posture stayed huddled, trying to protect her damaged arm.

"Look at me, Tif." Her eyes darted away from Hale and toward my voice, but they didn't linger. Immediately her gaze jetted back to him, wary he would move when she wasn't looking. "He isn't going to do anything until you're ready."

For whatever reason, she seemed to trust me. Her eyes found mine again.

"Good. Let's just sit for a minute. Talk." She still didn't relax, so I continued. "Is it all right with you if I hold your hand?"

She nodded. I picked up her left hand in both of mine, ignoring the filth embedded beneath the broken and jagged nails.

As usual, she picked one of the three physical traits most people noted about me. "Your eyes are amazing."

I smiled slightly and to keep her focused on me explained, "I'm not sure if I believe it, but my mom always said my eyes were how I got my name."

She looked baffled, so I continued. "You see, most babies are born with their eyes squinched shut tight and when they do first open them, most newborns have a sort of grayish brownish nondescript color to the irises. But according to my mom, I was born with my eyes wide open and the color like it is now. I say they're hazel, but well, you can obviously see there's a little bit of brown, a little bit of green, and then the golden flecks. Aurelia means gold and so. . ." I gestured to my face with a slight slanted smile.

"Huh." Hale cleared his throat and said with a bit of surprise, "I never knew that."

"You never asked," I said merrily and turned my attention back to Tif. "How do you like living out here? It seems like a peaceful place." It was in fact anything but peaceful. It was horrid and desolate and depressing. I had no idea how anyone could live in a place like this. Part of me thought what folks like Tif were doing *wasn't* really living, but I couldn't very well say so.

Her voice was small and timid. "It's all I know, so. . ."

"You've lived here your entire life?"

"I was born out in one of the bunker shacks." *Bunker shack?* What was a bunker shack?

"Oh? That sounds interesting. What's your favorite thing about the settlement?" I coaxed. Hale looked over her head and gave me a look I couldn't interpret.

"I dunno. Not much good to talk about." Her eyes drifted back to Hale, whose face had regained its placid neutrality. He sat patiently at her side, still one hand on her shoulder, the other on her arm just above the elbow. He hadn't moved them to prod or tug, just had them sitting there, allowing her to feel the warmth and weight of his touch.

"Tif? Look at me," I gently reminded her. "What about that awful dry lake bed? What's it like to live so close to it?"

She shuddered, grimacing with the movement. "Don't like it, but what can you do?"

"You all just stay away from it then?"

"Oh, the stupid kids dare each other to go out to the edge. Or if they're really thick, out into it. They always run home needing to change their shorts, though. Never met anybody who really went out across it or anything."

"Have *you* been out to the edge?"

"No," she said quickly. "The sounds that come from it, the crying and the screaming. . . Some say it's just the desert wind over the dry scales of earth, but I know different. This place? It used to hold all sorts of weapons and things. Way, way back. Those weapons must have made monsters of the people who used them. It's their ghosts or demons out there." She closed her eyes for a blink, and I nodded to Hale. "I think. . ."

She never got to say what she thought about the haunting voices from the lake bed. Instead, a strangled cry escaped her lips. Hale firmly pulled down on her upper arm and used his upper body strength to rotate her arm in a smooth arc to the side and above her head, which popped her shoulder back into the socket where it belonged. His exhale mixed with her whimpers. Tif's face had gone even paler, and a fine layer of sweat coated her forehead, the combination bringing the grime on her face into sharper relief.

I rubbed her other arm, trying to provide a small measure of comfort. In response, she cast a look my direction which was equal parts relief and accusation.

"It's easier if you don't know when it's coming," I said by way of apology.

Hale caught my attention, and his eyes asked a wordless question. *All good?* It reminded me of Roe, and I had to contain a smile. I nodded, and he unfolded himself from the stool he'd been perched on. Before he could make it to the door, Tif blurted, "Thank you!" More shyly, "For fixing my arm."

"No thanks necessary. It's our job." He offered the briefest of smiles.

I realized then the effect Hale's smile could have on a person. It changed his whole face. Even though he was just as handsome as Roe, it was harder to appreciate because he always looked so stoic. Looking from him to the pale and sweaty face of Tif, I knew she didn't stand a chance against the slight upturn of his lips.

Darting her gaze around quickly, like an animal hunted, she opened her mouth and closed it again. I registered a set of slightly crooked but otherwise well cared for teeth. Yes, she might have been pretty once. Before this place and that man had sucked it from her. She tried again. "I . . . I dint' fall," she finally managed.

I kept her hand in mine as Hale looked her in the eye, no judgment, simply a man trying his best to understand and to help. He was giving her a gift, a quiet strength. "I didn't believe that you had."

She looked down, and silent tears slid from under her lashes. Hale's jaw tightened, his mouth stretching into a tight straight line.

"You don't have to stay with him." My voice was also quiet in the small space.

"Don't I?" Her eyes were so hopeless. It was as if admitting to us what her life was really like was a relief, while knowing the relief wouldn't last. "There's nowhere to go. I got no family left here now. He's all I got."

I hadn't learned his name. Neither he nor Tif offered it when they'd shown up at the clinic tent an hour earlier, and I realized I didn't want to know it. It wasn't worth the space in my brain.

"I don't love him or anything," she added quickly, as if we would judge her if she did. "But it's tough here and it'd be tougher. Even than this"—she took her hand from mine and gestured at her face and damaged shoulder—"if I was alone. The desert isn't a kind place, for nobody, but especially not for a woman like me on her own."

"No. I don't suppose it is." I glanced at Hale standing by the flap and could feel the anger radiating from him. Dark pulses of it filled the arid air. "Even if you did though—love him, I mean—it wouldn't make what he'd done to you right."

"I know, but it does make it easier. If I loved him, I'd hate myself as much as I hate him. And who knows, maybe it won't happen again. Maybe it's outta his system."

"Maybe. But you don't really believe that, do you?"

She shrugged and winced a smidge at the motion. Hale excused himself and slipped out of the tent, giving me time to finish up.

I placed Tif's arm in a sling and gave her some tablets for pain and instructions to help the soft tissues heal over the coming days. I asked her permission to have a clergy member or a settlement leader check in on her after we left, but it probably wouldn't do much good. People here had to know what was happening, and no one had stepped in yet to help this poor young woman.

I saw a handful of other patients through the course of the afternoon, Hale doing the same on the other side of the tent. We handed out advice and medications in equal measure. The settlement, while eerie and odd, seemed to have the same mixture of gastritis, bloody noses, chlamydia, and asthma as any other place we'd been through. Sometimes I could give definitive treatment and sometimes I could only offer advice, education, or counseling. In those instances, I had to rely on the patient's willingness to take ownership of their own health and welfare. I knew, even this early in my career, this was often an uphill battle.

Late in the afternoon, after seeing a young man with what sounded like pneumonia, I wondered what it must have been like in the golden age of medicine, when "doctors" had a treasure trove of diagnostic tools and medications at their disposal. Imaging machines capable of showing detailed pictures of the insides of patients within minutes and pharmacies full of treatments to be given just as fast. It must have been glorious.

After we finished with all of the visits, we still had to wrap up all of the documentation of what we'd done. Every time the day was drawing to a close, and I still sat with a pile of forms in front of me, I vowed I'd be better about writing out my notes as I completed each patient. Maybe one day, I'd actually get the charting done in a reasonable time.

It was only after we'd finished up and Hale was pulling his stethoscope off to pack in his kit that I noticed the raw red scrapes over the knuckles on his right hand. He observed me observing him and shrugged. "He had it coming."

I gaped.

"What?" he asked. "Someone needed to do it."

"But. . ." I couldn't actually think of anything to say, how to voice what I felt without sounding shrew-like.

Hale kept packing his things, not looking at me. "Don't give me the whole professional detachment thing. I know you wanted to do the same thing."

"Maybe I did," I grumbled. "You were really great with her, you know. I think it meant a lot to her. To have you be so calm. So nonjudgmental."

"I guess Roe isn't the only one in the family who can hide his true nature when it suits him."

What was that supposed to mean?

"I shouldn't have said that." His voice was clipped. "What exactly is your point, Aurelia?"

I sighed. Why did everything have to be a fight with him? He was kind enough to Tif. Cared enough for his patient he thought it necessary to bloody up her abuser.

"You're right. I would have done worse if I thought it would solve anything. But it won't and. . ." I couldn't voice what I was afraid it might mean for Tif. "What about your hands? What if you had fractured a finger? Just because your forearm has been healing up nicely doesn't mean you're invincible."

He paused, and I could tell he was thinking about what I said. "Come on. Let's get back."

We exited the tent, and I inhaled a full breath of hot dry air. Even the wind tasted of dust and grit.

"Should we take it apart?" I asked, motioning to the flapping canvas behind us.

"No, Luc should be along soon to pack it up and stow it for the night." He tilted his head toward a group of men across the road, and I flicked a glance in their direction. "Let's keep moving, shall we?"

Three of them were standing there. Crusty, scruffy, desert rats. I thought I recognized the scrap of red and white cloth tied to the smallest one's head. It could have been a coincidence, but I noted the clothing on the other two just in case. The tallest was dressed in soiled green pants and a shirt which might have been white at one time. The other in jeans and an orange sleeveless vest. I didn't like the way they watched us as we moved down the road. I liked the wine red paint covering the left half of each of their faces even less.

Night settled over us again. It was simultaneously a welcome reprieve from the sun and a threatening, treacherous entity. Even the lights powered by the solar batteries could only reach so far into the darkness, providing a tiny globe of visibility around our camped trams and tents. The moon, which had been a thin sliver in the pale blue sky earlier that afternoon, now perched just above the western horizon—a fat yellow crescent like a disembodied toenail.

While Hale and I had been providing our services to the locals, the miracle wagon had caught us up and was now parked not two hundred yards from our camp.

"For the love of. . ." Hale didn't continue. He didn't need to. I think we all felt the same way.

Asher and Geneva were nowhere to be seen, but both Jude and Jake looked as if they would rather not have visitors camped so near. The tram masters had dinner laid out, a heaping pile of hot baked potatoes with warmed canned vegetables and chunks of hard cheese.

Helena, Phoebe, and Wade sat around the camp stoves, plates perched in their laps. I didn't see Roe anywhere, so I fixed myself a plate and sat in the open space to Helena's right. My muscles still ached as I settled in. Phoebe chatted quietly with her best friend, and Helena made attempts to respond, dragging her lips into the semblance of a smile at appropriate times. She had the same downcast expression she'd worn since we left Lita and Jonaten's home. My face might have held a similar one.

Rather than join us, Hale took his plate and stood near Jake, not talking, just taking up space in the silence.

"When did they get here?" I jutted my chin in the direction of the top-heavy wagon. Phoebe's face immediately turned from sunny to wary.

"An hour or so ago."

"Creeps," Wade added. He was letting his beard grow as we traveled. It made him look much older. It would probably serve him well at his new location. The people there might take him more seriously because of it.

"I thought the idea was for us to get ahead of them."

"I think it was. Maybe Asher's trying to figure it out now. He really didn't want them close on the road around the dry lake, but now he's concerned if we travel too closely together, the settlers from here to Devil's Meadows will think they're somehow affiliated with us. Medicus doesn't want to be associated with that sort of thing."

"But how did they catch up? They must have flown around the lake bed. They were nowhere in sight when we pulled in last night." Even though their wagon looked slow and cumbersome, maybe they had moved quickly today. As I pondered it, another thought occurred. Surely they didn't cross through the fog on the surface of the lake bed itself. The thought sent a cold shiver through me.

I was still thinking about it when Helena asked Wade, "Why don't we just wait them out? Let them get far enough ahead and we won't have to worry about it every time we stop."

"It's probably the plan. Roe told us he was going with Asher and Geneva to chat with them about their travel itinerary. I'm curious to see if they'll actually get any information though."

It explained his absence. Despite the ugly encounter the other day, Roe probably thought his charm would help make discussions easier. It was a gift really; he could talk to just about anyone and was so disarming, he could convince them to do things they had never considered before.

"Any good cases today?" Phoebe asked.

My mind flashed to Tif's downcast eyes, Hale's bloody knuckles, and the man who had been responsible for both. "Not anything worth talking about."

I picked at my potato, my appetite a fraction of what it had been. I was meant to spend years of my life as a Medicus Corpus practitioner. I had taken an oath dedicating myself to care for all who needed my particular knowledge and services. Yet here I was— not a month into my official service—and already I was flagging. My experience with Jonaten and Lita had struck a deep slice to my core, knowing about the cluster of similar children had widened the slice to a gash, and just when I thought I would be able to start mending that spot on my soul, Tif and her wretched story opened the wound. I wasn't naïve enough to think Hale's reaction would change anything. It was for his own benefit, lashing out in a way that could make it feel like he was addressing the issue. I didn't have the courage to share with him my biggest fear, that it would spark such anger in the man that he might take it out on Tif in a more drastic way. Push him to do something truly monstrous. I had no idea if it would, but even if it stopped the abuse for a day, a week, or even a month, there would always be other women. Other children. Perhaps even other men who would be treated in the same abominable way. Where was the medicine for that type of illness?

So the question remained. If I was already struggling under the weight of what I'd seen in the past few days, how would I bear it for a lifetime? Only time would answer the question, I supposed. Just then, all I wanted was for sleep to slam me into a place where the past handful of days would be removed from my conscious thought.

"I'm done in, guys. I'll see you in the morning." I rose and took my plate to where Minton and Hera were cleaning up. I smiled gratefully at Minton's weathered face, all too aware of how wonderfully they took care of us on the road. They allowed me to scrub up my own dishes and place them back in the crate to be used again in the morning. Then I was off to wash up. I fell into my bedroll before the water had fully dried on my face.

Some minutes later, I sensed a few of the others claiming their spaces around me, but I didn't bother to open my eyes to see who it was.

It felt like only moments had passed when loud voices cracked through my dreamless sleep, but the weak grey light of dawn was already upon us.

"What do you mean? How can no one know where he is?" Hale had an incredulous urgency in his tone.

Don't know where who is? Sensing it might be important, I rubbed sleep from my eyes and hauled myself up.

"Unfortunately, Doc, exactly what it sounds like," Asher growled at him. "He's your brother. Any thoughts on where he may have gone?"

"Shit, Asher. No. This isn't like him. Not at all."

They couldn't mean Roe. Roe was missing?

I searched blindly trying to locate my glasses. I always slept with them beside my head, knowing I couldn't function without them on my face. My fingers fumbled them on, and I stood, stumbling over my bedroll as I raced out of the tent. Surely there must be some mistake. Roe never would have slipped away without notifying someone. Not even for a few minutes, and certainly not for an entire night.

I hadn't heard him during the night. More often than I would prefer, I slept lightly and was aware of every snore and movement in our shared sleeping space. I knew the noises Roe and Hale made, as they were the two I slept closest to, but even Helena and Phoebe had kept me from deep sleep on more than one occasion. But yesterday, I was beaten down exhausted, and I had slept like the dead last night.

I must have *looked* like the dead as I stumbled over to them. The looks on Hale's and Asher's faces told me as much.

"How about you, Doc?" Asher directed at me. "Do you have any idea where your buddy might have wandered off to?"

My mind reeled. Where would he be? Where *could* he be? I'd seen a chunk of the settlement the day before and a good number of its residents as well. Nothing in this place would tempt him to stay out all night. No taverns or entertainment houses. No beautiful hiking trails or hot springs. Not even a brothel like I'd heard we might encounter. Even if there was. . . No, Roe would never visit one of those. It wasn't in his nature to wander, even if he needed air or space. If he needed a moment or two alone, he would have told Hale at the very least.

A large black bird flew overhead, pale powdery dust coating its wings. It settled onto a nearby wooden post, a long brown-grey lizard tail dangling from the side of its beak. I couldn't look away as it cocked its head to the side, studying me with its small beady eyes. In one swift motion, it threw its head back, opening its bladelike beak, and the tail disappeared into its craw.

"Doc?" Asher prodded.

"Sorry. No. I have no idea. Roe would never wander or intentionally disappear. Does anyone know how long he's been gone?"

Asher ignored my question and instead asked one of his own. "No spat or argument between the two of you?"

"What?" My mind was still foggy from sleep.

"Nothing come between you and Roe?" I almost didn't notice he'd used Roe's given name as he looked pointedly from me to Hale and back again. "Nothing that might have upset him or set him off?"

"For shit's sake." Hale sighed.

Understanding bloomed in my mind. "No," I replied emphatically. "Nothing like that. Roe and I are just friends and Hale and I are. . ." What were we exactly? I couldn't say friends, but we were more than acquaintances. "Colleagues. Nothing more."

I swear, if I didn't know better, I would have thought hurt flashed across his face.

Asher nodded and ran a hand over his shortly cropped hair.

"I still don't understand, and you didn't answer my question. How long has he been missing? He went with you last night on your diplomatic mission, then what? Did anyone see him leave after you returned?"

Geneva's face was troubled when she looked at me. "What diplomatic mission?"

"When you went to talk to Hollis. Roe went with you. Right?"

"We never went to talk to Hollis or anyone else in his camp. Why would you think we did?"

"But I thought—"

"Are you telling me Roe left here to have a chat with that bunch of trash?" Geneva sighed. "If that's the case and none of you spoke with him last night, the answer to your question is he's been missing for a little over eight hours now."

The air was knocked from me as I processed that. Eight hours was a long time. He never would have intentionally stayed out away from camp overnight.

Hale's eyes held a dark mix of misery and anger.

"Geneva and I had other business yesterday afternoon. It had nothing to do with the miracle folks. We had no intention of making contact with the occupants of that wagon again," Asher said.

He was in motion before I could even collect my thoughts. We would be packing up soon, but without a direction to go, I wasn't sure how we could.

"All right. Jake, you're with me. Jude, keep on eye on things here. Start getting everyone packed up. *No one*—and I mean not a soul—leaves your sight. We all clear on that?"

Jude nodded, no sign of his normal infectious smile.

"Wait, Asher!" Something had been tickling my brain, and I finally latched on it.

He gave me an impatient sigh.

"It's important, I think. Last night, near the tent, there were men with wine stains, you know"—I gestured to my cheek—"paint on their faces."

He looked at me blankly.

"Like the guy who bit Hale. They had the same maroon paint on their faces. They could have done something to Roe."

He placed both of his hands on the back of his neck and groaned while he looked up at the sky. "Yeah. I know. We saw them too. I'm not sure if it really changes much. We'll check the settlement after we chat with the miracle man."

Asher was already leaving when Minton jogged over to us. "Hey boss. You'll be wanting to look at this."

He shoved a scrap of paper into Asher's hand. His chestnut eyes scanned whatever was written there. His brows drew together, and the corners of his mouth turned down in hard lines. He studied it a moment more, tension building in his shoulders.

He looked up, and his gaze caught first on Hale before he turned his hard eyes on me.

"It appears we have a bit of a problem."

Only then did I notice the red and gold wagon which had been camped so near to us last night was nowhere to be seen.

14

ROE

Inventory was done. Surprisingly, the damage was relatively minimal. One box held the shattered remains of a set of glass slides, but those would be easy enough to replace. A few vials of lidocaine had been destroyed, and a jar of anise oil would need to be pitched as the base was cracked and the lid missing entirely. A shivering itch passed over me looking at it. I guess one less person would be getting treated for scabies. One of the water barrels had also cracked, resulting in a puddle but no real damage. We had plenty to last us the remainder of the trip. We'd also banged up the microscopes and autoclaves a fair amount, but Wade was a savvy technician and would be able to fix them up in no time. We carried spare parts with us for just such an occasion.

We transferred all the broken bits into a pile and reorganized the rest, once again placing the most valuable meds and equipment further back in the trams. If someone wanted to steal things within easy reach, let them have the box of anal speculums.

My back was tight and achy by the time we finished, and I thought again how glad I was Aurelia had elected to go with Hale. We were all worn from the journey, and I knew Auri wouldn't complain, but we still had so far to go. I wanted her—*needed her*—to be content, even though I was concerned she might never be happy. She was my best friend and had stuck by me all these years. It was the least I could do to make things as easy for her as possible. We would get through the rest of it by sticking together.

Loud splashing and quiet laughter drew my attention. Phoebe was using a pail and cloth to clean the sweat and grime from her face. No matter how we tried, none of us could keep the desert sand and silt from caking on every exposed—or at times unexposed—surface. My ears might never be clean again. Wade and Helena sat near her, Wade already tinkering with one of the microscopes—removing the lenses and inspecting them for cracks.

The three of them took turns describing the most inappropriate patient encounters they'd ever had. This ranged from a woman hiding food on her person only to find it rotting a week later to ridiculous attempts at flirtation to a verbally abusive patient who didn't get the medication they requested.

I looked up at a sky so pale and sun bleached it was more off white than blue. A thin sliver of moon hung toward the east, barely visible but there. It would set shortly after dusk, making for an intensely dark night.

I wondered how dark the nights would be in Devil's Meadows. Would they utilize solar power to keep the buildings lit as they'd once been or would we be bathed in light only from the stars and moon? We really knew so little of the place we would be calling home. Despite our questions, Geneva and Asher said relatively little about the settlement they'd lived in for their entire lives. They did at least try to reassure all three of us that the inhabitants there would welcome us, that the current practitioners there were all respected and comfortable. Still I had my reservations. Could we—*could I*—really be myself around strangers? Who knew? I suppose it was best not to think on it too much. What would be would be.

I was pulled from my thoughts by the high-pitched chiming of tiny bells. Really? They were still dogging our every move? At least this settled area was wide open and flat as it ran from the edge of the desolate lake bed to the towering mauve and toasted caramel mountains in the distance. It provided more than ample space for the lumbering wagon to pass by and keep moving. They could camp out toward the far side of what had once been a town and still be within the ring of the oddly geometric lumps of concrete and earth surrounding us.

It was likely this realization that made my temper flare so brightly when instead of moving on, they elected to rein in the horses and stop their wagon just two hundred yards from our own camp.

"What in all of burning hell?" I muttered to no one in particular.

Surely Asher or Jake would take notice and politely—or maybe not so politely—ask them to move on and give us our space. Unfortunately, both Asher and Geneva were not to be found. When I approached Jake to gain his insight, he informed me the two had been called away to deal with some issue with the settlement leader. He suggested I ignore the garish red and mustard wagon—at least for the time being.

I tried to take his advice. I really did. I fetched one of my packs and pulled a book from the top of the stack. Not a medical journal or textbook, but an old volume of ancient adventure stories.

Typically when I needed a break or distraction, the thick tome was just the trick. It was a collection of rewritten mythologies spanning thousands of years. I could immerse myself in trolls, gods, forbidden love, and bloodsucking creatures of the night. I was enamored by the fantastic imagery composing the tales of glory and death, vengeance, and the occasional rebirth from the ashes.

I thumbed to one of my favorites. Normally the tale recounting a drake and its hoarded treasure could take my mind to a distant place within moments of my eyes hitting the words, but blissful distraction eluded me. Instead of piles of gold and jewels, my mind continued to conjure the image of Hollis calling out to Aurelia, making her feel like a failure. After no less than three attempts at reading the same page, I snapped the book shut and threw it on top of my bag.

Hale and Goldie-Locks had yet to return from the day's clinic, and still there was no sign of Asher or Geneva. Hera was starting dinner prep, Luc was reshoeing a horse, and Minton was busy cleaning and stabilizing the solar panels that had been banged up the previous day. I had no interest in comparing healthcare horror stories with my colleagues, so I decided to take a little walk.

"I think the escorts went to chat with our neighbors. I think I'll join them," I told Wade as I rounded the tent. It wasn't a lie exactly. I was sure Asher would speak to them, I simply didn't know when. He nodded and refocused his attention on Helena and her description of a rather disturbing foreign body she'd removed from a delicate place.

Small clouds of powdery earth rose to envelope my boots with every step. I kicked along, watching the dust motes in front of me. As the sun sank lower and lower, the rays transformed the drab particles to a wonderful smoky golden orange cloud around me. Sadly the effect didn't last long, and soon darkness fell. My nerves settled along with the daylight, and I came to my senses, deciding to leave the camp's security to the people getting paid for the job. Time to head back. With any luck, Auri and Hale would have returned.

"I'm told wandering in these parts alone in the dark is not wise." The rich buttery voice seemed to emerge from the night itself. As my eyes caught the shape approaching me, I realized it was Nanette. I'd never heard her speak before. Hollis always seemed to do all the talking. "I am also told you *practitioners* tend to fancy yourselves wise. So . . . it would appear one of these is not quite true."

"I don't claim to be a wise man, and it does appear danger has been following me in the dark."

She held my gaze, and a smile curved her lips. She threw her head back and laughed.

"I assure you, there are worse things than me out here. In fact, I don't believe I should be wandering alone in the desert myself. Care to walk me back to my accommodation?"

A loud sigh escaped me as I shoved my hands in my pockets. I caught myself and plastered on my most congenial expression. Maybe I could convince her to speak with her—whatever Hollis was to her—and they would move on rather than torment Aurelia further.

"Of course. I'd be more than pleased to walk you back." Honey. Not vinegar.

In the dimming light, a quiet triumph seemed to appear on her face.

Nanette didn't speak as we strolled toward both our camps. Instead, soft desert noises filled the air. Murmuring brushing drew my attention upward. A small brown bat swooped drunkenly, chasing night-flying insects attracted by our camp's ring of light.

Like the insects, I veered toward the glow from our trams' solar lights. I opened my mouth to inform the woman strolling beside me this was where we parted, but she placed a slim hand on my arm and said, "A little further if you please."

I began to protest, but she smirked. "I may be dangerous, but I promise not to bite."

Perhaps this worked on other men. Perhaps she was lonely. Perhaps she wanted something I certainly was not going to give. It didn't matter. If I was going to get on her good side, I could manage the additional two hundred yards to her wagon. I intended to use the time to my advantage.

"If we are going to continue our stroll, we may as well chat. I don't suppose I could convince you to ask your friend Hollis to lay off Aurelia."

She raised one elegant eyebrow in my direction, and I noted again how practiced and insincere the expression was.

"Why would I do that?" Her tone implied it was less a question and more a bit of string dangling for a feline's pleasure.

"Because whatever he thinks she is capable of, I can tell you, she is not."

"So you don't even know what it is he suspects, but you can verify it does not exist? That does not sound like a very convincing argument."

"I know Auri. Better than anyone. I know she did everything she could for Jonaten. She used every tool in her arsenal. She would do the same for any child. Aurelia is no wonder-worker. There *are* no miracles."

"No miracles?" she scoffed.

"None. Not from her or anyone else."

"So you deny the entire aspect of thaumaturgy. Not just your friend's ability to wield it."

"I do." When she didn't respond I continued. "We are scientists. We study the things we can see and touch. We don't put blind faith in some convenient nonsensical healing power."

We'd made it across the expanse of desert brush to within a few yards of her wagon. A candle lantern hung from the rear of the rig, and a cloud of steam and smoke laced with the spicy tang of cooking meat filled the air.

"You insult me so casually." She seemed more amused than offended.

"It's not meant as an insult to you. It's more of an explanation." I heard the footsteps behind me and turned as a puff of something smelling of burnt oleander hit my face. I swayed on my feet and toppled forward into dirt and darkness.

15

HALE

The paper in my hands shook with a tremulousness one did not want to see in the hands of a surgeon. I took a deep breath and with force of will drove a stillness into them. It was something I'd been working on, commanding calm when all I wanted to do was thrash and tear. It was necessary if I was going to muck about inside someone's body. It was necessary now.

Once they stilled, I read the words again.

We have your charming young practitioner. He has come to no harm at this time. Whether this will remain the case four days hence is up to the lovely young wonder-worker. You will find another communication at the crimson and white tower.

—H

"Four days? Why so long? Why not let us negotiate with them now?" Aurelia demanded.

"There's an old mining town four days from here. It used to be a settlement where the Medicus trams would stop, but the few inhabitants it had have since thought better and abandoned it. We aren't likely to run into any prying eyes there," Asher explained.

"And it sits up on a hill. Lots of old rundown places to hide. They'll be able to pick a spot that suits them," Geneva added.

The son of a bitch had taken my brother. And for what? Some hopeless plan to get at Aurelia? I suppose he thought he could force her into performing his so-called miracle. And when she couldn't, what then?

Then he'd hand over Roe or else he'd die.

16

AURELIA

The water tower was clearly a relic from days gone by. It sat at the far west side of the settlement and was so decrepit I couldn't imagine when it had last held water. A gaping ragged hole had eaten out the base of the container, red and white paint flaking from what once might have been a checkerboard pattern.

It was out of our way to go there, but only by an hour or so. Asher had reasoned the communication had been placed there to delay us just enough to give Hollis and his companions a slight time advantage over us on the road. Despite its appearance, their rig was obviously quicker than our train of carriages, but any time they could gain would serve them well. They would be able to choose a location where our escorts wouldn't be able to simply overpower them and retrieve Roe.

The old mining site was on the road to Devil's Meadows, so we wouldn't lose too much time, *if* we could make a quick exchange for whatever it was he thought I could give.

I walked with Geneva—Hale and Asher were up ahead of the first tram. The other practitioners currently rode in the last carriage, not eager to be delayed any more than the rest of us but just as concerned.

It wasn't yet midmorning and already the temperature was climbing. My shirt showed rings of sweat in white salted waves. Again I was amazed at how harsh and unforgiving the landscape became a scant few days from the farming communities surrounding the valley bowl of Renfield. I had been told it would continue to worsen the closer we got to our new home. How was that even possible, and how could we live there for the rest of our lives? Already it was as if some long ago celestial being had taken issue with the earth and carved a burning scar across the crust in retribution. Where the scar lay, the vegetation was shrunken and crusty, the landscape just a shade this side of barren.

The two men in front approached the tower. It was difficult for anyone to make Asher look small, but Hale did just that. He walked to the dilapidated tower legs, rust clinging in great ugly patches where water had dripped down eons ago. He reached out and removed a scrap of white paper, read it briefly, and handed the note to our escort. Both men looked grim as they headed toward Geneva and me.

"This doesn't bode well," I observed.

Geneva grunted in agreement.

In truth, Hale looked more than unhappy. He looked murderous. I tried to catch his eye, but he wouldn't even look at me. Instead, he stared down the road to the southeast as if he could see Roe out there somewhere, just beyond his reach.

"Well?" I couldn't take it any longer. "What does it say?"

Asher looked at the battered sheet in his hand and read, "*The young man is well. He is eager to rejoin his companions. Continue your journey as planned if you please. The radiant young woman is to meet me at the appointed time at a location which will be made known to you when we deem it prudent. We will willingly exchange your smart young practitioner for the wonder-worker.* Signed the same *–H.*"

I knew something along this line was likely to occur, but the knowledge did little to stop my current trembling. No wonder Hale was furious. He must have thought the team would refuse the demand. It didn't matter what the escorts decided, though. Roe was worth more to the world. I would make sure to be wherever I needed to be in four days' time.

"Does it say I have to go alone?"

Hale's eyes snapped to mine. *Now* it seemed he could look at me.

"Whatever it is you're thinking, don't." Again his tone was clipped.

I wasn't asking him. I tilted my head and looked at Asher. "Do I have to go by myself? For the exchange?"

"Aurelia." Hale's voice was icy, commanding. I'm sure he thought I would somehow screw things up and get his brother killed.

I willed my voice to be just as cold and calm. "I'm not asking you."

Asher sighed. "It does not. I read it exactly as it's written." I started to speak, but Asher held up his worn callused hand. "But that does *not* mean we won't get more specific instruction. It says they will leave some other communication indicating a specific location. There very well may be other stipulations."

"Maybe, but for now we plan on moving forward with the exchange. I'm not sure I feel comfortable dragging everyone along, but if you or Geneva will accompany me, I think it would be for the best. Somebody's got to make sure Roe is actually released and unharmed, and, well . . . you guys have the guns."

"And then what?" Hale spoke each word slowly, as if speaking to a child.

"And then I don't know. They realize they're all deluded? That I have no miracles and they were wrong? They keep me as a pet chained to the wall? I. Don't. Know."

"Or they kill you for spite." He flung the words at me.

"What do you want from me, Hale?" I shouted, my emotions finally running away from me. "We can't do nothing. Leaving him there isn't an option."

He didn't answer, just glared at me as if I were some poisonous plant.

"Everyone calm down. We still have time to figure this thing out. Standing here isn't going to solve anything, however." Asher looked to his wife. "All right, Gen, can you get everyone moving? I want as many in the trams as we can fit, see if we can speed the horses up a little. We need to make up some time if possible. Start running through options in your head. Ask Jake and Jude to do the same. We'll get together on it tonight when we make camp."

Geneva gave me what I assumed was meant to be a reassuring squeeze on the shoulder and stalked off to do as she had been asked.

Minton, Luc, and Hera had the trams moving as quickly as they could, with only the escorts and Hale taking turns outside on their feet, keeping a swift pace alongside.

I tried not to think about the implications of the note. Tried not to worry about Roe and what he might be experiencing in the hands of those lunatics.

Only one other person might understand how I was feeling, but even if I had wanted to commiserate with Hale, I couldn't. He didn't acknowledge me for the rest of the day.

17

ROE

Stars. I woke to the glittering expanse of thousands, if not millions, of stars. Interspersed among the glowing, luminous dots were other celestial bodies. I recognized some—Venus, Saturn, the nebula that looked like a stallion's head—but others were a mystery to me. I must have still been dreaming as they were much too vibrant and appeared much too intricate to be viewed in such detail by my naked eyes. Stranger still, when I moved my head, the area around me swam in and out of focus. As it did, I witnessed the moon shift and blur from one phase to the next as it crossed the sky. At first glance just the barest sliver appeared to my right, and then a transformation occurred. By the end of my visual arc, I was looking at a fat glowing full moon setting to my left.

Nausea overtook me, and I squeezed my eyes shut—the afterimage of that impossible moon glowing behind my lids. Bile rose in my throat, the metallic tang of saliva filling my mouth. I turned my head again to the side and retched.

The earth beneath me rocked and bumped, bringing a ferocious pounding to my head with each small movement. Not the earth, I realized. This ground was too smooth. The motion too unnatural. My mind conjured the image of a rolling cart, and I knew I must be inside some sort of transport. This wasn't the true night sky; it was only meant to represent it. The quality of the paint and the artist's hand combined with my addled mind to fool me.

"Try not to move about so much. The effects of the powder will lessen with time." Nanette's voice came from an impossible distance away. At least I thought it was Nanette.

Turning my head, I looked in the direction the voice came from but saw only the shadow of a bent figure, hunched and withered with age. I jerked back at the image and blinked. My eyes focused, and I found the same gorgeous woman I'd walked with to my doom sitting no more than eight feet away. Searing my throat, I exhaled a breath as fury rose from my stomach at the sight of her.

I must be in their wagon, but the proportions were all wrong. One minute I could see for what felt like miles, the next the walls were only steps away.

Not trusting my senses, I croaked to her, "Where am I?"

"Your are precisely where you are needed most." Her cryptic reply was no answer at all.

As I regained my faculties, I felt ties around my ankles and wrists. I gave a slight tug; although my hands were near my chest, a long tether ran several feet behind me. Tied to what, I didn't know. The fury intensified.

"And where *precisely* is that?" I snapped back, but the words were slurred and sluggish—not delivering the same punch I had intended.

"You are our guest, Roe. It is Roe, is it not?" She didn't wait for a reply. "You are traveling now with one of the greatest wonder-workers to have graced this earth in ages, and we are now plunging deeper into the desert."

The greatest wonder-worker in ages? Hollis was simultaneously deluded and arrogant. A dangerous combination.

"What did he do to me?" My voice was stronger but still slurred. "The powder. What was it?"

"A simple mixture really. Oleander, a bit of peyote, and a little secret ingredient I am not at liberty to disclose. Let's just call it magic. Just enough to make you a bit more . . . accommodating to our needs."

"Why? What could you possibly need from me?" I scanned the space around me frantically, trying and failing to avoid quick movements which sent my head spinning. Nausea rolled through me, but this time I fought it down.

Candle lamps provided some illumination, casting light onto a comfortable-looking settee with a chaise placed next to it. There, Nanette reclined and watched me—lying on the floor at her feet. The restraints ensured I would be little threat to her.

She was wearing some sort of loose gown made of a thin expensive-looking fabric. It did nothing to hide the curves and swells beneath it. Her hair was similarly loose. A woman comfortable in her space and comfortable with others noticing her.

"Finally an interesting question. We need you to provide the motivation your plucky little friend needs to embrace the miracles within her."

"So I'm just the bait for whatever trap you have planned."

"Not a trap, Roe. You are an *enticement*. It sounds much more palatable that way. Don't you agree?" She stretched languidly and studied her nails. "She just needs to have a vested interest in doing the right thing."

"You are insane," I ground out—my voice still sluggish but better. "You and Hollis both."

A warm laugh sounded from deeper—further—in the wagon.

I took a steadying breath and with an effort hauled myself into a sitting position. I leaned my back and head against a heavy piece of furniture. It might have been whatever my bindings were tied to because the tension loosened a little as I did.

I strained my eyes in the direction I thought the laugh had come from and shuddered. It couldn't be but my eyes told me it was. A grove of trees lined a path winding away into darkness. Wind murmured through autumn-colored leaves and sent them shivering and shaking—a natural symphony in an obscenely unnatural place.

Autumn leaves in the middle of spring. Inside a moving wagon. *How the hell could this be inside their wagon?*

My mind latched onto the only rational explanation. Whatever they had drugged me with—the peyote and oleander and mystery powder—was causing this hallucination. I refused to believe any of it was magic—the powder or the expansive scenery surrounding me. I closed my eyes again, willing my mind to reset—to see things clearly—but even though my vision was now a plain black slate, the other sensations did not leave me. Still I could feel the cool breeze on my face. Smell the autumnal decay. Hear the whistle and rattle of the crisp leaves before they fell.

I scrubbed at my eyes with the heels of my bound hands, and when I opened them, Hollis was walking up the impossible path toward me—a downright spring in his step.

"Roe Belstrohm. So happy you could join us." His voice was as fluid and crisp as the unnatural wind in the trees. It rolled out before him, somehow trapped and amplified in the space of the wagon. It made me think perhaps the rest was merely an optical illusion, just like the stars on the ceiling.

I stared at him, not speaking.

"I understand you may not be as pleased with the situation, but I can assure you it is for the greater benefit of the very people you wish to serve."

"Perhaps if I hadn't been drugged and bound."

"Minor discomforts. The drug will exit your system soon enough, and the restraints can be remedied shortly as well. I just need some sort of good will gesture that you won't attempt anything rash." He leaned against an ancient-looking desk, his posture languid. Arms crossed over his chest. Feet crossed at the ankle.

"Rash? Does ripping your throat from your body constitute being rash?"

He tsked. "Now that is exactly what I mean."

"I told you he isn't nearly so gentlemanly as all those droll settlers would have us believe." Nanette purred the words from her place on the chaise.

"Indeed, my lovely. I of course believed you, but seeing it on display once more is quite . . . unfortunate. Isn't it?" He studied me, the candles causing his pale blue eyes to appear to be made of liquid mercury. "I had hoped the little display of chivalry you put on a few days ago was for your companions' benefit, but I see I may have been mistaken."

This was going nowhere. Instead of letting him bait me further, I tilted my head back and closed my eyes—settling in for what was surely going to be a long day. Or was it night? I had no idea.

"Am I boring you?" he asked and I startled, realizing he was leaning down next to me, his warm breath on my ear. In contrast to his companion, he was rigidly dressed in a formal jacket and tie beneath his starched white collar. Had these people not been traveling through the same desert we were?

"Is there nothing else you wish to know? We aren't keeping any secrets." He smiled, and it was so oily, I felt my stomach roil.

"What time is it? Day or night?"

"Inside the wagon it is always night, but out there"—Nanette flicked her hand toward what might have been the back of the rig—"it is midmorning."

"And I was only out for the one night?"

Hollis smiled and nodded.

"Nanette says I'm to entice Aurelia. Does she know? Do they all"—*Hale*—"know you have me?"

"We were kind enough to leave a note, yes. We have given your friend a total of four days to think on her future. You will remain our guest until then. If all goes well, you will be back with your group that very day to continue your journey—both in life and on the road."

"But not with Aurelia. You mean to keep her." It wasn't a question, but he nodded again all the same.

"Why? Even if she has whatever it is you think she possesses, why take her from her other given talents?"

Hollis had moved away from me on the floor, but now he bent down and placed his nose within an inch of mine. His breath smelled of peppermint and old coffee.

"Do you know how they treated us in that small farming spot?"

I sensed he didn't really want me to answer, so I kept silent.

"One moment we were welcome and treated with open arms. The next, we were practically run out as if we were murderous bandits, set on pillaging anything in sight. That woman? The boy's mother? After you left her in tatters and tears, I approached and offered our services. Told her we might be able to help. She said the most unflattering things to us.

Called us the most vile of names. And yet we weren't the ones who left her child to die when he could have been saved. We were trying to help, but she wouldn't even allow us entry to her sad little shanty. Wouldn't even listen as we offered her life for her child."

No words could combat this kind of lunacy. I silently raised my bound hands and swiped the spittle that had landed on my cheek during his rant.

"The very dismissal of our miracles creates its own poison. It undermines our ability to utilize our natural-born talents. I intend to awaken the wonders in your friend. Maybe then she will be an acolyte of the thaumaturgy and speak on our behalf to the Medicus Corpus and its practitioners. Then the staff and snakes will allow us to assist in your endeavors."

I couldn't help myself. A short barking laugh escaped me, and I realized a moment too late my mistake. Hollis delivered four short kicks to my ribs in time with each word. "Do. Not. Mock. Me."

The last blow glanced off my trunk and connected with the side of my head.

I tried to breathe, but unfortunately my lungs had other ideas. I must have resembled a fish out of water—mouth gaping—trying to get oxygen into my system.

Nanette rose from her lounge and placed a soothing hand on his chest. "Now don't let him get to you. He is nothing. His opinion means nothing. He is just a means to an end."

She looked at me as she crooned the words. Gone was the sultry siren bent on wooing those around her. Instead, this was a viper ready to strike, disgust and loathing in every hissing inch.

18

AURELIA

Those days on the road felt like weeks. Hale was still barely speaking to me. Asher was pissed he'd lost one of his charges. The other practitioners were edgy and quiet. And I was so torn up about being the reason—whether justified or not—for Roe's capture that I could barely stand my own company.

The farther we moved into the desert, the hotter it became. Because we were still trying to move as quickly as possible, I spent most of the travel time staring out the back of a tram, praying for any slight breeze to move the stifling air around me. The farther we trudged, the signs of any habitation became fewer, until they were practically nonexistent. If it weren't for the occasional ruin of an ancient road sign and the crumbling remnants of the asphalt beneath our feet, I could have been led to believe no person had ever ventured out this way. And why would they? It was arid and dusty and exactly the same temperature as the surface of the sun.

What kind of hell would it be once summer fully descended? I couldn't fathom the thought. It might be like how your brain doesn't remember the exact quality of pain you've experienced. You remember there was pain and it was annoying or terrible but not really what it felt like. Similarly, my brain wouldn't process what it would feel like to be stuck in the desert sun when the temps topped one hundred thirty as I was told they occasionally did. Forget heatstroke. A person could be cooked alive.

On the second day after Roe had been taken, we stopped mid-afternoon near a large crumbling concrete structure just off the road. I couldn't begin to tell what purpose it had once served other than as a spot for graffiti artists to take a break from the heat. Large patches of faded paint covered any bits that hadn't yet disintegrated into the ground. I could make out words like chicken ranch, shady, and hot springs but little else. In the distance, long abandoned mine shafts dotted the landscape. Closer to the road sat a series of rusted husks of some sort of transportation or mining vehicles. Everything was coated in varying layers of almond flour dust.

I'd sworn at one point earlier in the day we had passed the broken form of a boat on the side of the road. I had immediately thought I was finally losing my sanity to the clutches of the angry sun. I was about to ask Hale if he'd seen it too, but the set of his shoulders as I'd approached him suggested it would be better if I *were* going mad.

As I sat against the concrete, sweat soaking through my loose cotton shirt and cargo pants, I still couldn't guess why anyone would choose to live out here. Not just now, but ever. This place had no color. No vibrancy. No water.

The paltry number of fellow travelers suggested a scarcity of people dumb enough to live in these conditions. Even nonhuman life was stunted. The only vegetation was scrubby little weeds and the occasional jackrabbit or vulture. Oh and the string of ants marching past me through the dirt.

Devil's Meadows was a hub settlement built in the ruins of what had once been a thriving city—but still a city in the desert. I wanted to dry up and blow away in the desert wind if this was to be my life forever.

Unable to stand it any longer, I grabbed my canteen of water and walked over to Geneva, who was scanning the endless horizon.

"We'll get him back," she said as way of greeting. She must have read my discomfort and assumed it was Roe I was worrying about. I *should* have been worrying about Roe, but this seemed important too.

"I hope so. But that isn't what I wanted to ask you." She turned and looked sideways at me. Taking the silence as permission, I asked, "Is it like this?"

"Is what like what?"

"DM—Devil's Meadows. Is it like this?" I spread my hands wide and turned, encompassing everything within the huge open space around us.

"In some ways yes. In other ways no." She frowned. "It's . . . I don't really know how to say it. It isn't like any place I've ever been. Not as if that list is long, mind you. But not like any place I've ever heard about either."

"But is it barren and dry? Is there any beauty in it?"

"Well, I guess that depends on your perspective now, doesn't it? Some folks think these parts of the desert are the most beautiful thing they've ever seen. They love the way you don't feel closed in. They love the way you can see each and every shade from brown to peach and purple when the sun comes up on the mountains in the distance."

Was Geneva one of those people? A sort of disbelieving laugh erupted from me as I scoffed at the notion.

"Look at the range over there. What color are those mountains?" She pointed to our right.

"Tan. Just like everything else out here."

"If you say so." She stretched and walked back toward the trams. Luc and Minton were closing up the water barrels, and we needed to fill ours again before we set out. I trotted after her, needing the water but needing something different to slake this inner thirst.

"So if I don't think the desert is beautiful then I just what? Wither there until the day I die?"

Geneva set her canteen on the ground and placed her hands gently on my shoulders. She smiled a little. "Devil's Meadows may be in the desert, but it's more than just the sun and the heat and the sand. It's the people living there and the stars at night. It's the old buildings and all their colorful glass windows. It's the thunderstorms in the summer and the wildflowers in the spring. If you give it a chance, Aurelia, you might actually come to love it. Or at the very least, like it a little."

Then she did the most unexpected thing. She gave me a brief hug. I didn't really know how to react. No one had hugged me like that since I'd left my parents in Renfield. I think she could sense it, and she quickly said, "Grab your canteen and find a spot in the carriages. We need to get moving."

I rode there the rest of the day, but as the minutes ticked by, I got more and more restless. Convincing Geneva to let me walk for a while the following morning was easier than I anticipated. I promised her I would not lag in my pace. She gave me thirty minutes of freedom and then sent me back to the tram. I must have looked sullen because after lunch she told me I could walk again.

Everything looked exactly the same. Same desert scrub. Same washed-out sky. Same mountains in the distance. Same, same, same. Sun bleached, dried out, overexposed. Same.

I hated it. I hated Medicus. I hated Hale and Roe and myself. I stared at the dusty blacktop as my feet walked on. I only noticed I was crying when a fat wet drop splashed a perfect circle on my worn, dirt-covered boot. The tears were silent as they fell, and soon small puddles formed on the lower lenses of my glasses.

"Here." A canteen appeared in my line of sight. "Don't want you dehydrating yourself with all the crying."

Lacking enough energy to call him a jerk, I just took the proffered container from Hale's outstretched hand and unscrewed the cap. I gulped down a mouthful of the tepid liquid and handed it back. "Thanks."

"It's not your fault, you know."

I shrugged. The fact my best friend had been kidnapped and held for ransom—my ransom—certainly felt like my fault.

"Look. I don't know why he chose to single you out, but—"

Generally I could keep negativity to a minimum, but Hale hadn't even spoken to me in days. Now he wanted to make me feel better? He could keep his pep talk. I held up my hand, not letting him finish. "I think it's only fair you should know. Maybe there is something. Maybe this isn't just a coincidence and he didn't just randomly single me out."

"Aurelia," he scoffed. "What could there possibly be?"

"He said I radiate."

"Radiate?" He snorted.

I glared at him. "The first interaction I had with Hollis, it was the first thing he said to me. *You do positively radiate, don't you?*" The thought made me nauseous. The tone of his voice still felt slimy in my memory. "I figured he was just being creepy."

"It sounds creepy. But just because a man finds you attractive and has terrible pickup lines does not mean you suddenly have some miracle ability coursing through you." The implications of what Hale thought about Hollis and his motives toward me were clear.

"I know that. Its just there have been *other* things. . ." I wasn't sure how much I wanted to tell him. I'd barely put my suspicions together in my own mind, and even Roe seemed to shrug off the previous episodes I'd told him about. Hale surely would just mock me for being silly.

"What do you mean? Do you think you have miracles running through your veins?" His tone wasn't exactly mocking, but it certainly wasn't reassuring either. He wasn't going to make this easy for me.

"You're just like Roe." I sighed. "Or he's just like you."

"Umm . . . no. He's not. We aren't alike at all." He took a long drink from the canteen.

I laughed. "You honestly believe that? As much as you both hate to admit it, there are a few similarities." I used to think they were so different, but over the past couple of weeks, the similarities were becoming more apparent. "It doesn't matter. I tried to explain this to him the first time it happened, and he blew it off. Now look where we are."

"Tried to explain what? I have no idea what you're talking about." He was getting exasperated with me. I was only going to have one chance to explain this as best I could before he dismissed me too. Kicking a loose rock off the road, which went skittering into the scrub, I collected my thoughts.

"There've been a few times when I've gotten this feeling. The first was just before that man with the explosives ambushed us. Then it happened again the afternoon I met Lita and Jonaten. The day we skirted the lake bed. A couple of other times too."

"What kind of *feeling*? Like a premonition? You know what's going to happen?"

"No. Not exactly. It's more a sense of some kind of disturbance. I shiver or get a chill, I guess, and there's this really strange smell. I can't explain it really. It's like electricity in the air, but no one else feels the storm coming. I can't explain it any better than that."

"It sounds a little vague. Are you sure it isn't just random? Maybe you're having some sort of atypical migraine or something."

The same thing had crossed my mind more than once, and more than once I'd pushed it away. It didn't feel like the answer.

"Maybe. I don't have any history of migraines or seizures, and it might just be me connecting things that aren't really related at all. But what if it isn't? What if these episodes are why Hollis singled me out? Maybe he can sense whatever this is and is somehow drawn to it."

"I don't know, Aurelia. It seems like a bit of a stretch. You aren't actually using these episodes to benefit anyone, right?" He ran his hand over the stitches on his arm, a subconscious or conscious reminder that things could have gone very badly if the bite had been deeper. It also reminded me that we would need to remove them in the next day or two.

"You mean I'm not producing any miracles." I reached up and placed my hands on the back of my neck, arching and stretching the muscles there as we walked on. A long tired sigh escaped me. "Don't scratch at those anymore. I'll pull them out tonight when we stop."

He glanced down at his arm as if he hadn't realized he'd been rubbing the itchy silk threads.

"Do you want to be producing miracles?"

"No!" I responded quickly, but I thought about it for a moment. "Or yes, maybe. If I could have done something for Jonaten. What I wouldn't give to be able to have helped them."

Hale stopped walking and grabbed my shoulders. He turned me to face him, and I had to squint to keep the sun from my eyes as I craned my head back to look at his very serious face.

He sounded angry. "Do not let yourself think for one minute you could have done more. There is no magic cure, Aurelia. Don't fall prey to his delusions."

I dipped my head, but he continued. "Going down that road—even in your own mind—isn't going to help Jonaten or his mother or Roe. It certainly isn't going to help you. We do what we can." It was a similar sentiment to what he'd told me before. Now I wasn't sure who he was trying to convince.

"My mother believes in thaumaturgy." It was all I could think to say.

He let go of my shoulders and started walking again. I rushed to catch up, not wanting Asher to see me lagging and force me back into one of the trams. When I drew level with Hale again, I continued. "She never told me why she believed, what she had seen in her life to support such a notion. I might write to her when, or if, I can. I'm curious now, even though I never really was before."

"What do you mean *if?*"

I chose not to answer his question. "My father was never a believer. It didn't ever seem to bother her that he didn't think it was real, but I got the sense every now and then that it bothered her I didn't believe. I was too much into the science of healing to ever consider she could be right."

Some years after the Grand Divagation, word circulated of people claiming to have wonderfully magical gifts ranging from the ability to harness energy to healing others to walking on water. And everything in between. Because times were difficult in those years for the people who remembered having access to so much . . . *more,* it made sense to hope something better was possible. If you could dream of lighting your home without power plants or travel without fossil fuels, why not? If those dreams meant you had to invent an inborn magical ability to do so, so be it.

Many people still believed these tales even if they'd never witnessed a miracle before. People like my mother.

At least I didn't think she'd witnessed a miracle.

"There's nothing wrong with that. You were training to help people. It's your job to focus on the science."

"I think part of me wants it all to be this made-up fantasy. Because if it isn't, that means I could have helped Jonatan and Lita. It means I let them down. But what if it can help Roe?"

"It can't, so stop."

"No, Hale. Really. Listen. What if whatever this buzzing might be can help us get him back? So maybe I'm not a wonder-worker, but if something is there, we can use it to our advantage. I can worry about myself after he's safe again."

"No." He looked like he was going to run away from me again but changed his mind. "I know it isn't my decision to make, but we still have time to figure out a better plan. I am asking you not to do anything we will all regret."

The urge to argue was overwhelming, but he was being fair. I didn't agree with him, but I kept my mouth shut for the time being. He disliked me enough as it was. It was pointless to make him hate me enough that he would refuse to help me when the time came.

Sounds from ahead drew my attention, and I stepped off the road into the scrub to see around the trams. Coming toward the train of carriages—several miles up the road and over the next rise—was another group of similar horse-drawn trams. We'd seen so few travelers, at first I wasn't sure if my eyes were deceiving me.

Unlike the presence of the miracle wagon, this new group didn't seem to alarm the escorts. I realized why almost an hour later as our slow steps drew the two groups closer together. The carriages of their trams were marginally smaller than ours but were emblazoned with the same large staff and snake insignia in bold blue and yellow paint. The escorts or tram masters must have had some idea about the schedule of groups traversing across the barren landscape on Medicus missions. No need to raise an alarm if you knew which groups had no mind to plunder our supplies.

Sure enough, as soon as the approaching group was within shouting distance, Luc raised an arm in recognition. This seemed to satisfy Asher and Jake further, and the call was given for us to stop for an early break.

"Won't be making camp just yet, but let's at least see if there's any news from down the way." Jake smiled as he informed us of the plan.

Minton and Hera signaled to the horses and pulled their rigs up behind where Luc had parked. They were as far to the right of the road as possible without being in the low-lying ravine just off the shoulder. The three trams facing north were in a similar arrangement off the east side of the road. The six drivers came together in a small huddle along the center of the surface and exchanged handshakes, smiles, and in the case of Hera and a burly older man, a warm embrace. I'd heard bits and pieces of the interconnected network of drivers who ran the various routes. Occasionally, if timings worked out, they would camp together on the road when crossing paths and maintained friendships when they were in between routes, stationed in Renfield.

This group was returning from a run to deliver supplies to sites south and east of Devil's Meadows. They had no practitioners with them, and rather than escorts, they were accompanied by two guards who ensured the supplies and the trams themselves were secure along their journey. Having already delivered their loads, they were running virtually empty, making for markedly swifter travel.

The guards exchanged greetings with our escorts while the tram masters exchanged travel updates and gave the horses a brief respite. Phoebe, Helena, and Wade took the opportunity to stretch their legs and sneak off behind various bushes to do what needed to be done after hours inside the carriages.

I drifted over to stand by Geneva and Asher as they spoke with the guards.

"We saw that wagon just this morning," the younger of the two guards was explaining to Asher. "Maybe five, six hours ago. It was this side of the old solar farm. The driver made a big stink over letting us pass. Real ass."

He chuckled and then seemed to notice me standing there. He nodded and winked at me. He wasn't the most attractive man I'd ever seen, but his smile was absolutely gorgeous. I imagine he knew it too and used it every chance he got. An uncontrollable grin bloomed on my face in response.

The second guard shrugged when he saw Asher frown as he looked at me. He was older than his companion, and judging by his expression, this was something he dealt with frequently.

Asher returned to his conversation. "Did you notice how many were traveling with them? See anyone besides the driver?"

"There was another guy, might have been in charge," the older guard answered. "He popped out the wagon's window to yell at the driver. Had him make way for us. I didn't catch sight of anyone other than those two."

"And this was outside the solar farm? How far? That's a big stretch." Asher directed this to the younger guard.

"Well, we slept the night in that old mining settlement on the hill and had been traveling maybe two, certainly not more than three, hours when we crossed em." He looked from Asher to me and smiled again.

"Enough of that crap now, Rog. You don't need to flirt with every pretty girl you see," his companion scolded him mildly.

I blushed and looked at my toes as he replied, "Yeah, but this one is pretty *and* smart."

"Pretty, smart, and headed far enough away you'll never lay eyes on her again. Sorry ma'am," he directed at me.

"No apology needed. Thanks for the information."

I walked away but couldn't keep the smile from my face. It had been a long time since anyone had called me pretty. Cute. Smart. Wow, look at those eyes. You have amazing hair. Petite, or worse, short. I got those on a regular basis. But not pretty. Not beautiful. Only Roe called me lovely with any routine. And he didn't count. *Tiny Goddess*? That was just him teasing me.

As I joined my colleagues waiting to load up again, Hale narrowed his eyes and asked, "What's got into you?"

"Nothing," I replied as the smile left my face. "But I need to talk to you."

If the guards were right, Hollis and his friends would be at the meeting location by now. If they were roughly four hours ahead of us, we could be there tonight if we pushed it. The exchange was meant to take place the following day, and we still hadn't come up with any kind of solid plan. Maybe we would never have a solid plan because there wasn't one to be had. Maybe taking them by surprise was the best option. Maybe I needed to do what everyone told me not to. Maybe I needed to do something stupid.

19

HALE

Asher's lips were moving, and words were probably coming out of his mouth, but the roaring in my head made it impossible to translate the sounds into a coherent conversation. Aurelia looked up from where she'd been plucking the black threads out of my arm. She held tweezers in one hand to get under the thread and a small pointed blade to snip it in the other. From the look on her face, I knew she felt, if not the same as me, then very damn close.

Geneva glanced nervously from Asher to the petite ball of energy next to me. Jude and Jake wore matching expressions of anger mixed with alarm. They didn't seem to like this either, but apparently allegiance to Medicus and its chain of command would prevent them from voicing any objection.

"You can't be serious," Aurelia sputtered. The sun was melting behind the mountains in the west, turning the sky to liquid fire, and its reflection in the lenses of her glasses gave her added fierceness. I wasn't sure about Tiny Goddess. Tiny Badass seemed more appropriate at the moment. "I can't for the life of me think you are serious."

"I'm afraid I am," Asher voiced calmly, trying and failing to placate both of us. "I know you don't like this. None of you like this"—his gaze scanned his fellow escorts—"but it makes the most sense."

"It makes zero sense," she yelled back, her voice shaking and on the verge of breaking. Her eyes, always astonishing, were blazing a vibrant hazel and gold. "We cannot just leave him."

"We aren't just leaving him. You aren't understanding what I'm saying."

"Oh, we understand all right." The cold calm in my voice was a dead match for his own. "You are sacrificing Roe so Medicus doesn't lose both a practitioner *and* more time."

Losing practitioners didn't seem to be an issue when Luc had given us that bullshit speech before we skirted the lake. Obviously getting off schedule was really the big deal to these people.

"No. I'm making sure we don't lose *two* practitioners. I will make every attempt to retrieve Roe without also risking Aurelia."

A couple of hours after we'd parted ways with the other Medicus train, we'd found a communication strapped to a length of gold and purple cloth. The cloth was attached to an old signpost on the side of the road. It was even with a turnout to a partially destroyed and abandoned solar farm tower, a mile or so off the main road. Whether Hollis had placed it after he'd met with the empty Medicus trams or if the tram masters from the other group simply ignored it was anyone's guess.

We made camp not long after finding the missive and were positioned at the base of a long incline that led up to the remains of a small mining town. It looked like maybe a two hour walk from there to where the old buildings were nestled at the apex of the climb, tucked between matching rocky outcroppings.

Night had fallen and our fellow practitioners were getting ready for bed when Asher explained he and Jake were going to the rendezvous spot alone. Aurelia was to stay with the rest of us as Geneva and

Jude led us around the old town via a mostly disused mining road to the other side. We would meet up with them half a day later further down the way. It was Asher's hope he would have Roe in tow when they caught us up.

"What happens when they won't negotiate with you? Hollis has been pretty clear. I'm the ransom."

"I've got it covered, Doc," Asher told Aurelia as he patted the rifle he was cradling.

My heart was pounding, and acid burned deep in my stomach at the thought of leaving Roe's fate to these virtual strangers. I was responsible for him, regardless of the contract I'd signed with Medicus. "There has to be another way."

"I'm open to suggestions."

Aurelia started to speak but was cut off by Asher. "Suggestions that don't involve handing you over."

She had that look on her face that meant she was going to argue, but suddenly she stopped and simply walked away.

I didn't like what I suspected her silence meant but knew I would agree to whatever stupid plan she had. Throwing one last scathing look Asher's direction, I followed her into our tent.

20

ROE

My ribs were on fire. A deep searing pain lanced my chest any time I took a breath deeper than a sip.

For the first few hours after Hollis had used my body to shine the toes of his boots, I had been convinced at least one rib was fractured. Later, when the pain began to improve, I realized they were likely just bruised, not broken. My ear, however, was another matter.

In his rage, one of those kicks had ricocheted off my flank and connected with my left ear. Thankfully it hadn't been a direct blow to my head, but the swelling and throbbing in the helix of my ear was still substantial. I'd felt it several times with the fingers of my bound hands and each time noted the firm, taut, painful mass wasn't improving. If the hematoma didn't get drained soon, I was at risk for having a misshapen cauliflower ear forever.

Time passed slowly after those blows, but for the life of me, I had no idea how much. Inside the wagon, it remained perpetual twilight. Nanette rarely left her place on the chaise, and I spent the unending hours tied up at her feet like some supplicant. A hateful and murderous supplicant perhaps, but my place remained at her feet nonetheless. I was given an ornamental bucket reminiscent of some long ago chamber pot, but I used it only when I couldn't take the pressure in my bladder any longer. I hated the idea of her watching me as I used the frilly flower-covered thing even if my back was turned to the chaise.

Hollis came and went at random intervals. I never saw the driver—who I finally learned was named Darner. First or last, I have no idea. They gave me water and bits to eat here and there. If the meals held a pattern, I couldn't discern it. I assumed this was to keep me confused, but it could just as likely been from laziness or lack of caring for my comfort. I could tell when we stopped moving for long periods, and I figured those periods were true night when Darner needed to sleep and tend the horses.

I slept poorly if at all. My senses were hyperaware of every creak and footfall. I worked at the ropes on my wrists, but every time I made progress in weakening them, an unnatural fatigue would settle over me and oblivion would claim my mind. It was like a tap got turned on and all the energy in my body and soul simply flowed out and away. When I would awaken minutes or hours later, the bindings were freshly tightened. The second or third time this occurred, I awoke with a start to find Nanette standing over me, licking her lips as I pulled on the freshly snug ropes. An antique mirror dangled from one hand—the silver of the filigree handle tarnished and worn, the glass cloudy and dark.

"Please. Keep struggling. I find it most delicious to witness."

I'm not sure what flashed across my face, but whatever it was caused her to erupt into wicked laughter. The sound sent a chill down my back, and I stopped pulling on the tethers. That one moment almost broke me. I could sense something in her, a darkness I had yet to fully grasp, and it made me want to disappear into myself.

The feeling lasted only a short time though. Before long I was worrying at the ropes again, the cycle of loosening and tightening on repeat.

During my waking hours—and they were almost all waking hours—I studied the wagon around me as I rubbed the skin on my wrists raw. It was full of both new technology and ancient arcane relics. Mixed together were solar stoves, battery-operated fans for cooling the wagon, a hand-crank music box, sets of crystal orbs, several gilded picture frames, and a mechanical printing press. The wagon also held a collection of creepy porcelain dolls and the skull of a large reptile that might have been an alligator or a dragon.

Some of the items I'd heard stories of but had never seen save for illustrations in old books. Most intriguing was a scattering of candles that burned in a variety of different colors—these seemed to change in tune with Nanette's mood. Bright violent pink when she was pleased, a dull nondescript yellow-orange when she slept, and mint green when she grew bored. They flashed indigo only once. That was when she grew angry at something Hollis told her. He'd said it in a low whisper, so I wasn't clear on the words, just her flash of temper and the candles changing hue to let me know she was unhappy with it. The flames never reacted to either Hollis or me, so I assume they were tuned to her exclusively somehow.

Occasionally I would notice an item of interest, and when I looked for it again, it either wasn't there or it had been relocated to a new location within the shelves and furniture of the wagon. Because the light was dim in the night wagon, and the flickering of the candles often played tricks on my eyes, I could never be sure if the movement of the objects was a complex series of optical illusions or the deliberate acts of someone trying to drive me mad.

The planets overhead continued to glow among the painted stars, but I never witnessed the moon changing phase again. It remained a thin crescent in the corner of the wagon's night sky.

The mirror with the tarnished handle was always within Nanette's reach. I don't recall if I ever witnessed her peering at her reflection, but it was often in her lap or on the settee where she lounged as if at any moment she would need to check that her perfect features were still perfect.

Of all the strange, wondrous, or terrible items in the wagon, the one that horrified me the most wasn't actually an object I normally would have found upsetting. In fact, it was something I generally found solace and comfort in, but here, in this place, it was simply wrong. A simple set of books. Text books to be precise.

I was once again trying to move my hands and feet to keep the blood circulating. I'd found I could lie down or sit comfortably, but when I attempted to stand, the bindings would pull in such a way that my balance would shift and I would topple forward. The best I could manage was a sort of kneeling position. I was rocking back and forth on my knees when Hollis approached from the front of the wagon. The trees were gone—replaced by a couple of rows of what I took to be church pews arranged for a small service. Candles, flickering with mundane yellow flames, littered tiered candelabras among them. He sauntered closer, his crisp white shirt practically glowing in the mix of candlelight and manufactured starlight.

"I suppose it might not be the most comfortable position, but you must understand our need for caution." He reached down, and with a flick of his wrists, the knots binding my legs were slackened. I slipped the loops from my ankles and stood on shaking legs. My hands remained bound in front of me and tethered to the heavy piece of furniture, but at least now I could hobble within the small space. The tingling of a million pins racked my lower extremities, and I grimaced as a tight knot formed in my lower back.

"It's only for a short time, mind you," Hollis said. I didn't know if he meant I'd be allowed to stand for a short time or if the period between now and when we were to meet the others was drawing to a close.

"She won't be there, you know," I told him as I stretched and shook my legs in front of me. "If it was up to her, she'd trade herself in a heartbeat, but her decisions aren't her own. They'll never let her do it."

"Perhaps." He cocked his head as if contemplating what I said. "I suppose we shall all have to wait and see."

I turned in arcing circles—first clockwise as far as the tether would allow and returning counterclockwise. As I did so, I saw the piece of furniture to which I was bound. The heavy oak writing desk was capped with three rows of bookshelves. The shelves were crammed with a multitude of books, journals, and thickly bound texts. Many lacked any identifiable titles on the spines, and several others were labeled in languages I didn't recognize. A few had symbols—stars, suns, flasks, and skulls—in lieu of language I could understand.

I rolled my neck and shifted back to face Hollis. He was watching me with mild interest and expectation.

"I've been waiting a very long time to find a practitioner with your friend's gift." He sat down in a high-back chair with deep indigo cushions. I didn't recall seeing the chair before, but it must have been there. "Would you trade your place with her?"

"With Aurelia?"

He nodded.

"Never."

Hollis chuckled softly. "You enjoy our company so much? Enjoy being a guest in our home?"

"I despise your company, but I would rather she forget I ever existed than subject her to even a day of this." I turned again, willing blood to flow into my cramped feet, thighs, and back. "This wagon . . . your home. It makes no sense and hurts my head. What even is all of this stuff?"

I tried to lift my hands to encompass the troves of bizarre and arcane items surrounding me, but the ropes burned along my wrists with the movement.

"This *stuff* is the culmination of lives lived, secrets found, and miracles worked." His words, while typical for the fanaticism I'd come to expect from him, lacked the conviction. He sounded almost morose. Or scared.

"It appears to me like a pile of useless ephemera." As I turned back to my left, my eyes fell on the bottom shelf of the writing desk. Nestled in the corner was a trio of books I knew better than any others. The first was a standard pharmacopoeia. The second a thick tomb of anatomy—filled, I knew, with hundreds of artist-drawn color plates depicting every nerve, muscle, blood vessel, and gland in the human body. The last—its spine worn and cracked—was *An Introduction to Patient Care.* Each spine was embossed with a tiny staff and snake.

They were the standard introductory texts given to, and pored over by, every first year student at the Medicus Corpus schools.

I was so absorbed in the titles and what they implied, I never heard him move from his chair. Hollis stood next to me and whispered into my ear, "I would think, Mr. Belstrohm, after your time with us these past days, you would understand not everything is always as it seems."

When I didn't immediately respond, I sensed him turn from my side and knew he was following my gaze to the books on the shelf.

"That will be enough movement for the day." His voice was no longer morose or scared. It was tight and trembling. No gentle pull of energy lulled me to sleep this time. The blow to the back of my head came swiftly.

When I next awoke, my head was pounding out the rhythm of my heart. The wagon had stopped moving, and I was bound even tighter than before.

21

AURELIA

We snuck away from camp well before dawn. It had been surprisingly easy to convince Hale to go with me. Some small part of me had hoped he would balk at the idea and try to convince me not to go. He didn't so much as utter an argument though. When he'd sensed my mood and plans the night before, he'd cornered me and insisted that if I was going to do something inadvisable, he was going to do it with me.

Hale understood retrieving Roe was paramount. His safety was far beyond any sense of duty either of us had to Medicus and its time lines or financial obligations. Even if his skills alone weren't worth the risk, his life certainly was.

Asher would be livid of course. So would the other three escorts. I felt the tiniest bit of guilt for putting Geneva, Jude, and Jake in a bad spot, but not enough to further jeopardize my friend. We didn't know Hollis well enough to predict his actions should Asher and Jake show up without the one bargaining chip we had—me.

Hale didn't like my idea of a simple straightforward exchange, and he liked my second idea—winging it—even less. We'd briefly entertained the notion of pilfering a rifle from the escorts, but rationality won out on that point at least. Neither of us had ever handled one of the old weapons, and the prospect of us accidentally hurting Roe or ourselves seemed just as high as not.

I tied a note to our tent flap, knowing someone would find it when the other practitioners were up and moving. The tram masters often took early morning watch duty as they were generally up to tend the horses and prepare for the road anyway. We waited as Minton made a loop away from our tent, and then we scurried off into the brush.

Neither of us uttered a word as we hurried toward the base of the road's incline up to the old mining town. It didn't take long for us to reach the outer ring of light the solar lamps provided to the camp. In the desert, the darkness before dawn was thick and complete. Not wanting to lose the road in the dark, we walked along the side where the ground was relatively smooth and devoid of hazards. It was still too risky to turn on a lamp, as even the smallest light would be a beacon in the dark.

The temperature was balmy. No breeze shifted the air. Despite this, a nervous energy had me jittery and shivering. My teeth chattered as I jogged to keep up with Hale's long striding gait.

Once any trace of light from the camp was gone, Hale slowed a fraction, and I was able to calm my breathing enough to speak comfortably. "When they release him, where do you plan to meet up with the others?"

He looked at me with confusion.

"Do you think you'll need to backtrack? I think Asher will stick with his original plan more or less. You should be able to catch them on the other side of town, right where he originally planned for us to wait."

"Don't you mean where will *we* meet them?"

I shrugged. "I guess I'm just not overly convinced I'll be with you when this is done."

"Why are you so damn set on sacrificing yourself?" he demanded. "Is this some great romantic gesture on your part?"

Despite the force of the question, his stoniness told me if I had been able to see his face, it would have held the same cocky calm expression he favored. I couldn't think how to respond.

"You do love him, don't you?"

"He's my best friend, Hale. He's been by my side since I was an awkward, scrawny, nerdy kid. And still now when I'm less scrawny but still an awkward and nerdy adult. Through school and life. I've seen him at his best and his worst, and we've learned some life lessons side by side. He knows all the ugly parts of me as well as the good, and he still wants to share in our journey together. Of course I love him."

"Believe me, I am well aware he's your best friend, and I'm sure there aren't as many ugly parts as you'd like to make it sound. I'm happy he has you to rely on." He paused, as if weighing whether or not to say more, and added, "I think you want something more."

So this was the most important conversation to have on our way to trade me for his brother?

"I can see it, Aurelia, and I understand. Roe is outgoing and fun, and I would do anything for him. But as well as you think you know each other, there's something he's not telling you. Believe me, he isn't . . . he won't—"

I cut him off. "You're right, Hale. I do want something more." Although I couldn't see his expression, I imagined it well enough. Hard lines would be making his handsome features grim. "I want him to be happy. I want him to live the life he chooses and to feel like he's accepted. I love him. *Like a brother.* I love him, but I'm not in love with him."

I heard his steps faltering in the dark.

"And Roe will never be in love with me either. That's what he's not telling me. We are best friends. Nothing more."

"He would love you if he could," Hale said simply.

"Maybe." I sighed, knowing what I was about to say would not come as a shock to Roe's brother. "Hale, I *know*. He'll never love any girl in that way. He's into guys."

"He told you that?" Shock and maybe a little anger colored his words.

"No, he hasn't. But he doesn't need to. I just know." I could feel the confusion radiating off him. "I assume you also *just know*."

"Well, yeah . . . I mean no. I don't just know. He told me. But even before that . . . I've known for a very long time." His arm landed on my shoulder, and he turned me toward him. In the dim starlight, I could just make out the shape of his face. "Why didn't you ever say anything?"

"Because it isn't my truth to tell. Or yours for that matter. It is his and his alone. And until he is ready to tell me, or the world, I will be here for him as his friend. After too. I will always be his friend and give him whatever it is he needs from me."

"That's a big promise to make. *Whatever he needs?* Even if it means you're living a lie?"

"How is it a lie?"

"Because people see you and think you're more than friends. Even I thought something more was going on. Or that *you* thought there was more, I mean."

"Why should I care what people think?"

We had started walking now, and for a change I was pulling a little ahead of him.

"It doesn't allow either of you to find someone else. Doesn't allow you to be happy."

"There are lots of ways to be happy, and I will find someone when I want to. So will Roe, I hope. We know what we are to each other. I could give a flying rip what other people think they know."

For once Hale didn't seem to have anything to say.

"For the record," I said without looking at him, my voice sad even in my own ears, "I'm glad he told you. Glad he has someone he cares about enough to share things with."

A whistling breeze carried over the sands and stones, singing a quiet arid melody and sending tiny shivering tingles up my neck where the baby hairs moved and shifted. When it was quiet like this, and the sun hadn't yet scorched all the joy from the world, I could see how some might find this place beautiful. It was a muted pastel type of beauty, so different from the bright white of the snow-topped mountains and green pine forest I had grown up with.

"When our dad skipped out—or more correctly—when he was thrown out, my mom seemed so much happier. But Roe . . . he seemed to take it harder than I would have thought. It was his blood after all that sent the bastard packing."

I didn't want to speak. Hale never opened up to me like this, so I just waited for him to continue.

"We were just kids. And Roe was a *great* kid. He was a lot like he is now. Funny, charismatic, quick to smile and tell a story. Everyone gravitated toward him, but he wasn't rough and athletic like the other boys. I knew even then he was different, but not in a bad way, you know?"

I nodded. The movement sent my glasses slipping to the end of my nose. It was a reflex movement to push them back up.

"Well, for good old Wendell Watt, that difference was a bad thing. At times you could see him visibly cringe when Roe would tell a story—get up and walk right out of the room as if it physically pained him to watch my brother be who he was."

Again my heart ached for little Roe, and again I wanted to throttle this man who I'd never even meet.

"It was a doll. Roe was brushing the hair of a doll that morning. I don't even know where he'd gotten the damn thing from. I knew the bastard was going to hurt Roe because he had no capacity to feel anything for him other than disgust." Hale's already quiet timber became little more than a whisper. "There was no way I was going to let that happen. I'd die first. Even though I was just a kid myself, I wanted to do some real damage to my father in the process."

He was quiet for so long this time the stars were fading before he spoke again. "After that, Roe changed. I think he honestly believes he's responsible for that shitbag's behavior." He looked at me, perhaps to judge my reaction to his language. Still I kept quiet. "He started playing ball with me and the other kids at school. Stopped being quite as outgoing—though that soon wore off. Transformed into one of the guys as we got older. Then in secondary school he started bringing you around all the time, and I just thought it was another way for him to kind of deny who he really was. I didn't like it. I want him to always be who he really is."

Finally I spoke. "And you will always be who you are."

"What's that? A stone-cold asshole?"

I grimaced as my words came back to me. "No. You will always be his big brother—the one who defends him and looks after him."

"Even if he doesn't want me to," he agreed.

We walked on in silence for another few hundred yards. The light was changing in earnest. There'd be no more hiding from anyone who bothered to look, so we migrated back to the blacktop where the walking was easier. I only hoped we'd put enough distance between the others and our meetup with Hollis.

Off in the distance to our left, the silhouette of a great hulking tower was just visible in the gloom. It was surrounded by a vast sea of darkness I could only assume were the remnants of thousands of solar panels. Such a shame. That plant alone could power every settlement in this vast and unending wasteland. The equipment remained, but the infrastructure was gone in the wake of the Grand Divagation. The tech for small solar panels was available for use by whoever could afford it, but gone were the days of freely flowing power to every inhabitant on the planet.

I finally decided to ask a question that had been chewing little bites into my brain for months, if not years. "Is that why you hate me? Because you thought I was keeping Roe from being happy?"

His eyes went wide. "What? Why would you. . .? I don't hate you, Aurelia."

"Well, you clearly don't like me very much."

"That's not true at all. I–I–I don't even know how to respond to that."

"Hmm. Hale Belstrohm at a complete loss. I never thought I'd see the day."

"I don't hate you, Aurelia," he repeated. His words held an earnestness I didn't often associate with him, and I warmed toward him just a bit. Who knew? Maybe we could manage to work and live side by side after all. The thought made me smile inside. He continued, "I apologize for making you think I do."

It was so unlike the Hale I knew, I said the only thing I could think of. "Apology accepted."

The hills in the east glowed with the promise of the sunrise to come. But before the fat orange orb made its official appearance, a series of faint pops sounded from the direction we'd just come. Worry washed over me. Hale didn't stop but turned to walk backward, squinting down the slope toward where our friends were still camped. Even facing forward, I had to hustle to keep up with him.

Concern etched his brow. " I can't see much. We've made good time."

Another series of pops peppered the air—this time followed by a considerably louder bang. A shiver ran up my spine as Hale slowed finally and stopped. I turned and stood near him, straining to see in the weak silvery light. A minute passed. Then two.

A faint smudge of grey rose above the clump of tiny trams at the base of the hill. Smoke. Something at the camp was burning.

The subtle concern on Hale's face blossomed into full-blown conflict. Something was happening down there, and we had no idea what it was. Did we stay with our plan and continue to the rendezvous and hopeful reunion with Roe? Or did we abandon my friend—Hale's brother—to rush back into whatever was happening down the hill in an attempt to assist those we'd left behind?

I looked to Hale, but his face held no answer.

"We keep going," I said. " I don't know what all that is, but there isn't anything we can do to help now. It'd take us over an hour to get back to them, even if I could run the entire way."

He nodded, but the unsettled look never left his face.

I started walking, and within five strides Hale was at my side again.

"The note said to look for the ruins of an old hotel and to turn left at the intersection. From there we should approach an old mine shaft." He nodded again.

I sighed. "It looks like there are old mine shafts all over the place. How are we supposed to know which one?"

He rubbed a hand over his face with a long exhale. "My guess is it'll be pretty clear. Or at least I hope it is."

Hale threw one last look over his shoulder, and I mimicked the gesture. The smoke was thicker now, and movement appeared in at least one of the trams.

I couldn't imagine what had happened and could only hope if everything worked out, I'd see them all down the road.

Several long minutes later, after passing a handful of crumbling buildings and at least one rusted out ancient gas pump, we came to a building standing taller than anything else in the old settlement. In its glory, the old hotel must have been five stories of relatively clean accommodations. Now the only overnight guests were apt to be desert rodents and the tormented ghosts of long-dead miners. The glass was missing from the first three floors of windows, but when I looked up toward the top, a set of grimy handprints stood out in the dust coating the pane of an upper floor window. A shiver ran down my spine as I imagined the child who stood there looking out at the vast surrounding landscape.

"Aurelia?" Hale's expression was somberly quizzical. He tilted his head. "It's this way, I think."

I rubbed my hands down my arms. Checking I had everything in place as we'd planned, I set off in his wake up the hill and toward a pile of cracked and rotted wood supports. Another fifty yards past it, the red and gold wagon perched, waiting for our arrival.

22

HALE

What the hell?

What the ever loving f'ing hell!?

She knew. Aurelia *knew*.

I couldn't decide if I should be elated or mortified she knew about Roe. On the one hand, I didn't have to worry about things going ridiculously bad when she found out, but on the other hand, she knew. All this time. How many other people knew? Not that it mattered. I personally never understood why it mattered, but for whatever reason, Roe had obviously been trying to keep this part of himself to himself. Aurelia and I shouldn't have even talked about it. For that I felt the slightest bit of guilt.

Of course I knew. We'd talked about things briefly a few years ago, but it never seemed necessary to discuss it again. It never made any difference to me, just as my being attracted to women had never been a topic of conversation for him. We were who we were.

Aurelia was his best friend, and I understood more now than ever before what that kind of friendship meant. She was willing to be his friend with no thought of anything more. I felt bad for assuming she wanted him in other ways, but all this time, she too was just protecting him. Aside from Roe, I'm not sure I've ever had a friend like that in my life.

It made me feel all the worse for how I'd treated her since . . . well, forever.

It was no wonder she thought I hated her. In truth, I admired her quite a bit. She was smart and funny but also modest and hardworking.

It really wasn't the time to dwell on the particulars of what an ass I was or what I did or didn't think of Aurelia, however. We had more important things to focus on at the moment. First, how were we going to make sure this exchange wasn't an exchange at all? And second, what the hell had just happened down the hill at camp? It wasn't the first time on our trek the popping noises had sprung up. Something with a very similar sound had spooked Asher into hurrying us around the dry lake bed. I thought at the time it might have been gunfire. I thought the same thing now.

One thing at a time. Roe first. We weren't going to know what happened to the others. Hopefully we'd all hear the story later that night. Hopefully.

23

ROE

No sooner had my eyes adjusted to the weak watery light did I wish I hadn't been able to see at all. By the looks of things, it was fairly early in the morning. Still I wasn't sure how many days had passed inside the magical hellish space. Surely not more than a handful, but I would be willing to go back and spend the next hundred weeks in the wagon if it meant the sight before me was different.

Nanette had signaled to Hollis a few minutes earlier, and he'd appeared to untie me and help me to my feet. Pins and needles shot through my legs as he'd half escorted, half carried me down the few wooden steps to the rocky ground beneath. Some sort of wooden structure stood off to the right, and a dilapidated mine shaft was boarded up about fifty yards below where we were parked. Standing next to the shaft were the two people I wanted to see the most in the world.

I simply did not want to see them here. Not now. Not this close to the oily wrongness of Hollis and Nannette.

The watery light, weak as it was, made the pounding in my head all the more intense. Using my hand to shield my eyes, I cringed. A whimper might have escaped me. "No." My voice was barely more than a breath.

"Oh yes," Nannette's purring voice replied. "Oh yes. Yes. Yes."

Aurelia had actually come here. To meet with Hollis and presumably trade herself for me. I could not wrap my mind around it. What was she thinking? For that matter, what was Hale thinking bringing her here? Where the hell was Asher? He should be here. He was getting paid to be here. To protect us and get us to our destinations. To protect Auri. None of this was making sense.

"I won't do it."

"Won't do what, pet?" Nanette crooned.

"I won't trade. I won't let you have her."

"As far as I see it, Mr. Belstrohm, you have no say in the matter," Hollis answered. "You could, I suppose, refuse to leave, but then we'd have the both of you. I see no reason to deny you if that is your wish."

Spit flew from my lips as I whirled and screamed into his face. "You don't need her. Just let her go." The pressure in my face sent my head booming again.

"Temper, my boy. Your temper," he said smoothly. "It was you who suggested it, not me."

I could feel the blood pounding in my temples. Hear it rushing in my ears. Within seconds, the sound of footsteps pounding over the dirt mingled and harmonized with my pulse.

"Roe. Are you hurt?" Hale slid to a stop just feet from where the three of us stood. He caught sight of my mangled ear and raw wrists and grimaced.

Darner was nowhere to be seen. Thankfully Aurelia remained where she'd been, down next to the ruins of the mineshaft. Far enough away to be safe for the moment. I could sense her distress, but she needed to be smart and stay the hell away from these people.

"Fine." I glanced at him and back to Auri. "I'm fine, Hale. What are you doing here?"

"Making a trade."

Nanette's laugh was throaty and full. I hated that laugh.

"Oh, Roe. Your brother is just divine. I'm so pleased he chose to join us."

I stared at Hale. I was aware he didn't particularly care for Auri, but to knowingly sacrifice her to these filthy people? It was beyond anything I would have thought him capable.

"I suggest we walk." Hollis inclined his head down the slope toward Aurelia. Hale began casually walking toward the wooden mine supports—leaving me no choice but to follow. Both Hollis and Nanette strolled along with us—in no hurry or rush—as if they possessed all the time in the world.

"Run, Auri," I yelled. She merely looked at me, planted her feet, and lifted her chin. "Please."

She didn't know. Didn't understand what it was like in that wagon. How they could shift and change reality. Expand and shrink the space. Make you see things that weren't there.

"Roe." Hale moved closer and placed his arm around my shoulder. I shook him off.

"I knew you could be a bastard, Hale, but this?"

A flash of emotion crossed his face—disappearing almost instantly. He might have shook his head. I wasn't sure. My eyes were fixed on Aurelia, standing like a lamb to the slaughter. And for what? A talent she didn't even possess.

Movement in the shadows to Aurelia's right caught my eye, and Hale muttered a curse as Darner stepped out from behind the timber structure to stand next to Auri. She went from calm and resigned to stricken in the span of a few heartbeats. She and

Hale seemed panicked at the unexpected presence of the driver.

Darner was only a few inches taller than Aurelia. I would have felt sorry for him and his lot in life had he not been holding a knife so near my friend's neck.

Hollis stopped walking perhaps five yards from where Aurelia and Darner waited. Hale continued a few feet further and placed himself between Aurelia and me. Nanette, however, continued to meander down the slope. Dust rose where she stepped, and it coated the bottom six inches of her eggplant-colored skirt. She circled the two of them, looking up and down at Auri, tutting—disappointed in what she saw. She finished her circinate path and retuned to stand beside Hollis.

"So, Ms. Morris. Are you ready to show us what you are really made of?" Hollis asked.

"All I am made of is right here. There really isn't anything else to see."

"You deny then you have moments of . . . *insight,* shall we say? Moments when you feel the miracle rising up through your body, tingling under your skin? Enlivening your senses?"

Aurelia's eyes flashed to Hale and back to Hollis. Recognition glowed in her beautiful multicolored irises. Something in his words had sparked a memory, but I couldn't imagine what it was.

"There is nothing to deny. I am a Medicus practitioner. Nothing more."

He cocked his head and looked at her. A raptor studying its prey.

"I'm afraid I don't believe you," Nanette said matter-of-fact. "And neither, I'm sure, does Hollis."

"None of us gives two shits what you believe." Hale's voice was calm and just as direct.

"Your big brother to the rescue. It seems his temper is much more restrained than yours, Roe." Hollis stood with his hands behind his back, rocking up and down on his toes. He seemed to contemplate his words and then spoke with the same greasy condescension I'd come to associate with him. "Ms. Morris. It's quite simple actually. You could have saved the child. I realize you don't know the particulars of how at this moment, but I will tell you once again. You have it in you. The thaumaturgy. How many other children, or parents, or best friends"—his eyes flicked to me—"will die because you aren't courageous enough to reach inside yourself and provide what they need?"

Nanette came to stand next to me. Bile rose in my throat as she ran her hand down the front of my dirty shirt. "Perhaps this task is too great for the little one, Hollis. We could keep this one instead. He might come in handy in other ways."

"You're disgusting." I heard the soft mix of loathing and amazement in Auri's voice. I felt the same. Did people really behave this way? How was it possible to live with yourself when you behaved this way?

"Don't you judge me, darling." Nanette's eyes flashed first in Aurelia's direction and then in mine. I saw a fierceness there, on the verge of madness. I couldn't look at her any longer.

"You keep speaking of thaumaturgy, Mr. Hollis." Aurelia directed her comment at him, ignoring Nanette completely.

The shake of his head was almost imperceptible. "Not Mr. Just Hollis."

"My misunderstanding. So thaumaturgy?"

"Miracles and wonder-working yes."

"Let me tell you what I know of miracles and wonder, *Hollis*. The human body is its own wonder. Its own magic. Lots of people take that for granted, don't you think? Every second of every minute of every day, the body performs small acts of magic you can't see. Blood and sunshine. Water and air. It's a magical balance of chemical reactions making you who you are and me who I am. Your skin is processing sunlight right now to help your bones. Your blood is transporting oxygen from the air to keep you alive. It's all intertwined. Your heart beats, your lungs inhale, your eyes see wonders. All without you thinking about it for more than the briefest of moments or only when they stop functioning. If that isn't magic, what is?" She drew a breath and then said, almost to herself, "The kidney! My heavens. I still don't understand the intricacies and the magic within the kidney!"

I hid my smile. Nephrology had never been her strong suit, but I didn't think now was really the time to discuss it.

Nanette snorted. At least she'd stepped away from me for the moment.

"You don't believe me? How else do you explain how meat and bone can be animated? How the brain processes information? How electricity can course through us with the drive to move muscles and whisper information to us? How we dream and how we feel and how we love. How everything just . . . stops, the moment those processes cease. Back to meat and bones and water and gas. Just like the flip of a switch. Miracles indeed. I do study miracles. Just not the kind you think I do."

"Well, wasn't that a snippet of pretty poetry?" Nanette had the most unflattering sneer on her face. I'm sure she wouldn't have been happy to see herself in her fancy little mirror just then.

Hollis's expression was harder to read. One moment he had the glassy eyes of a fanatic and the next all I saw was . . . regret? Sympathy? Sadness?

As none of those made any sort of sense, I elected to worry about it later.

Instead, I needed to worry about getting Aurelia away from Darner and hope she and my brother had some sort of plan. Perhaps Hale wasn't as big of an ass as I had mentally accused him of being just minutes before. I was confident the two of us could take Hollis and Darner. That would leave Goldie-Locks to outrun Nanette.

"It was." Hollis was frowning slightly. "Quite lovely."

Nanette whipped her head toward him, daggers firing from her eyes.

Using the moment to step closer to Auri, I looked further downhill to a trail of dust rising on the other side of the hill where the settlement crumbled permanently into the desert brush and sand. Was that our train of carriages? The trail of dust gave the impression they were moving at a pretty decent clip.

My attention was forced back to Aurelia by a not-so-gentle elbow in my ribs. Hale, also taking advantage of the silent argument between Nanette and Hollis, had edged up right next to me. He dipped his head toward Auri and the short, pot-bellied driver. She stood with her back to him, arms crossed over her chest. Her eyes bore straight at Hale, no one else. He watched back just as intently. If I wasn't watching her so closely, I would have missed it. A quick double blink. And then she was in motion.

For a moment, I was sure I was still hallucinating on whatever drug I'd been exposed to, so unreal was the sight. Auri's right hand moved quickly and smoothly—drawing the scalpel from the cuff of her left sleeve. In one sweeping motion, she ducked below the level of Darner's knife and swept her arm in a less than elegant arc. It didn't matter if it looked smooth, however. It connected with his groin and cut smoothly through the canvas of his pants, drawing a spray of blood as she whirled around. Clearly not anticipating any type of resistance, the disgusting little man doubled over and squealed like a stuck pig. Auri barely managed to stay on her feet, the momentum of her movement carrying her slightly downhill. She pinwheeled her arms and ran toward the buildings at the bottom of the incline.

Within a fraction of a second, Hale was also in motion. He grabbed my arm and yanked me after him. I tried to get my feet moving, but my mind was still playing catch up and I stumbled into the loose gravel and dirt. Unlike Aurelia, I couldn't salvage my balance and ended up splayed on the gritty dirt. I didn't have long to appreciate the turnabout in seeing my clumsiness competing with the Tiny Goddess and her ability to stay on her feet. Hale was there in a blink, but as he drew me up from the right, another set of hands hefted me on the left.

I turned to see Hollis, his face inches from my own. "Remember what I said. Not everything is always as it seems." His voice was quiet but frantic. His eyes wild. "Now. Go."

Auri was already to the bottom, turning left past a tired-looking building. It took me a few strides to gain my legs, and then I was running full out, Hale next to me. When we rounded the corner, I almost tripped again over ancient signage resting on its side along the walkway. Broken letters—OTEL— lagged next to the remains of a bronze horse statue. Aurelia was ahead of us, but only by a short distance. Running definitely wasn't her thing. In the moment, however, I didn't care. She had risked her life to get me away from Hollis and Nanette.

I'd never been more relieved or more furious.

24

AURELIA

"They should be here." I spun in a circle, causing dust to rise into the air. "Hale? Right?"

Adrenaline had flooded my body when Roe was running behind me through the derelict mining town. I had been elated to see him. Now, all happiness dried up like a puddle in the summer sun. Left behind was only dread and horror.

I looked at my best friend. "We were going to meet them right here."

"According to you, I was going to meet them right here," Hale deadpanned.

"Now you're a comedian?" My voice cracked as tears sprang to my eyes.

I clenched my fist, and a wave of nausea crashed into me. My hand was tacky with the reminder of what I had done. Blood coated my palm, and the memory of squeal-like screams rang in my ears. I'd broken my vows and had injured a man. On purpose.

"It's—" Hale stepped toward me and started to put his hand on my shoulder but stopped abruptly as Roe enveloped me in a crushing embrace.

"What were you thinking?" Roe's voice was in my ear.

I had no time to answer before Hale urged us into motion again. "We need to keep moving. Maybe this isn't the right spot. They could be waiting further up the road."

Rather than running as we had been, we walked, albeit at a relatively brisk pace. Nanette and Hollis hadn't shown any signs of pursuit, likely choosing to stanch the driver's bleeding rather than leaving him. Still, it wasn't as if it was a mortal wound, and they could be after us within the hour. Plus, they had horses. I pushed myself a little faster—taking nearly two steps to each of the brothers' one.

My mind and soul were still reeling from what I'd done.

When we'd first reached the mineshaft earlier that morning, Hale had lifted a handful of the loose gravel and tossed it between the rotting planks. The small pebbles skittered and slid for several long seconds on their way into the darkness. He took one booted foot and pushed on the lower planks. It didn't take much effort before splinters were also following suit. He warned me to stay as far from the hole as I could but suggested if push came to shove, I should use my lower center of gravity to *shove* one of the trio into the darkness. I'd scoffed at the idea, but now, knowing they could pursue us indefinitely, I almost wished I'd taken his advice.

What was *wrong* with me? First, I'd slashed a man, and then I was regretful I hadn't committed murder. My instructors would be mortified. I should be mortified. I wasn't though.

"So, what's the plan?" Roe asked. He sounded—not angry—but irritated.

"I think we should stay off the road if we can. Their horses could manage the brush, but that wagon looks like it might shake itself apart if it hits anything rougher than the hard pack," I said.

"You don't know the half of it," Roe muttered.

Hale glanced at his brother and looked as if he wanted to say something but thought better of it. Instead, he looked at me. "I agree. Let's get to the base of the hill and then head a couple hundred yards out to the west. We should be able to see them coming if they stick to the asphalt, but with any luck we'll be mostly hidden from them."

No one said anything more as we made our way down the remaining descending section of road away from the old town. Heaps of slag rock reached toward the sky on both sides, throwing the road into shadow. The tips of the piles were a vibrant umber color and a deep burgundy brown at eye level. When the road began to flatten out, one of the monstrous piles created a tight channel as the asphalt made a turn to the left. Then, within the span of a few yards, the view opened up dramatically. The rock hills petered out to the left and right, but straight ahead the valley became a wide-open expanse of ochre and khaki. It stretched on for miles and miles.

"Ummm. We might have a bit of difficulty staying out of sight."

Hale and Roe both nodded, but neither immediately spoke. They must have been just as awestruck as I was. The broken asphalt trailed down in a relatively straight shot across the open expanse, diminishing into the barest thread as it climbed another small hill at the edge of the horizon.

I raised my hand and pointed. About a quarter of the way across, a set of tiny black blocks were moving on the road. Although I wasn't sure how they had gotten so far ahead of us, presumably that was our tiny convoy. Our friends and escorts. I knew Asher would be upset about our ill-advised plan, but I never would have believed he would simply abandon us and keep traveling.

Had Geneva asked him to stop? Had Jake or Jude? Or had they all agreed it was best to let us perish for our folly?

"I don't understand." This time Hale did place his hand on my shoulder.

"Let's keep moving."

I nodded dumbly, and he gave me a brief hug.

"I feel like I missed something," Roe said, looking back and forth between Hale and me.

"We *missed* you," I offered weakly as I grabbed his hand and started walking.

We'd gotten just around the outcropping when Hale let out a harsh chuckle. "Shit. I almost missed it."

I followed his gaze to a small pile of items tucked into a slim crevasse facing the road. Hale reached in and handed out a pack of supplies, two hand lamps, and two bedrolls.

"Looks like someone didn't think your rescue mission would be a success," Roe said dryly as he strapped on the backpack. He handed me one of the bedrolls to strap over my shoulder.

Hale shook his head. "Not so fast." He produced six canteens of water, handing two of them to each of us. "My guess is this is Asher's way of telling us to sleep in shifts."

He had a point. Two bedrolls meant one person would be awake and watchful at all times. But still, why not wait for us? They'd left enough water for only a day, maybe two. What would happen if we couldn't catch up?

"There's a note." He handed me a slip of paper he'd removed from the bedroll he was securing to his broad shoulders.

"*Catch up. Will explain when we see you,*" I read aloud. "That's all it says."

Hale finished tightening his straps. I was embarrassed as I caught myself staring at the muscles of his shoulders. I looked away as he explained to Roe, "I think they had some sort of trouble this morning. Auri and I heard a commotion after we split from the camp."

"*Auri* and you?" Roe asked. The way he emphasized my name made me uncomfortable.

I shot him a quizzical look.

He shook his head at me. "I can't recall him ever calling you Auri. It has always only been Aurelia. I definitely missed something."

"Don't worry, little brother. I have no intention of stealing your girlfriend." Hale used his most condescending tone. Roe hated that tone. At the moment, I hated it myself.

"I just for the life of me can't figure out why it's the two of you here. Someone could have gotten hurt. Or worse."

I frowned at him. "Roe. Enough already. Hale and I have spent the past few days trying to figure out how to get to you and Asher didn't. . . Look. It's a long story, okay? I promise to give you all the gory details, but for now can we just get out of sight and try to make up a little time?"

"Sure. Sorry. The last few days have been . . . rough." He looked genuinely appalled at his own behavior. "Sorry," he said again.

"Looks like there's a wash or something over to the right. We should be able to use it for some cover." Roe pointed toward what appeared to be a slight, ribbon-like depression running parallel to the road.

Hale nodded. "Let's go then."

From the vantage of the asphalt, the desert scrub and sagebrush looked like fluffy tan cotton balls. The land seemed flat and even. It wasn't until we were several yards off the road's surface and heading toward the depression in the landscape that I realized most of the vegetation came up at least to my waist—some of it as high as Roe's shoulders—and rather than being smooth and flat, the ground was uneven and rough. Even worse, what I had up until that moment assumed were soft feathery leaves and petals were in actuality thorny prickly barbs and burrs. Each and every plant was poised to cling on my pant legs and sleeves. Sharp barbs threatened to embed in my hair and claw at my face as the ground was ready to send me sprawling.

When I grumbled about it, Roe only said, "The sagebrush is a pain, but from what I've heard, you really want to avoid the jumping cholla." He pointed to a golden-colored plant born of a nightmare. Long stiff stalks were coated in hundreds, if not thousands, of inch-long serrated daggers. There'd been nothing like this close to the road. Or more correctly, I hadn't seen anything like this. If I had, I never would have suggested our off-road route.

When Hale saw my expression, he chuckled. "Try not to fall."

I'd never walked so carefully in my life.

Once we made it to the wash, another obstacle presented itself. What for all the world had looked like the barest depression in the earth was actually a small canyon, perhaps twenty feet deep. The sides were near vertical and it took a fair amount of time to find a washed-out slope where we could descend without falling in. The loose dirt slipped and slid under my feet, but I managed to make it to the bottom with only one slide on my butt.

I rose and dusted off the seat of my pants and found a large rock to rest on while dumping buckets of chunky sand from my boots. At least both Roe and Hale also needed to shake out their shoes before we were walking again.

The wind was blowing in earnest. Rather than cooling us, however, it simply felt like a furnace blowing grime into every nook and cranny of my body. I could even feel a thin layer of grit coating my teeth.

I checked over my shoulder every few minutes, knowing eventually a garish maroon and gold wagon would be on our trail. From the bottom of the ravine, however, the view was limited. Perhaps one of the boys would have better luck, not being as vertically challenged as I was.

We made our way south, and Hale explained what had transpired with Asher and Jake. I kept mostly quiet, partly because I was embarrassed by my own role in this and partly because I was ashamed of the decision our escorts had made. I still could not believe they would risk him that way. Roe, however, sided with Asher.

"Of course that makes the most sense. What were you thinking, Goldie-Locks?" It seemed a rhetorical question, so I didn't bother answering. "What I witnessed in that wagon. . . You never should have put yourself in a position to barter like that."

I couldn't remain silent. "What would you expect me to do? Let them keep you without even trying? Maybe I should have just strolled on into good old DM, knowing you were either suffering or dead. Does that sound good? Damn it, Roe, it's not like I asked for Hollis's attention."

"What I *expect* is for you to be smarter than him. Or them. And you"—he pointed a finger at Hale's chest—"I don't even know where to start."

"Why don't you start by explaining how you ended up in that wagon in the first place?" Hale leveled back.

"Is that all you care about? How I managed to screw up again and you needed to come save me?"

"You know that isn't all I care about, but don't put all of this on us. You don't want to talk about it right now, I get that. How about an easier one? What the hell happened to your ear? Or easier still, why'd you just say *'them'*? Smarter than *them*, plural. From what I saw, the only one with anything between the ears is Hollis."

"Way to change the subject," Roe said.

"There's nothing to say, Roe! I couldn't stop her from going. It was better to stick with Aurelia rather than risk having neither of you return." Subject closed. "Now, tell me what you meant earlier."

I'd had enough of the bickering. "I'm still here too."

"Tell *us* what you mean," Hale amended.

Roe glared at his older brother. "Okay. I will. But this isn't over."

"Yes, Roe," I said quietly. "It is."

Hale glanced at me, and for once he looked more appreciative than annoyed.

"Wow. I'm gone for a few days, and you've switched sides. Pretty fickle, huh, Specs?" He said the words lightly—a joke between friends.

"Watch it," Hale ground out.

I didn't want to look at either of them but particularly not at Roe. I couldn't take the risk of seeing pain glimmering in his eyes. It would likely end in my own frazzled nerves breaking and I'd be weeping as I walked. Instead, I slowed and looked over my shoulder again. I still couldn't see above the edge of the ravine. I hoped it meant we were still well hidden from view.

"It's fine, Shrimpboat. Nobody back there." I exhaled but he added, "Yet."

I shoved my elbow into his side.

"Who knows? Maybe he's given up the chase." I wasn't sure if he was trying to reassure himself or me.

"They've been dogging us every mile of the way. I doubt Hollis will want to give up now." Hale was always so optimistic. "You didn't tell us what happened to your ear either. We need to get that drained. Soon."

"I'll give you one guess, and it rhymes with Hollis. I realize we have all been working under the assumption he's the chief whack job in that happy little band, but after the past few days, I'm really not so sure."

"You don't think Hollis is calling the shots? But he's the miracle man isn't he?" I asked.

"Well, it certainly isn't the weird little guy you stuck your scalpel into," Hale said.

"No, not Darner and not Hollis," Roe agreed. "I think Nanette might be in charge."

The sun had moved further toward the west, and the shadows within the ravine were lengthening dramatically. The ground was already on the treacherous side—with all the loose gravel and chunky melon-sized rocks. Adding in the shadows, I wasn't sure how much longer I'd be able to navigate the terrain without snapping an ankle.

I grabbed Roe's hand and gave his fingers a brief squeeze, looking over my shoulder one more time. "Maybe we could find somewhere to stop for the night and then you can tell us what the hell you're talking about."

25

ROE

"Keep going, Goldie-Locks." My voice was tired.

I was tired.

When was the last time I'd slept for any decent length of time? The last time I hadn't woken in sheer panic at who might be watching me? How long since my mind wasn't confused or addled thanks to the drug they'd hit me with?

My side still ached, and taking full breaths was still a chore. Resting sounded like paradise, but this wasn't the best place to lay down our weary heads.

"But it's softer here," Auri replied.

"If this is soft, I don't want to know your definition of hard." I threw her my most charming grin. Just because I was miserable didn't mean I needed to act like it.

She raised her eyebrows and shook her head.

"Keep walking, Ms. Morris. I have no desire to sleep on top of that." I pointed at the massive mound and the multitude of large black ants coming and going from the hollow in its center. If they were this busy with the sun setting, I could imagine they'd be all over us when the sun rose in the morning.

Auri made a slight strangled sound when those gorgeous hazel eyes focused where my finger led. "Yikes. Maybe a little further."

The light had turned from the harsh glare of day through the beautiful shades of dusk. We were in the brief slot of time when the atmosphere was silvery and weak, and it would be in our best interest to set up for the night before it was gone altogether. We walked for perhaps another two hundred yards until we came to an area of looser sand piled up against the side of the wash. The bend in the wall must have been created by rushing flood waters hitting the dry packed earth and flowing through at tremendous speeds. The inlet was relatively devoid of brush and succulents, and there didn't seem to be any burrows or hiding spots for desert predators. It was the best we were going to find.

The wind had been wicked all afternoon, and it showed no signs of letting up for the night. It was most unfortunate.

Groaning, I threw down my pack and opened one of my two canteens. I had drunk sparingly through the afternoon and was parched. After three long swallows, closing the cap filled me with no small amount of sadness. Another groan escaped as I lowered myself and leaned up against the side of the ravine wall and opened the pack.

Asher—or Geneva more likely—had packed a good stash of dried fruit, cereal bars, nuts, and jerky for us as well as a lighter, extra socks, and a small pack of first-aid supplies. Luckily the latter had alcohol and some sterile syringes. I unwrapped one of the bars as Auri rifled through the other packets and handed Hale some fruit and jerky. It might have been my imagination, but I swear he looked at her with a softness I'd rarely seen on his face before.

Aurelia sat next to me and put her head against my arm. "My glasses are filthy. I can barely see."

"Give them here, Specs." I held out my other hand in front of her face and cleaned the thick lenses with the bottom of my slightly less filthy shirt. I worried the grains of sand would scratch the lenses, but desperate times meant less than perfect spectacles.

When she had them securely back on her face, she said softly, "I want to hear what happened."

She applied some salve to my wrists. I could just make out a whiff of cocklebur and camphor as she spread it in a thick goopy layer and wrapped my wrists in clean dry gauze. When she picked up the syringe and a vial of liquid antiseptic, I cringed a bit. The relief I felt when she handed them to my brother might have made me feel guilty, but Auri knew Hale was much better with procedures than she was.

"Me too," Hale said.

I caught the reflection of the moon in the depths of Hale's eyes as he studied me. It was going to be no use. I could never hide anything important from him, and this story was no exception.

So as he cleaned the bulging mass of blood trapped in the cartilage at the top of my ear, I talked.

I told them—my brother and my best friend— how I came to find myself in the wagon. I told them of my stupidity in trusting Nanette and of the magical mystery powder that had dropped me like a stone. Of waking in a wagon full of night and the universe, about the stars more beautiful and vivid than those on display tonight and of the shifting moon and the vibrant planets. I tried to build the image of the candles and their multicolored flames, the church and the forest of trees, the glass globes and the unrelenting twilight, knowing my words were falling short. I spoke of the tedium of loosening my bonds just to fall asleep and find them snugged up tight once again. I hadn't quite captured the sense of imbalance and wrongness, but I didn't really need to. Hale had always understood me better than I understood myself and from the sound of Aurelia's hitched breath, I sensed she understood as well.

Tension filled me as Hale lined up the large bore needle close to the throbbing lump on my ear. The pain was intense but thankfully brief, relenting as the pressure left the trapped space. I paused my tale long enough for Hale to apply enough pressure to the surrounding cartilage and ease out the buildup of fluid. He assured me I could get a nice silver hoop for the hole he'd made.

I left out the more humiliating parts—the chamber pot, Nanette's constant attention, my inability to control anything around me. Some things are best not discussed with those we love. The beating Hollis had given me was impossible to skip, but I played it down as much for their sake as my own.

"It sounds"—Auri struggled for the right word—"unpleasant."

I barked a laugh. "Indeed. It was." I grimaced, knowing she couldn't see my face. "I'm sorry for my earlier behavior. I really am grateful you two managed to spring me. It's just the thought of you, with them . . . I'd rather die than have you experience how vile it all felt."

She squeezed my arm in the dim light. Hale shifted his face away from us.

Turning on the hand lamp on I'd been holding in my lap, I swung the beam in a wide arc around us. Between the two lamps, they should have enough charge to make it through the night. The sun would do the work of recharging them for us as we continued walking the next day.

Hale scratched at his head and stretched. "I still don't understand why you think Hollis won't come after Aurelia."

"I never said I didn't think he'd trail us. I said I wasn't sure he was in charge."

"Okay." He drew the word out. "Care to explain?"

"It's what he said when I tripped. Did you hear him?"

"I was too busy trying to drag you down the road and keep an eye on the little troll with the knife."

"He told me not everything is as it appears. Or something roughly along those lines. Then he pushed me after you and told me to run."

Auri made a grunting noise. "Suddenly he has a conscience? I don't really see how that means anything, Roe. It was probably just another play. This one just didn't work out."

"When did you become the cynical one? What did you do to her, Hale?" I meant it to be funny, but part of me really did wonder what had gone on between the two of them. "It was the second time he'd said it to me. The first time was after I noticed a small stack of Medicus books in the wagon."

"Medicus books?" Hale asked.

"Yeah. A few of them. All together. I'm not sure why, but I think they might have belonged to Hollis."

"Medicus books?" he asked again, clearly not believing such a thing was possible. "Are you sure? You said yourself, you thought they were messing with your head."

"I did and still think they were. But this was different, and they were for sure Medicus texts. I saw *Intro to Patient Care*, our anatomy atlas, and our big pharm book. There might have been more. I didn't get a chance to peruse the shelves. They were older editions but still our books—snakes and staffs on the spines."

"Aurelia sat up straighter and turned her body to face me. "And you think this is important because. . .?" It wasn't a condescending question, more of an I really want to know what you're thinking tone.

"It might not mean anything, but I am almost positive Hollis was embarrassed I noticed them."

"Maybe he took them off the last person he kidnapped?" Hale's tone wasn't kind.

Auri frowned at him. It was too dark for him to see, but I appreciated it nonetheless. "Maybe he failed out or maybe he picked them up on his travels somewhere?"

"I think maybe they were his," I said, continuing quickly when Hale made a noise like he thought this was an inane suggestion. "It just seemed . . . I don't know. Like Nanette was toying with me. Always trying to get under my skin just to see me squirm. Hollis, while vile, was more direct. A time or two I even got the faintest impression he was trying to distract her from her games."

"So they're both screwed up in the head. Maybe she gets bored easily. It doesn't matter. We stay together. We get back to the others, and we get this whole damn journey over with." Hale would never stop being my older brother, but I wished he wasn't such a prick all the time.

"I guess." I sighed, not wanting to fight with him on something neither of us would win. We couldn't know what Hollis was thinking, and right now Hale was right. We needed to catch up to the others. "We should probably try to get some sleep. I know a fire is risky, but it's already cooling off. We should light one."

Hale got to his feet and gathered up chunks of dry yucca, dead brush, and whatever branches he could find that weren't covered in needles and spines. I said a silent thank you to Geneva for including the lighter and watched as the flames sprang to life.

"Aurelia? You think this will make you feel better when the coyotes and bobcats come around?" he teased her. I had never heard him tease her before.

"Not funny." She spread out a bedroll a safe distance from the tiny bonfire, but within the ring of light.

He held his hands up in mock surrender. "Hey. I don't like the thought of wild animals anymore than you do."

I stared into the flames. They burned an intense coppery orange—the smoke thick and greasy in the cooling air. I felt my best friend curl up on the bedroll beside me, clearly not intending to move anytime soon. My eyes shifted from the dancing licks of flame to the face of my brother. He didn't notice me looking—too focused on the form of the petite girl beside me.

He stood by the fire and crossed his arms, all business once again. "You both look exhausted. Get some sleep. I'll take the first watch."

Despite my exhaustion, I didn't sleep well. None of us did. The wind. The rocks. The threats of predators, both animal and human. Take your pick.

By the time the first light of morning cracked over the eastern hills, we'd been trudging through the loose sand of the desert wash for at least an hour. Grit was in my eyes, in my ears, up my nostrils. My feet hurt and my back hurt. Auri looked just as miserable, her eyes red behind the thick lenses of her glasses. The dust was so thick in her braids, they were more of a mud color than the luxurious chestnut locks I was accustomed to.

Hale shouldered the pack this morning. He seemed more like himself though. Quiet and brooding. It came as somewhat of a relief to me. I knew what to do with this version of my brother.

Sometime before noon, a cry rent the air. Auri jumped but calmed down as Hale stopped and pointed to the creamy tan underside of an enormous hawk against the blue of sky. It sailed in large concentric rings, rising and falling on the thermals, barely needing to flap its deep umber wings. I imagined every desert cottontail bunny and scampering chipmunk for miles around was as frozen in place as we were.

It might have been that hawk that saved all our lives.

Lost in the monotony of the march—heads down against the wind—none of us had been paying much attention to the landscape around us. More importantly, none of us had noticed the gathering thunderheads behind us. Watching the hawk, I realized the normally pale robin's-egg blue was now a deeper slate.

I looked over my shoulder and stumbled. Ahead and to the south the sky was still clear, but behind? Towering grey and charcoal clouds swallowed the horizon.

"Do you both see this?" I asked. "I've never seen storm clouds like that."

"They say the thunderstorms in the desert can get intense but don't generally last very long. Maybe it'll blow itself out before it hits us." Aurelia had a hopeful look on her face.

"Maybe." Hale didn't sound convinced. "Probably best if we try to make it to some shelter though."

"Ummm . . . I don't think shelter is going to happen," I replied.

"Maybe not, but we at least need to get out of this wash." Hale wasn't panicked, just practical.

Damn. He was right. If that thing broke open, even miles away, most of the water would funnel down through this wash. Flash floods were a true threat out here. Jude had told me about the floods they got in Jave in the summer. The water could travel up to ten feet per second when it really got rolling. What was worse, the power of the water was intense enough to push mounds of debris—even hundred pound boulders—like they were children's toys. People could easily be caught unaware and pay the price from either blunt force trauma or drowning.

We moved at a much faster pace. Not running, but close.

I kept my eyes open for a spot where we could climb out of the ravine, but the walls were just as steep as they'd been for the past few miles. Even worse, the dirt was crumbly and soft. There wouldn't be any good footholds to scramble up if needed.

We didn't make it far before a solid wall of deep adobe orange rock replaced the soft crumbling dirt on our left. It would have been beautiful if it hadn't made me feel even more trapped down here. Whose stupid idea had it been for us to travel in this wash?

Just as the wall of the ravine transitioned, so too did the ground beneath our feet. Gone was the chunky loose gravel. It was replaced by more of a hard pack. Still dirt, but firmer and easier to walk and possibly even run on. Finally, something in our favor.

"Maybe here," Hale said as he stepped closer to the wall on our right. It was marginally less vertical than any other spots we had passed, but I wasn't optimistic. It loomed at least fifteen feet up and had only the smallest grips for hands or feet. Even if he made it, I doubted Auri would be able to scale the wall.

My brother didn't seem to think of these things however. Before I could voice my concerns, he was digging into the face with his booted feet. If there had been a rope or some decent handholds, he might have made it. There weren't and he didn't. When his feet were just above the level of Auri's head, he grasped a chunk of loose rock and it was over. The rock came away from the wall in his hand, and he didn't have the leverage to cling to the cliff face. Luckily he realized what was happening and pushed back with his feet. The fall was neither graceful nor quiet—he let out a rather ugly expletive as he tumbled—but at least he managed to keep his legs under him. Hale landed feet then ass in the dirt but was up in no time.

"Maybe not here," he grumbled as he readjusted his pack and kept moving.

The going was a little quicker now that we didn't need to plod through the shifting gravel—all three of us scanning for an area we could easily climb. Still nothing.

"Do you smell lightning, Auri?" Hale asked. He was sounding a little more winded and a lot more concerned.

She shook her head.

"Good." He kept moving down the wash.

"I don't think the storm is close enough to worry about lightning right now," I offered.

"It's not. I just want to know how much trouble we might be in."

My confusion must have shown on my face. Hale pointed another fifty yards ahead to where the wall on the right also became bright rusty orange and converged with the wall on the left, leaving a gap of perhaps two feet across.

"If things are going to get bad, Aurelia might sense it. And to me, that looks like it has the possibility of being trouble."

Aurelia looked at him with a mixture of shock and sheepish pride. I decided not to unpack what it meant that he was suddenly a believer in this ridiculous train of thought.

Thunder cracked in the distance, and I looked back to see the mountains and desert behind us hidden by a veil of charcoal grey. Long vertical brush strokes pulled downward from the heavens. The storm was still a good distance off, maybe ten miles, but that curtain of rain looked intense. Even if a single drop never descended on our heads, all of that water needed to go somewhere, and that somewhere was into this wash. If Jude was to be believed and the water could get rolling that quickly, by my estimation we had maybe thirty minutes to get out of here.

We approached the crevice in the wash. Hale first. Then Auri. Me in the rear.

Hale cursed loudly and with passion.

I edged around to Aurelia's right and looked down. The red stones made a staircase of sorts, but the space was tight and we were talking stairs that would be comfortable for a giant. It was a bad vantage, but I could see three drop-offs. It was easy to tell the first step was at least six feet down. The others though? I couldn't guess from this angle. The crevice opened up after the first drop at least, but negotiating that first one was going to be tricky. The last thing any of us needed was a snapped ankle.

"Maybe we can backtrack, find another way out?" Auri asked, but we all knew that wasn't an option. I didn't blame her though. Those drops were taller than she was. At least she had the advantage when it came to squeezing between the rock walls. Both my brother and I would be a bit more scrunched.

Hale took a deep breath. "Right. I'm going down first. I'll check for good grip points. If I get wedged, Roe, you'll need to help me back up."

He took the pack off and handed it to Auri. She stepped aside so I could be close to the gap should he get stuck. The light dimmed as clouds shifted over the sun. Where shadows had been, now the light was diffused and soft. Again, it would have been gorgeous had it not added to the growing sense of calamity.

Aurelia shivered. The slight groan that escaped her told me she was convinced the chill meant something else. Damn Hale for suggesting she would sense our doom.

I registered the flicker of a white flash behind me several seconds before thunder boomed through the ravine.

"That's my cue." Hale placed one hand on either side of the crevice and stepped downward, placing his right boot on the wall. I could see the strain in his trapezius and biceps muscles as he pushed outward with his arms in the small space. Slowly, he moved his left foot inward and down as well. He shuffled a few inches at a time until he could easily drop the rest of the way.

I let out the breath I'd been holding when he turned around and motioned for the pack Auri had been holding. I threw the bedrolls and canteens down after.

"I think you should go next," I told her. "I can help lower you down, and then Hale can grab you from the bottom so you don't fall."

Relief washed over her face. "I was afraid I was going to have to do that." She pointed toward Hale in a vague sort of way. Thunder rumbled again, more overhead now. She winced.

"Don't worry about that. Turn around and face me."

After pushing her glasses up on her nose, she did as I asked. I took hold of her arms just below the elbows. "All right, Shrimpboat, grab onto my wrists and step backward. Just walk down the wall until Hale's got you. We won't let you fall."

She nodded and blew out a breath and stepped back. I hadn't counted on the strain of trying to keep her weight even as I squeezed my shoulders into the cramped space. My injured ribs yelled at me, and I gritted my teeth to keep a groan from escaping.

Thankfully, it took only a few moments for her to be low enough for Hale to lift her easily to the ground. Then it was my turn.

I was halfway down, ribs and shoulders singing, when thunder clapped through the air, reverberating off the red walls surrounding me. Within seconds, fat drops of rain were falling. The storm was quicker than we'd anticipated.

Hale and Aurelia had already scooped up the gear by the time my boots hit the red outcropping. It was roughly four feet to the next drop but the ravine had widened up considerably.

Hale dropped to his stomach, swung his legs over the edge and shimmied down the next drop.

The air smelled fragrant and comforting. Petrichor. It was a lie. This rain would hold zero comfort. The pitter-patter of the shower lasted only a minute before it became an unrelenting tattoo.

"Come on, Aurelia. I've got you." Hale had to yell over the din as she scooted over the edge. I was right next to her, blinking water from my eyes as I scrambled over the drop. The rough stone scraped along my forearms.

We hit the next level, and I nearly cried. The wash ran on for hundreds of yards beyond the last drop. I didn't see a slope or depression in the wall anywhere.

Lightning flashed against my retinas, and the accompanying boom of thunder was deafening. Water was coursing over the rock above us and through the gap we'd just traversed, like a tiny rushing waterfall. Only a couple of inches wide but a waterfall nevertheless.

Hale was already swinging his legs over the side when Auri shouted, "It looks like steps."

She ran to the left and scampered down a series of lumpy boulders. Not quite a pristine staircase but functional at least. My brother and I followed, and we hit the soft gravel once again. The rain made the loose pebbles more of a slush, but at least no gaping holes waited to twist an ankle.

The sky above continued to dump bucketloads on us, but it wasn't the sound of the thunder or deluge that made my heart sputter. It was the rumbling from behind us I didn't like. That rumble meant a wall of water was barreling down the ravine.

26

HALE

My ass hurt from the fall in the rocks. As a matter of fact, I was pretty sure I was going to have gravel patterned bruising on my left cheek. It didn't stop me from moving quickly though.

We ran like hell, jumping over rocks and dodging the scalpel blade ends of yucca.

The rain lashed at my face, and the ground made slurping noises in some spots and grinding wet slurring noises in others.

There had to be a way up and out of this wash. There had to be.

I'd never seen earth like that before. It was so dry it soaked up the water quickly at first, but soon water was running past us in rivers over the concrete-like rock and desert pavement. We made it through the crevice. At least that was something. When I looked back, a steady spraying flow of water was gushing out of the gap. It wouldn't be long before it became a rushing river.

Thunder cracked and I flinched. Aurelia yelped, and I swear off in the distance answering voices cried out as well. It must have been a trick of the acoustics in the gully walls. Either way, it didn't matter. If we couldn't find a ramp up out of here, it might as well be the full Medicus Corpus faculty, Hollis and his wagon of trolls and harlots, *and* the entirety of the population of Devil's Meadows combined for all the difference it would make. We'd be drowned before we ever saw another breathing soul.

The water was definitely moving more quickly. My boots were soaked and bits of desert debris flowed past my calves. Then came a sound like nothing I've ever heard before—the crush of thousands of gallons of water headed down the narrow chasm.

"Hale, to the left. The left." Aurelia's frantic calls rose above the noise.

In front of us by about twenty yards, the canyon's wall had crumbled on itself, making for a steep but climbable ramp out of this hell and into the purgatory above.

Water flowed down the side and eddied where it joined the rest of the deluge flowing down the valley. I stood in the swirling turbulence and pushed first Aurelia and then Roe up the incline. I followed once they were both safe.

Not two minutes later, we watched a wall of water, earth, and debris rush past, filling the space at least four feet up the sides.

"Thank the hawk," Roe croaked.

I looked at him blankly.

"The hawk. If I hadn't looked up to watch it, I wouldn't have noticed the storm. We wouldn't have started moving faster. We would still be down there and most likely dead."

"Well then." Aurelia smiled at him. "Thank the hawk for sure."

Something twisted low in my gut. I sometimes wished she'd turn that smile on me.

27

AURELIA

"I'm filing a formal complaint."

Hale kept walking, not bothering to acknowledge my statement.

"Do tell," Roe replied.

"With Medicus Corpus. When we get to DM. I am filing a complaint."

He cocked an eyebrow. "On what basis exactly?"

"Undue duress. That's three times now I've had to run for my life since we left Renfield. I don't recall anyone from Medicus mentioning running."

I was joking, but only a little. The truth was, I needed to make a joke of it or else I would probably lose it once again. I simply hadn't anticipated this level of danger when I'd applied to Medicus Corpus for training all those years ago. I wanted to be a practitioner, but the practicalities of leaving my home, family, comfort, and security to pursue this dream had been completely lost on me at the time. And to be fair, during all the discussions about the match and our contracts to serve our oath, no one— not one person—had mentioned bandits or lunatics or kidnapping as part of the deal. The escorts had been merely an insurance policy to make sure we stayed on track and our supplies intact.

Roe was nodding sagely. "There's a lot Medicus left out of those brochures."

The rain disappeared as violently as it had arrived. Having collected and run off for many miles behind us, the water still flowed through the wash, but the sun shone brightly overhead once again. It made the air sticky and heavy, but I was sure it would be dusty and dry again in no time. On the upside, it had washed off at least the topmost layer of dirt from my hair and skin. My clothes were a lost cause.

"At least we came up on the left, closer to the road. I might have just sat down and died if I thought we had to cross that chasm again."

Hale grunted in agreement.

"What do you think it was like, before?" I asked.

"Before what, the rain?" Roe responded.

"No, before Medicus. Before the Divagation."

He let out a long breath and looked at Hale, who shrugged. Roe spoke slowly. "There was a time when I dreamt of what that kind of tech might have been like. Pushing a button and getting an actual picture of organs and vessels. But now, well, I don't let myself think about it. What good would it do to wish for something we don't have?"

"Doesn't it make you angry though?" The past days had filled me with frustration, and now it bubbled up and overflowed.

"A little, I guess." He looked at me sideways, a wariness in his eyes. "It would be nice to have better medicines, better communications, better imaging. It would make the healing easier, and I'm sure we'd save more people without having to work as hard or think as much."

"That's an interesting take," Hale muttered.

"Come on, you know what I mean," Roe said quickly.

The trouble was we really didn't know. Some texts detailed the kinds of medicines and ancillary services that once existed, but the Grand Divagation made sure we didn't know too much. At some point, the global community—or at least those in power to make the decisions—felt things were too good. Too easy. Folks were living too long and leaving nothing but abuse and consumption in their wake. Excess got the better of people. Those decision makers determined it needed to end. Major changes swept the world, limiting the technology for all sorts of things, not solely medicine. But our forbearers had taken a huge hit. Over the span of a few decades, medicine had stepped backward centuries. And there we'd stayed.

"I guess what I mean is, why worry about something we can't change. Let's just do amazing things with the tools we have."

"Because," I said fiercely, "if we had all those things, we wouldn't need miracles."

Hale continued walking, not looking at either of us. His thumbs were hooked through the straps of the pack, his face thoughtful. "While I don't agree with my dense little brother, human nature is what it is, Aurelia. Even if you could cure cancer, they would always want more. They'd still want miracles."

I couldn't say anything to that, so I simply walked ahead in silence until movement caught my eye toward the road. We'd finally made it across the valley and had a clear view back the direction we'd come. We hadn't seen anyone, but now we were once again out in the open, I wondered if we'd just been foolish the entire time. If we had been able to hide our movements, so too could someone else.

Hale and Roe were at least two dozen yards behind me, having a quiet conversation of their own. Had they seen anything? I strained up to my toes, trying to see the road as it gently curved toward what appeared to be a small group of worn-down buildings—perhaps a long-forsaken service station.

I'd nearly convinced myself the movement had been a simple jackrabbit or some desert birds, but I didn't see any wildlife that could explain it. Maybe I should have found a hat to wear or gotten some sun-reflective coating for my glasses. The light had to be playing tricks on me.

Then I saw it again. Splashes of color—orange and blue, maybe even some scarlet and white—moved against the never-ending taupe and olive. It wasn't bulky or vibrant. Not the miracle and wonder wagon with its crew full of loons then. It looked more like a . . . a couple of people on the road. On foot. I crouched down on instinct.

The Belstrohm brothers were at my side immediately, conversation forgotten. I don't know if they saw what I did. It was possible they were just responding to my posture.

I started to speak, but Hale shook his head and placed a finger over his lips. He gestured for Roe and me to stay put while he ran ahead, crouching low among the desert plants. I lost sight of him as he made his way closer to the road.

The sun was beating down on the top of my head, causing a pounding in my temples and through my eyes. I looked to Roe. He was motionless save for the twitch in his jaw where a tiny rivulet of sweat ran along it, traversing from his temple to his collar. Crouching there, I became more and more convinced it had been people I saw. One tall and the other wiry and small. Both in disheveled clothing and the shorter one wearing a grime-coated cloth to keep the sun off their head. Something was so familiar about the image, but I couldn't get my mind to pick out what it was.

We waited and then waited some more. Finally, after what felt like hours but was probably no more than ten minutes, Hale returned, a grim look on his face.

"Whoever it was, they're gone now or hiding somewhere," he informed us.

"But you both saw people?" I asked. "It wasn't just my imagination or a coyote or something?"

Roe was the first to answer. "I thought I did, but the optics out here can get pretty weird. Maybe it was just an unusual heat shimmer or something."

Hale agreed with his brother. "I thought so too, but Roe's right. It was probably nothing."

I nodded. Maybe we all needed more water and a good night's sleep.

"Do you think it's safe to keep going?" I wasn't sure what our options would be if we didn't.

Again, Roe spoke first. "I don't see that we have much of a choice. The sooner we catch the others the better."

Hale nodded. "I agree. I say we head back to the road, hit those buildings to see if there's any sign of the trams coming through, and come up with a better plan."

The house was made of bottles. Green and brown, clear and even the occasional red. The rounded ends of a thousand bottles—mostly chipped and cracked, but some miraculously whole—peeked out from the mortar holding them together as walls. The roof was gone and most of the front wall lay in a shattered and jagged mess on the ground. The broken bits of glass glittered like gems over the littered ground.

Across the road and down the way, a iron plate fashioned into the shape of a donkey sat next to the shell of an old camper, its wheels gone and windows shattered.

It wasn't the bottle house or the metal donkey or even the dilapidated camper wagon that concerned me though. It was the legs sticking out from behind one of two rusted windmills that slowed my steps.

"What's wrong?" Roe asked at the same time Hale said, "Do you feel something?"

Roe shot his brother a look, but Hale merely shrugged, *she's been right before* in his gesture. My eyebrows rose as I willed them to be quiet and pointed at the legs.

Roe's face broke into one of those gorgeous smiles I loved so much. "Jude!" he exclaimed and jogged down the asphalt.

Jude? He could tell from dirty pants legs and scuffed boots it was Jude in the shade of the stout metal structure?

He wasn't wrong. As Roe neared, the resting man stood, surveyed the surrounding area, and only when he was convinced it was just the three of us, returned the smile. He stepped forward and grasped Roe's hand with his large brown one. The other clapped on Roe's shoulder.

"So you're alive then? Good." He turned to Hale and me as we approached. "And with Auri-Girl here to boot. Well now, that is a win win."

I looked around, noting the obvious absence of Jake, Asher, Geneva, and more importantly the three trams with the rest of our group and provisions.

"Where's everyone else?" My voice was a little more breathless than I would have liked.

"Good to see you too." Jude frowned at me. "There was an incident. Unfortunately said incident has led Asher to push on to Devil's Meadows at a rather accelerated clip. I asked to wait here for you three—hoping it would be three—while they kept going. I'll explain more on the way."

"How far ahead?" Hale asked directly.

"Not much. We hit this place a few hours ago. Thought it was the best stopping off point. I've got enough food and water for three days—give or take."

My back was aching and my feet were tired, but I got the impression none of my companions would be happy if I asked to sit and rest for a few—in particular, Jude.

I opened my canteen and drained the rest of the tepid water down my throat. "By chance, do your supplies include any sun block?"

He reached into a pocket in his pack and handed me a small jar filled with thick white goop. I smeared it on any exposed skin and cringed as the texture went from dense and pasty to a gritty cement in no time. Apparently the rain hadn't gotten me quite as clean as I had hoped. The idea of a cool bath nearly brought tears to my eyes.

"I've got protection from more than the sun." He bent to the pile of items next to where he'd been waiting. As he rose, he strapped the long rifle across his back.

"Did you see anyone just ahead of us? We thought maybe we saw people on foot a little way back." It bothered me how they had seemed there and then . . . gone.

"No ma'am. Just you three."

Admitting to myself I was seeing things was hard, but not as hard as believing someone could just vanish into thin air.

I helped Hale redistribute the things Jude had for us, while Roe filled all six of our canteens from a larger drum and strapped it to the top of his pack. We were traveling heavier than we had been, but at least I didn't worry about dehydration as much now.

"If we hustle, we might catch them up before the next settlement. I don't imagine they'll stop there for any length of time, but it's the last one until we hit Devil's Meadows." Jude looked to all three of us and when we nodded continued, "Good. We've got maybe three more hours of daylight left. I think we should use every second of it."

I didn't want to know what catastrophe had hit the others to take the jovial smile from Jude's face, but we were about to find out.

28

ROE

According to my watch, we ended up walking four hours and twenty minutes before we camped. Other than the day going around the lake, it was the longest day on our feet this entire journey. The sun had set and the stars were out in all their brilliant glory by the time we made camp.

During that time Jude gave us the horrifying details of what had gone wrong enough to cause Asher to leave us to fend for ourselves.

"To start, both old Asher and Pops were pretty well ticked you two just headed out on your own," he leveled at Hale and Aurelia. "Don't get me wrong, I understand why you did it. I too am happy to see Roe alive and in one piece, but Asher was bent when he got up and found your note. He'd just come to our tent to yell at us to get a move on when we heard the first flash bang.

"It was pretty clear from the start we were dealing with the same kind of human waste that typically try to hit us on the road. The noise was meant to be a distraction to get us moving away from the trams so they could get at the supplies, but Asher yelled at me to stay with Phoebe, Wade, and Helena. He didn't want to lose another one of you if this was some sort of ploy from the miracle man. I didn't argue, just did what I was told.

"I wish to all that is holy I hadn't."

He was angry. At who, I didn't know. Maybe Asher. Maybe himself. Maybe at Hale and Auri.

"The kids were all right." I smiled to myself that he thought of us as kids. He couldn't have been more than five years older than most of us. "They seemed a little dazed, having woken to find you both gone and now an explosion somewhere close. I told them not to worry, not that it did much good. You'd never have thought it, but Phoebe got the other two moving better than I could. They just needed to put themselves together. Collect up their things. I was planning on taking the three of them with me to pitch their belongings into Hera's tram and then I could help figure out what was what. That was when things started getting really ugly.

"A second flash bang went off, this time on the other side of the camp. It caught some of the brush on fire and really spooked the horses. Luc needed to get them calmed and hitched up and that left only Hera and Minton to mind the supplies. We've been through this sort of thing before, bandits trying to make off with the good stuff, but with everyone already being distracted and all, we just weren't on like we should've been."

I don't think Jude meant to make us feel guilty, but he did just the same. I felt guilty for being dumb enough to get nabbed, and judging by the look on Little-bit's face she felt much the same way. Hale? Guilt trips rarely worked on him, and Jude's story was no exception.

"I urged your friends to hurry and of course they did. Within two minutes everything was scooped up and we were standing behind the tram just as I planned. Luc was still busy with the horses, and when I saw Hera, I told her the kids were with her. She nodded and I was off to help with the real trouble. I could see a dust up over on the side of the rigs where the first explosion had come from. Looked like Pops was going after some scraggly piece of desert trash and handing it to him good. I left him to it and looked for Asher. That's when I heard the first gunshots. There was maybe five or six of them coming from a little further up the road. I took off in that direction at a run. A careful and watchful run, but still moving as quick as I could without running into a bullet on accident. That's when I saw him kneeling in the dirt, blood splatter all over his face. One body was in front of him, moaning and writhing around, and two others lay still in the rocks. I caught a glimpse of some movement further out in the scrub, where the ravine was traveling parallel to our position, and made to take off after them, but Asher screamed at me. Not yelled. Screamed at me to help him. I've never heard the man like that before. All composure and calm steel gone and replaced by this wildness and terror."

My stomach dropped as the picture became clear. It was obvious where this was going.

"That's when I knew who he was kneeling by. When I knew whose blood was coating his hands. It was Geneva."

He stopped talking, and Aurelia made a noise between a squeak and a sob. She'd always been fond of Geneva. "No," she whispered. "No."

My blood ran icy as Jude stopped and drew a breath, unfastening his canteen from his hip. His hand was shaking as he brought it to his lips, and the deep brown of his handsome face was a little shy of ashy.

"She'd taken a knife to her side." His voice was thick.

"How bad?" Hale's voice was urgent. Demanding. "Was Wade able to patch her up?"

His meaning was clear. *I wasn't there. The surgeon wasn't there. Was anyone else able to save her?* Arrogant as that train of thought was, he was right. He was the best with a needle and thread. Wade would try, but he wasn't Hale.

"It isn't good. Wade got the bleeding under control and stitched up as much as he could, but he's worried there might be some bowel perforation he couldn't find."

Hale shook his head. "We need to move faster. We need to catch them. I can get in there and take a better look."

"They were amazing really. The ladies got an IV into her and pumped her full of antibiotics. We were packed and on the road not an hour later. They made a space in Luc's rig for a stable bed and all the equipment the kids needed to keep her comfortable. We've been hauling ass for the last day and half. We did go to the meet-up location on the other side of the mining town, but we didn't wait long when you weren't there." He didn't meet any of our eyes when he said this. "Sorry."

Hale had picked up his pace a little, silently pushing our little band of travelers a bit faster.

"But as of this morning, Helena told me the wound didn't look good and Gen's been feverish.

"Asher decided then and there, we were hauling flat out for Devil's Meadows."

"Makes sense," I said. "Better equipment and experienced practitioners there."

"It was Geneva who took them down. The two dead bodies in the road. She shot them both after she took the hit."

"She should have shot them before." Aurelia's voice held more venom than I expected from her.

"*I should* have shot them," Jude said. "If I hadn't been assigned babysitter for folks who decidedly don't need one, I would have been there with her. I could have prevented it from happening."

I don't think I'd ever heard any of the escorts question Asher or his decision-making.

"Last time I checked," Hale said, "Geneva is a complete badass. If she couldn't take care of them, you might not have been able to either."

"Maybe." He blew out a long breath. "Maybe."

Aurelia's head snapped up, and she had that light in her eyes that meant she'd thought of something. "Were they wine stains?"

A deep furrow formed between Jude's eyes. "Was who what now?"

Auri shook her head. "The attackers. The bandits. Did they have those creepy wine stains on their faces?"

"Ooohhh." Jude drew out the word, understanding blossoming on his face. "Like the little cannibal that got a hold of Hale here? They sure did. In fact"—he became dead serious again—"one of the ones Gen popped was the very same scumbag."

Breath exploded form Aurelia, and she stopped walking. "If I had let you. . ."

If she had let us kill him the first time, maybe Geneva wouldn't be injured.

"It would have been some other asshole," Hale finished for her.

She was quiet for a long time as we talked about other things. When she spoke again her voice tremored. "Was he still wearing the same clothes?"

Jude gave her a half shrug. "I'm not sure. Don't really remember what he had on. Why?"

She looked a shade paler but shook her head. "No reason, just . . . on the road today. I thought I saw him, but if he's dead, that would mean. . ." She looked uneasy. Shaking her head she mumbled, "never mind."

The rest of it was just bits and pieces. Our trio of colleagues were doing their best to keep Geneva comfortable—and more importantly, alive—until the group could make it to DM. Asher was trying to keep his shit together, sometimes succeeding and sometimes not. He was also both livid we'd left the camp and thankful he'd stayed, given the attack that happened. Had he and Jake been heading up the hill to make the meeting with Hollis as planned, things would have ended even worse for our little band of travelers.

Jude was the first to suggest someone wait for us to catch up, and if we didn't, to backtrack for a day and see if we were alive. Why no one suggested this sooner he didn't say. He seemed the obvious choice and was happy to do it. He hadn't needed to wait very long, but by his best estimation, the caravan was a good three to four hours ahead of us. He'd been told they would stop to rest the horses but would keep moving at as much of a steady pace as possible. I didn't think Asher was fool enough to really push it, as bumping and jostling would be bad for Geneva. Add in the risk of an accident and it was likely they would be moving steadily but not break neck. We could move just as fast on foot.

When we really started to flag, Jude called a halt to our day's travel.

Every part of me hurt and every bit of me smelled. The combination was terrible, and I felt sorry for not only myself but also for the three human beings who had to share space with me. To be fair though, they were all also fairly fragrant, and I presumed at least Auri and Hale had comparable aches and pains.

I unfolded the lightweight tarp Jude handed me from his pack and used the small stakes bundled inside to pitch a makeshift tent. Not perfect but better than we'd had the night before. Jude took the first watch. I fell into sleep almost immediately.

For two days we pushed as far and as fast as we could. It was a monotony of cracked graying asphalt, dry dirty landscape, and pale cloudless skies. We talked when the mood struck, but at times the only sound was parched hissing winds and the calls of the occasional carrion bird.

I marked the time and distance by counting steps between the rotted out wooden poles spaced along the roadside. Some had lengths of useless cable and wires dangling from them, and others were toppled over completely. Presumably, when the power stopped flowing through here, so had any thoughts of maintenance. I wouldn't be surprised if folks thinking to use it to shore up their homes and to burn in their hearths hadn't carted off the wood and cabling.

We slept in bursts too short to suit my tired body and soul, but lingering wouldn't help anyone. Not us and not Geneva.

Hale hadn't voiced it again, but I knew. Knew he drove us as hard as Jude. Jude because it was his job to see us safely back with our group. Hale because he thought his surgeon's hands might be of some use when we caught them.

We saw no sign of Hollis and Nanette. Perhaps they had given up the chase in favor of other prey. Or perhaps Auri had done more damage to Darner than she had intended. Were they also going slow and steady in an effort not to bring pain to an injured friend? It didn't seem likely.

Similarly, we saw no sign of any other wine stains, as Auri had labeled them. If there had been more than the four who'd launched their attack on the camp, it seemed they were off licking their wounds.

The longer we walked, the lighter our physical burden became. I worried we should ration the water better, but every time the thought hit my brain, my tongue grew thick and dry.

The light was fading toward night and the temperature was beginning to abate when we crested the top of another of a thousand small hills. That was when I saw the donkeys.

"Close now," Jude said. "We push on until we come to the next set of buildings. It's too small to be called a settlement, but there's some folks who live there."

Auri nodded but couldn't seem to take her eyes off the hundreds of four legged creatures grazing on both sides of the road. Dozens stood or walked lazily on the blacktop itself. "There must be water here."

"Underground springs," Jude confirmed.

I understood then what my eyes had seen but my mind had dismissed. It was grass. Actual green grass growing along both sides of the old road. Thick and lush and the perfect buffet for the incredible number of donkeys.

Not fearing us as predators, the animals barely took notice as we strolled among them.

"I've made this trip a good number of times now, and I always get a kick out of these guys." Jude was smiling. Not the big bright, easy smile he'd worn when we first met, but a smile nonetheless. "They'll be in amongst the buildings too. I've never seen another place quite overrun by them like here."

He was right. As we made our way into the tiny group of buildings, the donkeys—I was later informed they were actually wild burros—meandered up and down the road and rested in the spaces between shacks and trailers. I wasn't sure how well I'd sleep that night knowing one could walk up and bite me on the rear or try to steal food from our packs. It seemed I could do nothing about it. Clearly they owned the place. I trusted Jude had a plan to camp us where we'd be out of their way.

As it turned out, sleep would be a long time coming. As we passed an old worn structure—larger than the others—we came to a dead stop. Just ahead, and blocking the road completely, were three large fiberglass trams, snakes and staffs painted boldly on their sides.

29

AURELIA

The gravel under my feet sprayed up as I slid to a stop.

As soon as the caravan came into sight and my brain registered what it meant, I'd torn off as fast as my short legs would carry me. I needed to see her. Needed to help her. Geneva had always been kind to me, and the thought of her injured or possibly even dying filled my belly with an acrid sensation I couldn't escape.

As the back of Luc's rig came into view, however, my gaze didn't catch Geneva or Asher or even Jake. It was Hollis. Bound and disheveled yes, but here. Where he most certainly did not belong.

More gravel flew as I spun around, searching for the cumbersome red wagon.

"Don't fret, Ms. Morris. They aren't here." His voice was less than it had been. Not polished and refined but harsh and worn. The voice of a man who'd been endlessly speaking. Or screaming.

His hands were tied together with what appeared to be long strips of bandaging. A leather strap secured his waist to one of the rungs of the metal steps.

"How?" I whispered.

"How what, my dear?"

I shook my head. "Actually, never mind. I don't have time for this."

He nodded as if he understood. "When the time comes, I'll be waiting right here." He chuckled at his own joke and gestured to the thick piece of leather around his torso.

Raised voices from the large stucco-coated building alerted me to the others. Hale, Roe, and Jude were already heading in that direction, and we arrived at the gruesome scene at the same time. I clamped down on the groan threatening to erupt from me.

Geneva was on a makeshift bed. An intravenous catheter had been placed in her arm, the rubber tubing connecting it to a bag of fluids hung above her on a wire hanger. Phoebe was holding Gen's wrist in one hand, not looking at her but rather at the watch on her other arm. She shook her head slightly. Asher paced back and forth, clenching and unclenching his fists in time with his steps.

Gen's color was all wrong. Gone were the gleaming golden skin and shiny sun-kissed hair. Now she was all sallow grey and limp strands. Deep bluish circles bloomed below her eyes. A towel had been draped over her bare chest to protect her modesty. A thick pad of bandaging clung to her side, stained yellow, brown, and red.

After two steps, the odor hit me. It was not the smell of a person who was going to survive. It was fetid and thick and made me gag involuntarily. Hale—never the squeamish one—must have smelled the same thing, but instead of making him pause, it seemed to snap him into action.

"I need my kit."

Asher's head whipped around at Hale's voice, and the fog cleared from his eyes almost instantly. His gaze flicked to each of us in turn, counting perhaps. Satisfied four additional people were in the building, he didn't waste time with reprimands. "We'll talk later. Can you help her?"

Although the escorts were supposed to assume all practitioners equal, even a fool would have noticed Hale's skills in the previous weeks. Asher was anything but a fool.

Hale made no false promises. "I need to look at the wound first."

Helena materialized at our side. "I've got your things. And I woke Wade. It was his turn to sleep, but he did the initial patch up."

Hale took the kit and set it on the least dilapidated surface he could find, a squat metal bench. He pulled several canvas rolls from the kit and unfurled them one at a time. Each contained a series of pouches, and within each pouch, a paper sterilization packet contained one of a hundred different surgical instruments. He didn't remove any of the packets or instruments yet—that would come once he knew what he needed and once a relatively clean operating space could be established.

The snap of the latex gloves hitting his palms was deafening in the quiet space. Phoebe remained at Geneva's side murmuring soothing words, but otherwise no one spoke. She offered Hale her stool, but he gave a brief shake of his head and flipped a five-gallon bucket on end and used it to sit next to Gen.

"What's she got on board right now?" he directed at Phoebe.

"We've been giving her morphine for the pain. Last dose was maybe thirty minutes ago. As far as antibiotics, we've given her what we have, but you know it's not much. Just the cefotaxime we had ready for IV, and we have only one dose of that left. Wade's done what he can, and it's better than anything I could have done, but the wound . . . it's not good."

His brow was furrowed as he studied the dressing. "How often are you changing this?"

"Every four to six hours. I was about to do it now." A handful of hours wasn't very long considering how stained and damp the material was.

"Okay." He breathed out. "Let's take a look."

Geneva moaned louder as Hale applied the slightest pressure trying to get a grip on the edge of the tape. As he lifted the edge, he winced at whatever he saw. When he removed the remaining dressing, I peeked over his shoulder. The flesh over her left hip was tight and discolored. The sutures stretched, forming tense divots in her skin where they pulled. Leaking from between the silk threads, purulent drainage oozed out.

"Where's Wade? I'd like to know what I'm going to see in there."

"Here. I'm here." Wade looked how I felt. Dark circles hung below his eyes, and his beard was more grungy than manicured professional. At least he was making an effort, unlike the rest of us—tucking in his shirt as he walked into the building.

Wade nodded at both Roe and me, grabbed a pair of gloves, and joined Hale beside the makeshift bed. "Obviously those sutures need to be released, then you might be able to get a drain in. I thought we might make it to Devil's Meadows before I needed to, but . . . well, I should have done it at the time. I don't know what else is perforated. I'm not as good with surgical stuff as—"

"Wade." Hale said his name calmly, and Wade stopped rambling. "So you think there might be a bowel perforation? Judging by the odor, I agree with you."

He looked around. I didn't need to be a mind reader to know what he was thinking. This place wasn't an ideal operating space. It wasn't just dirty, it was filthy. Old linoleum peeled and cracked under our feet. Boxes and cartons were stacked along two of the four walls. The roll-up doors forming a third wall were bent and crooked on their railings, and the wind whistled through, bringing with it not just an insanely annoying sound, but also loads of desert dust. I didn't even want to think about what sorts of animals might call the space their home, but the moment the idea came to me, it wouldn't leave. As if in answer, a long braying cry startled me into looking toward the door where one of the smaller burros was sticking its head in as if to investigate our presence.

"Why'd you choose to set up in here?" I asked Helena.

"We didn't really have any other options. Asher says it's another four days at least to hit Devil's Meadows. Unless we could make it to some abandoned prison down the road, we'd be out in the elements if anything else needed be done. We were going to do what we could here tonight and then get moving at first light again." She looked at Roe and seemed to realize for the first time he was there. She gave him a weak smile. "Phoebe was worried sick about you."

"Thanks. I guess I should see what Hale needs to get set up."

I turned back to her. "I know we shouldn't have left, but—"

"Don't apologize," she said. "It was bad, and I'm sure things could have been handled better, but we all know you did what you felt you needed to do. It isn't your fault or Roe's. It's *their* job to keep *us* safe, remember? Not the other way around. I know that sounds harsh, but if they didn't see the attack coming, neither could you."

"Yeah, but if she doesn't survive. . ." I couldn't bring myself to finish the thought.

Helena didn't seem to know what to say either, but she gave me a brief squeeze on the shoulder. Her eyes were full of sorrow as she watched Asher pacing back and forth again. Jude and Jake would travel on with her team, but that didn't mean we hadn't all grown attached to one another.

There wasn't much for either of us to do. Phoebe remained next to Geneva, wiping her forehead with cool cloths. Wade and Roe were busy setting up a surgical area, but without enough space for us to assist we'd only be in the way. Hale was still studying the wound.

Jude and Jake stood by the doorway, speaking in hushed tones. Only the three tram masters were missing. Presumably they were monitoring the supplies and keeping a wary eye on the prisoner tied to one of their rigs.

I wanted to ask about Hollis, but now was not the time to bring it up. It boggled my mind though. We'd been as watchful of the road as we could be and had never seen the wagon. As hard as it was to miss, we hadn't seen the wagon near the dry lake bed either, and look how that had turned out. Had they passed us in the night while we slept in the ravine? That was possible, but if so, where was it now? Why was Hollis here without his accomplices? Perhaps he'd made the journey alone on foot. If I had done real damage to his driver, perhaps he'd left Nanette to tend to the wounded man. Fat lot of good it did him, to catch his target only to be apprehended by our escorts and tied up like the criminal he was.

Maybe that was what Jake was filling his son in on. I'd ask one of them later. My focus needed to be on helping to heal Geneva in any way I could.

As if thinking her name had somehow roused the sleeping woman, I heard her thin and reedy voice. "Well, look at this. Are we having a party?"

"No parties until you can get up and dance with me," Hale told her. Looking to Roe over his shoulder, he said, "Let's get some more morphine ready. Oh, and make sure you grab the chloral hydrate. I don't want her to wake up halfway through."

30

HALE

The escaping gas made a wet hissing noise as I snipped the sutures.

When we were young, Roe had a thing for blowing up balloons and letting them go to race around the room. He always seemed to get as much saliva in there as air. Geneva's wound reminded me of one of Roe's air-propelled wet balloons. Not good. Not good at all.

The gash was only two inches at most—not nearly enough room for me to get in there and look around. It needed to be opened a good bit. After scrubbing off as best we could given our location, Wade and I donned sterile gloves and gowns to cover our soiled clothes. He stood across from me on Geneva's other side. Roe was next to me, and Phoebe—tasked with monitoring Geneva's breathing—sat by her head. We'd rolled Gen's body so her wounded side was up, and placed rolled blankets around her to prevent as much movement as possible.

I caught myself before I started. I couldn't think of the woman lying in front of me as Geneva. For this to go well, she couldn't be the person who kept us in line, the woman who chatted with Aurelia every evening, the friend and mentor we could rely on. It was time to turn off the familiarity and think of her as a patient. If I didn't do that, I would never be able to focus completely on the procedure.

Roe handed Wade a retractor, and Wade inserted it delicately into the gash and held it in place, gently pulling the wound back on one side. The skin and subcutaneous tissue were friable and filled with crepitus. I ran my gloved fingers along the edge and gently under the tissues, feeling for bogginess and other signs of infection. A small puddle of cloudy fluid ran out. My initial assessment seemed about right. Not good at all.

Time to do what I could. Without saying a word, Roe handed me a scalpel, knowing what I needed before I had to ask. I cut further through the skin and muscle, doubling the size of the opening. Our patient moaned a little but didn't move. Once the incision was wide enough, I slowly poured sterile saline into the cavity while Wade used the small battery-powered suction machine to pull it out again. After several rounds, the fluid transitioned from thick and murky to something closer to the saline we irrigated with. She shuddered once. I needed to speed things up.

I located the glistening loop of bowel and methodically inspected it. Most of it was the pearly pink grey of healthy tissue, but several patches showed darker, more worrisome colors. As bad as those spots were though, none of them showed signs of rupture. A hole in the bowel would mean trouble. The bacteria and contents within the gastrointestinal tract were meant to stay within the gastrointestinal tract. Feces did not belong in the abdominal cavity. So I looked and looked again, not wanting to miss anything.

After a time, I began to hope the knife had missed the bowel and the signs of infection were simply related to local external bacteria infecting the wound. That we could deal with. Before stitching her up, I took one last measure and poured more saline into the opening, this time instructing Wade not to suction it out just yet.

There, coming from the back of the thick rope of intestine, a series of bubbles rose to the surface. I couldn't control the curse that sprang from my pinched lips.

Roe loaded a driver with our smallest needle and thinnest thread and placed it in my waiting hand. It took some maneuvering, but eventually I located the laceration and sutured it up as tight as I could, while still hoping to save the fragile tissues around it. We irrigated again and placed a small tube to serve as a drain.

"Her breathing is getting really erratic, and her pulse is thready." Phoebe's voice was laced with worry.

"Almost done." Perspiration collected along my hairline, the rank aroma of stress rolling off me.

"Helena, can you bring another bad of fluids?" Phoebe asked.

I sewed faster than I ever had before. I didn't think she would mind a few ugly stitch scars if she made it through this. If.

We placed clean bandages and wrapped her in warm blankets, even though it wasn't cold in the little building. Night in the spring desert meant huge temperature shifts. We needed her to stay warm.

I cleaned up my instruments as the others tended to the patient—Geneva. Now that my part was done, I could think of her as the person I knew and admired. She got the last dose of relatively strong antibiotics hooked up to her IV and another small dose of morphine. Asher kissed his wife on the forehead and came my way, hope gleaming in his eyes.

He didn't even open his mouth before I said, "We need Aurelia." The hopeful light in his eyes extinguished almost immediately. I knew he understood, so I added, "And we need to talk to Hollis."

31

AURELIA

The desolate little building contained only so much space, and even my small frame meant more crowding, more breathing, more germs circulating and primed to infect an open surgical site. Over the past few weeks, I'd come to realize I enjoyed watching Hale work. He was a machine—methodical and efficient. Even so, both my heart and my head told me I didn't need to be present to gawk at his skills that evening.

Helena had taken the opportunity to use the time for sleep. It would be her turn to monitor Geneva soon, and a few hours of rest would help her stay relatively alert during the watch. Leaving with her, I elected to find something to eat.

Minton must have been in charge of feeding the team that night. A small camp table was set up with a pot of warm red beans and rice along with cornmeal bread and honey. I meandered over to his rig and sat down alone with my plate. Despite not having a warm meal for the past three days, I didn't enjoy the food and had to force myself to get even half of it down. Rather than risk a revolt from my stomach, I set the dish aside and leaned back to stare up into the heavens.

The glorious wash of white stretching across the night sky caught my breath once again. The sheer number of stars made me feel small and insignificant. I'd seen them every night for the past three weeks, and each time I reminded myself they'd always been there, I just hadn't noticed them until we were in the middle of nowhere. Maybe I'd been too focused on the wrong things. Instead of letting my attention catch on the billions of pinpoint diamonds shining down on us, I'd spent my days and my nights with my face buried in books—trying to rush through my education so I could get on with my *real* life.

Was it possible I'd missed real life? Perhaps I hadn't paid enough attention to all the other little things that were just as important as the pharmacology lab and the microscopes and the endless hours with the textbooks. Maybe I should have talked to Roe about *his real* life. Maybe I should have watched Hale and his amazing skills in the operating room before. Maybe I should have made more friends. Maybe, maybe, maybe.

No matter what happened tonight, tomorrow, or next year, I would take the time each day to look up at the sky and allow myself to marvel at the stars, clouds, moonbeams, and rainbows. My stargazing was cut short. Asher and Hale were headed my way. I hoped it meant the procedure had gone smoothly, but the hard set of Hale's face and the desperation on Asher's didn't lend themselves toward optimism.

I didn't need to be a marvelously talented surgeon to know Hale was worried about Geneva. His concern meant things were likely not good.

As the pair walked from the desolate stucco building over to the back of Minton's tram, neither spoke.

Minton dished each of them up a plate. Asher looked at his and handed it back. Hale fueled the machine that was his body by downing the food quickly and efficiently.

I never would have thought Asher had defeat in his vocabulary, but as he looked at Hale, it was written all over his face. "Tell me," he finally managed.

"I've done what I can." Hale sounded tired and drained. "Her insides are patched up, but I'm worried about some necrotic areas I saw while I was in there. And I think she might already be septic. She needs stronger antibiotics if she's going to stand a chance."

"Can we send someone ahead? Maybe on one of the horses to make better time?" I asked.

Asher looked like he was doing the calculations in his head. "Jake could probably get there in the next day and half . . . if he goes all out. You can write out what you need, and he could head back. Might save us a day, two at the most."

Hale shook his head. "It won't be good enough. She needs them now. Phoebe gave her the last dose of cefotaxime as I was closing her up. She'll need another in eight hours. Twelve if we push it. It isn't enough."

What he wasn't saying was that even with more of the same antibiotic, she might not pull through. Injuries like hers led to infections that required special medications. Those meds were rare and in limited supply. Again I cursed the lack of tools once so readily available that we could only dream of having.

"We can't just give up," I told him. I tried not to sound angry. This was far from Hale's fault. In fact, he was the currently doing everything he could to help Geneva.

"I'm not suggesting we give up, Auri. *We* will do everything we can. Which brings me to my next point." He looked at me, green eyes serious and blazing. "I want you to talk to Hollis."

"What good is that going to do?" Asher asked.

"I want Aurelia to hear him out."

"Hear him out?" I hated that my voice sounded shrill. I paused and composed myself. "If I'm not mistaken, not a week ago you were trying to convince me he was full of crap. Now you want me to see if he'll give me parlor trick lessons?"

"Let's think about this." He took my hand and held it in both of his. "I know at first it sounded ridiculous, but you can't deny you've been feeling little zaps of something for a while now. I didn't say anything before, but I'm not entirely convinced you didn't help heal my arm. Something was there when you stitched me up. I felt it, but at the time, I just blew it off."

"That's ridiculous, Hale. Your arm healed because you got the right care."

"Maybe, but I never took any of my antibiotic pills. At first, I just forgot and then it seemed like it was healing on its own and I didn't want to waste them."

I squinted at him—shocked by his admission. An infection in his arm could have meant the end of his surgical skills. "Well then, you're an idiot. But still, it doesn't explain anything more than you got lucky."

"Please. Just talk to him. I'll go with you." Then as an afterthought, "Or ask Roe to."

My stomach was roiling with nausea and fear. The beans felt like they were going to make a return appearance, but I fought it down and looked at Asher. Nothing there swayed me one way or the other. And that was what decided it. If he had looked too hopeful, I would have refused. If he had looked angry or disbelieving, I would have refused. He didn't look either. He just looked . . . gone.

"I don't want it to be Roe. Let's go."

"Go ahead and stretch out those legs of yours." Jake, like his son, seemed to have lost his infectious smile somewhere in the past three days. He had not, however, lost his calm courtesy, even when dealing with less desirable people.

I'd asked Asher to allow Jake to accompany us on our errand. Not because I thought he was quicker or more competent than Asher, but because if Hollis withheld anything—anything at all that might help save Geneva—I knew Asher would hurt him. Badly.

Jake had been more than willing to oblige as I was sure he would. Before we spoke with the miracle man though, I wanted Jake to tell us how Hollis had come to be tied to the tram.

"The fellow's been with us for more than a day actually." When Hale and I expressed our surprise, Jake smirked. "Lot has happened since you two took off on your secret little mission."

I opened my mouth to protest, but he didn't let me. "Now, don't get your feathers ruffled. I'm not scolding or anything. I realize why you did what you did. You're just lucky it worked out.

"Anyhow, your man Hollis stumbled up to the camp last night, just as we were tucking things in. I damn near shot him on sight, but he looked so pitiful, I took mercy on him.

"You know, for a time, I think we were all believing the miracle man and his friends were the ones taking things outta the trams—using the supplies to help cure their own patrons. It was pretty clear after Gen took those two goons down that wasn't the case."

"We saw them on this side of the dry lake bed." I gestured between Hale and me. "In the creepy little settlement where Roe got taken. Hale and I saw a group of them. Faces all stained to match. Like a weird tribe or something. They must have been tailing us for a while before they took the shot." Another flash of shame passed through me about not alerting anyone of the wine stains' presence, but then I reminded myself we all had a lot on our minds.

Jake did me the favor of alleviating some of that shame when he said, "Yeah. We saw them there too. Asher and Gen went off that day to see if they could scare the buggers off a bit. Guess it didn't work so well."

"So, Hollis?" Hale prodded, effectively changing the subject.

"Right. He just sort of stumbled up on us at camp. Said he let you all go and thought you'd be with us."

I scoffed. "I wouldn't exactly say he let us go, but whatever."

"I figured as much. He was rambling on about knowing we would need him and if we would just wait, it would make sense to let him live. We found a little of that mercy somewhere and tied him up. I haven't spoken to him since. We've all been a little preoccupied, you might say."

"Weren't you worried about his companions?" I asked.

"The thought crossed my mind."

"But you haven't seen them?"

"Not a glimpse of the wagon or the other two. I'm still not sure how he made it as far as he did on his own, but. . ." He shrugged.

It was getting late, and if we really were setting out at first light, we needed to get this conversation over with.

Hollis looked up as we approached. His face was pale, and without the characteristic dapper appearance, he really did seem diminished.

"Ah. My petite wonder-worker." His smile was tired but just as unsettling as before.

"I'm not your anything."

He shrugged one shoulder. "The time has finally come for you to seek what I offer. Better late than never as they say." His eyes slid from me to Hale and then Jake. "And where is my favorite Belstrohm brother?"

"Otherwise engaged. I guess you're stuck with me." The calm clear timber of Hale's voice was a fortifying balm I wasn't aware I needed until he spoke.

"Pity." Hollis smirked, and again the oily feeling rolled off him. He focused on me. "So, it takes a friend dying to do what you should have done long ago?"

The accusation stung, but not because it was untrue. I still wasn't sure I believed what he said, but I *was* only entertaining the notion because it was Geneva in there hanging on.

"Where are your friends, Hollis?"

"I have no friends." He spat the words at me with such venom, I took a step back before he schooled his features into the smug bastard I'd experienced before.

"Do you know my name isn't even Hollis?" He chuckled. Almost to himself, he added, "Silly of me. Of course you don't." He refocused and explained crisply, "She didn't like Holdan Listerman. Said it sounded too ridiculous. Too *simple* yet too much of a mouthful. Was worried the Medicus folks would track me if I used it. So she took it from me when she took everything else. From that day and every day after I have been Hollis."

"What are you talking about? *Who* are you talking about?" I was tired of this stupid game. Of all of it.

"Nanette of course. Not that Hollis is much better than Holdan now, is it? It was just something for her to take from me. She took my name because *she could*."

When none of us responded, he continued, "Ask your friend. Ask him what it was like in that odious wagon. Ask him what he felt. What he saw. *He* was there for only four days, yet he'll tell you he almost couldn't bear it another minute." His voice dropped and became darker—sinister. "Then ask him to imagine it wasn't four days he was in that purgatory, but seven years. Seven years of questioning his own sanity, of trying to maintain a sense of who he was, what he was meant to do. Seven years of bowing and scraping to her every whim." It was clear we were no longer talking about Roe.

Was he actually trying to convince us he wasn't an active part of all this? That Nanette was somehow to blame and he was merely an innocent pawn? How would Nanette even been able to keep him, hold him hostage for that length of time? It was difficult to believe.

"Oh please, Hollis. Or should I now call you *Holdan?*" I didn't like the sarcasm in my voice, but this was too much. "Why would I believe this isn't just another ruse to get me to let down my guard?"

"Actually, I prefer Dan. It's what my friends used to call me. When I had friends, that is. I've always hated Holdan, but I hate Hollis even more." He paused and for a moment the shining lights seemed to catch tears on his pale lower lashes. "Anyway, does *this* look like a ruse to you?"

He raised his bound hands to the front of his shirt, and both Hale and Jake reacted. Hale stepped in front of me, and Jake raised the riffle at his side into firing position at his shoulder.

Hollis froze. "May I?" He still hadn't lost the condescending tone, but he at least looked wary.

Jake nodded. "Anything funny and it's your funeral."

Seated as he was, and tied to the tram, it took a moment, but Hollis reached up to the dirty front of his shirt. The ties didn't encumber his fingers. As he released the snaps, I realized with mounting horror that what I had taken for bits of dirt and debris marring the cloth of his shirt were actually smears and speckles of dried blood. He chest was a patchwork of crisscrossing linear abrasions. No, not abrasions. Burns. Long thin slashing burns. Some blistered, some pearly tight and pink, others scabbed with dark eschars.

I winced when I saw the damage, but he didn't seem to notice. That amount of trauma should have been terribly painful, yet he didn't stiffen or cringe as he moved his arms. In fact, his face never lost its haughty air.

Hale whistled low through his teeth. "Someone certainly did a number on you, yet you were able to move quickly enough to catch the trams. Explain."

"I disobeyed. She got angry. This was the result. What else is there to say?"

"You're telling us Nanette did that to you?" It was brutal, certainly. But he was a good five or six inches taller than the curvy beauty and probably outweighed her by at least fifty pounds. The driver, Darner, hadn't seemed in any shape to hold him down. Not after my scalpel had finished with him. "Did she somehow knock you out?"

"No."

"You just let her do it?" That seemed unlikely, but they were all a little wrong in the head. "What did she use, a hot iron poker?"

"No and no. None of this is helping your friend right now, you understand."

"Yes, I do understand. But if you think I'm just going to blindly let a viper into that building with her in the hopes its venom is a balm rather than a poison, you're even crazier than I previously thought."

One side of Hale's mouth twitched upward before he returned to giving Hollis—or Holdan, or

Dan, or whatever we were going to call him—the infamous Hale Belstrohm death stare.

Sighing loudly, Holdan fastened the snaps of his shirt. When he was done, he sat up straight and frowned, attempting to brush off what little of the grime from the front he could.

"Nanette neither wanted nor needed me to be incapacitated when she administered her chastisement of my behavior. Additionally she neither wanted nor needed anything as crude as an iron poker. She possesses a well of power much deeper than any other we have encountered. A flick of her power, magnified in my direction and . . . lesson completed."

He was so direct about it, but I noticed he'd used the words lesson *completed*. Not lesson *learned*.

My mind was reeling not only with the implications of that kind of ability, but also with horror of a person being quite that brutal. And Roe had been subjected to her for those long four days. This man for seven years, if he was to be believed.

Jake was the first to speak. "You've had this experience before? These lessons?"

Holdan lifted his chin, refusing to be embarrassed or shamed by what he was admitting. "Many, many times. It's quite a long and sordid tale. One I don't feel like regaling you with at the moment. Suffice it to say, I initially went to her willingly but realized the error of my ways quite harshly and quite quickly. Once I did, I fought her at every turn. But after a time, it became abundantly clear any effort at resistance was not only futile but also seemed to excite her. She likes it when someone puts up a fight. I decided not to let her win that from me as well."

"So if you have this magical healing ability, why not use it on yourself?" My voice sounded ugly and accusatory. So much for being a caring healer of the sick and injured.

He sighed again and cast his eyes down. "I can't. It doesn't work when I try. I'm not sure if it's the same for anyone with our gifts or if Nanette simply chose not to educate me how it's done. Her lessons would be less educational if I didn't have to suffer after."

I had so many questions, and to be honest, I wasn't entirely convinced any of this was actually true. The man I'd know as Hollis did however make one good point. None of this was helping Geneva. Time was drifting away from us like sand in the desert winds.

Hale must have read the thoughts on my face. When I glanced at him, he gave a brief uptick of his head. Time to get on with it.

"You still haven't explained how you caught up to the trams."

"I didn't. Nanette's wagon did the catching and I along with it. She has a very deep well of power, as I said, and is able to utilize it in a myriad of ways. One of which is pushing that wagon of hers from one place to another quite rapidly. I don't know how, so don't ask. Just suffice it to say she is capable of dark wonders. Wonders which are vastly different from your notion of the word, or mine for that matter."

My brain—usually one of my better attributes—still wasn't processing what he was trying to tell us.

"If Nanette holds all the power of thaumaturgy, why did you tell me to find you when you knew I'd need to access a miracle? How can you help?"

"I never said she holds *all* the power." The condescension was back once again. "I said her well of power runs deep. Mine may be a shallow dip in comparison, but I do know how to wield it. I believe you contain wonders within you far beyond my capabilities. But until you learn how to access your skills, they are useless."

"And you believe you can teach her in time to save Gen?" Hale asked. "Why not simply heal Geneva yourself?"

"Oh, I could." He frowned. "I simply do not want to."

"Why not?" I blurted. "Roe told us about the books he saw. You used to be in Medicus Corpus, didn't you? Or at least study with them? Have you given up on serving your oath or did you never take it?"

"Oh, I took the oath. I lived for that oath." His voice was the strongest it had been since we'd begun this insane conversation. "But if I heal her, you will have learned nothing."

"And then"—Roe stepped around the back of the tram Holdan was tied to—"Nanette might not be convinced of your skills, when he betrays you to her to save himself."

32

ROE

How had I missed it? The pieces should have clicked long before. When it hit me while cleaning up the operating equipment, I'd looked around for Hale and Auri to share my delayed brilliance. Neither of them was there. Wade was busy chucking surgical tools into a washbasin where they could be cleaned prior to placing them in packets for the autoclave and surely wouldn't care about my discovery. Phoebe looked up from the notebook serving as Gen's medical record. She'd admire my genius—delayed as it was—but she wasn't the person to tell. She gave me a sad smile, and I hustled out to find Auri.

Hearing Hollis's voice, I slowed my steps. I was going to kill Hale for allowing Hollis to get close to her again. They'd gotten lucky—*we'd* gotten lucky—in the mining town. I didn't care that he was tied up and looked like he'd been drug through hell and half the desert. I didn't care that he had pushed me up and told me to run. The man could not be trusted, and as I heard him confirm he wouldn't heal Geneva on his own, I knew I was right.

Aurelia and Jake looked at me in complete bewilderment when I called him out, but not Hale. He raised his hands behind his head and exhaled long and slow, understanding dawning in his eyes.

"You are still planning on handing her over to Nanette in exchange for your own freedom, aren't you?" I demanded.

A slow, sly smile spread across Hollis's face. "Aren't you the clever one? I had considered it, yes. I do have one other bargaining chip, but it may not be enough."

It wasn't clear who was more surprised at what happened next—me or Hollis. Hale had always been the calm water compared to my swirling tempest. So when he took three long strides forward and drove his fist into the bound man's jaw, I just stood there gaping. Not that I could have stopped him if I'd wanted to. Good thing I *didn't* want to.

Aurelia yelped and Jake grabbed Hale before he could inflict more damage. "Okay, you got your shot in, now that's enough."

Hollis smiled again and spit a gob of blood to the side. "Careful. You might become my favorite Belstrohm brother after all."

Auri looked at Hale with a mixture of shock and gratitude. She took a deep breath and said to Hollis, "Enough of the games, Holdan."

Holdan? Who the hell was Holdan?

"Yes, yes, yes. I agree, Ms. Morris. We have bigger things to do."

"If you plan to give me over to Nanette, why bother coming here at all?"

"I said I had considered it. It so happens I've changed my mind. Oh, don't look so surprised," he said to me.

He was right. I was surprised. "You said you'd been looking for someone with Auri's gifts for a long time."

"I did, yes. And I have been. It became clear to me long ago. I may have been Nanette's favorite toy and the tool she used to exert her influence on the poor ignorant fools we treated, but she would trade me in for a bigger, brighter star the first chance she got. When we encountered your lovely little group, she took one look at Ms. Morris and I knew my chance to escape had finally come. Nanette had no need to keep two underlings with the same ability, and it would have been much too taxing trying to subjugate the both of us. She would have let me go."

Aurelia's brows were furrowed. "I don't understand. If she holds as much power as you claim, why does she need you—or me—at all?"

"Because of what we *are,* dear little girl. I too am a practitioner. Without one of us trained in healing, the patrons see only a witch or fortuneteller. A charlatan." He smirked at Auri. She didn't bat an eyelash at the term she'd used to describe him. "She is the power without the prestige. It . . . *bothers* her. Without a practitioner, she's just a magician. Not a wonder-worker. There are no miracles within her. But with you or me, she can claim to be the greatest of healers."

You are traveling now with one of the greatest wonder-workers to have graced this earth in ages. At the time, I'd assumed Nanette was speaking of Hollis. It never occurred to me she was referring to herself.

"She wants a stronger conduit and I want . . . out."

Hale, Auri, or I could have told him where exactly he was going to get with this plan, but as it turned out, none of us had to. Jake did the honors for us. "You can shit in your own hand and call it honey. Not gonna change anything. There is no way in this life or the next you are walking away from here if it means harm comes to this young woman."

"Your friend might disagree if his lovely partner is to die."

He was banking on Asher choosing to save Geneva. In other circumstances with other people, it might have been a safe bet.

"If you think that's true, you don't know Asher at all. As much as he loves Geneva, he would never allow anything like that to happen," Auri explained.

"And if he did?"

"I wouldn't." The finality in the words matched the steel in Jake's eyes. I wished we were going with him and Jude to Jave or they were staying with us in Devil's Meadows. They were the kind of people who could become family.

Hollis pursed his lips and ticked his head from side to side—studying our little group and coming to some sort of decision.

"I expected as much, and whether you four believe me or not, I'd already come to the same decision. I only ever wanted to become a practitioner, you know? How I came to be in Nanette's employ is an ugly story, but one best saved for another time."

"And?" Hale drew the word out, not flinching at the violent light in Hollis's eyes as he did so.

"I have what you all need. Knowledge and the bargaining chip I'd mentioned. You have what I need—transportation and the possibility of joining Medicus once again." He studied us each in turn and asked, "Do you care to make a deal?"

Asher's face was pale and drawn save for the red blooms covering his weathered cheeks. His normally kempt hair stood up in fits and swirls from the countless runs his fingers had taken at it. He might have aged ten years in the past four days.

"Absolutely not." The words were meant to hold authority but came out grave and tired.

"She needs more than we can give." Hale motioned between him and me, encompassing our skills as practitioners. "Right now, our best bet is on Aurelia, and she needs Listerman to have any chance."

They'd explained to me who Holdan Listerman was on the way to find Asher. Both Hale and I agreed calling him Dan wasn't going to happen, so we elected to use his surname instead.

"Even if I thought it could work, Medicus Corpus has certain rules that even I can't break. Transporting a nonessential—not to mention potentially dangerous—person, amidst our cargo and team, is terms for termination. Add in what might happen to Aurelia should word of this get out once we make it to Devil's Meadows, and I just can't justify the risk."

"Despite the potential reward?" I asked as gently as I could.

"Yes. Even despite that. Gen would say the same if she could."

Color flooded Auri's cheeks, and her voice trembled. "But she can't and that is the point. She is septic, Asher. She is going to die if we don't do anything. You might be willing to take that on for the sake of Medicus, but I am not."

"We can dump him before we roll into the hub. As far as word getting out about Aurelia, who is going to say something? None of us, I can assure you." Hale was using his most calm and reassuring tone, but a muscle was ticking in his jaw. If this didn't get settled soon, it wouldn't matter what Auri did or didn't do. We were wasting time, and we all knew it.

Holdan Listerman had posed a simple trade. He would assist Geneva's healing, walking Aurelia through the process so she could use her own power—which he insisted was stronger than his own—to heal the infection coursing through Geneva's body and systematically shutting down her organs one by one. It sounded insane and ridiculous to my scientifically trained mind. But really, what was there to lose?

According to Asher apparently quite a bit. It had been discussed during our training that Medicus had a well-established and long-held doctrine that no practitioner of the healing arts in their employ was to use anything outside standard practice to treat patients. As students, we had all assumed that meant not trying out untested treatments or experimenting with procedures that weren't proven effective. Because none of us took any stock in wonder-working or miracles, it had never crossed our minds the Medicus policies would include those things. Apparently they did. Explicitly.

According to our escorts, a Medicus practitioner could not only be thrown out of their position but they could also be reported for malpractice, resulting in terrible repercussions including but not limited to serving prison time.

If Asher actually thought either Hale or I would report Aurelia to the Medicus Corpus officials in Devil's Meadows, he was grossly mistaken. When I said as much, he scowled at me. With a tone indicating exactly what kind of an imbecile he thought I was, he said, "It's not you I'm worried about."

"We've already discussed it. We're planning on asking the others to step out for a while," Aurelia said.

None of us thought Phoebe, Helena, or Wade would say anything, but we also didn't want to involve them in something potentially career wrecking. If they didn't know about it, we couldn't feel guilty asking them to keep it a secret.

"Again. Not them I'm worried about." He actually rolled his eyes when he said it. He'd never seemed like the eye-rolling type to me. Asher ticked his head to the side in the direction of Listerman, and I understood. Holdan Listerman might claim to be a changed man, but none of us actually believed it.

He could roll into the settlement and throw down an accusation at any point. It would be his word against ours. At the very least, it might garner an investigation. None of us wanted that, but the alternative was to let Gen die. Auri would never forgive herself if that happened.

"Right," I said. "I think we all understand it's a risk."

"It's a risk I'm willing to take," Auri said. "Please, Asher. Let me do this."

Whether it was the weeks on the road, the pain and suffering he'd witnessed in his years as an escort, his love for his wife, or something else altogether, Asher finally relented. Aurelia Morris—Goldie Girl, Shrimpboat, Tiny Goddess, Specs—was going to try to work a wonder.

33

HALE

The wind was a fierce thing, out there in the dark of the desert night. We got windstorms in Renfield. This was something else entirely. This was a dust storm. It scoured me as I walked—millions of sharp grains taking microscopic bites at any and all exposed skin. I could see the haze of it in the solar lights scattered around camp and hoped the dressing on Geneva's side was good and tight. Thinking of cleaning out the myriad of minuscule crystals from the granulation tissue of her surgical site filled me with less than pleasant thoughts.

Phoebe swayed on her feet as she adjusted the clamp metering the flow of fluid into Gen's arm. From the entry, I could see things hadn't improved. A slick sheen of sweat coated her pallid skin. The rise and fall of her chest was too shallow and much too rapid—her breaths attempting to compensate for the acid building up in her blood as her body simply shut down under the burden of infection. No amount of rapid breathing would keep the balance. Soon she would tire and her breathing would slow. After that, it would be only a matter of time. It was simply too late.

"Hey, Phoebe. Why don't you go try to catch some shut-eye?" I pulled up the same bucket I'd previously used as a stool—resting my elbows on my knees as I watched Geneva's eyes move behind their lids.

"She's pretty fitful, but I've already given her more morphine than I probably should have." She stepped around the bed to leave but caught herself. "If it looks like. . ." Tears rolled down her cheeks, and she took a deep breath. "If it looks like it might be the time, will you please come get me? I'd like to be here when . . . when. . ." A sob racked her body.

I stood and wrapped my arms around her shoulders. "It isn't going to come to that." I put every bit of confidence I had into the words, but she wouldn't take any comfort from them. She could see exactly what I could and didn't have the benefit of knowing what we were planning. "But if the time comes, I promise to make sure you're here."

She wiped the tears from her cheeks and ran her palm up her nose. "Thanks."

As she was leaving, I called out, "If you see Wade and Helena, tell them to get some rest too. Roe's on his way with Aurelia. We should be set for the night."

34

AURELIA

I've never understood people who can sleep for only three or four hours per night and be just as productive, just as alert and peppy, just as normal as if they'd slept for hours more. I was, and will always be, an eight hours a night girl. Any less than eight and I get cranky and irritable. If I need to stay awake longer than eighteen or nineteen hours straight—to study for an exam or to care for a patient—the physical effects hit me hard. I get jittery and shaky. I have a difficult time staying warm and need to bundle up in a thick sweater and socks. My eyes burn and no amount of cleaning my glasses keeps my vision clear.

When we were finally ready to attempt our ludicrous plan to save Geneva, it was well past midnight and I hadn't slept for more than a few hours at a stretch in several days. My body was in serious revolt. I needed to ingest a highly caffeinated sugar-filled drink, but I'd vomit if I attempted it. My head was pounding and my ears were ringing. I had absolutely no idea how I'd be able to offer anyone anything, much less cure a woman on the verge of total cardiovascular collapse as the result of septic shock.

When I voiced my concerns to Roe, it was Holdan who answered. "If you think you feel poorly now, just wait. If things go as planned, I wager you won't be able to stammer your mother's name in about an hour."

Not reassuring in the least.

Roe gave the ginger a look to kill thousands but didn't say a word. He just squeezed my hand and told me he'd meet me inside in five minutes.

Jake walked with his hand on Holdan's shoulder. The meaning was clear. He might be free of the bindings, but any attempt at violence would be met with swift and decisive action.

Our solar torches threw straight beams of white light into the never-ending darkness of the desert, and my eyes took a moment to adjust when we entered the small ramshackle structure serving as Geneva's sick room. Hale glanced up from his vigil at her side. He hadn't bothered to collect any medical equipment other than his stethoscope. None of us had any idea what to expect, but Hollis—Holdan, I reminded myself for at least the tenth time—had insisted not so much as a syringe, a scalpel, or an otoscope would be needed. The stethoscope would be useful though. Hale could listen to her heart and lungs to assess if she was fading or recovering.

Roe entered and pressed a pouch of apple juice into my hands. "It's not much, but hopefully the sugar will help."

I nodded my thanks and walked toward Gen's bed. I stopped halfway there, the full weight of what was happening hitting me.

Her face was just as beautiful, just as lovely, even with her color being all wrong. She didn't look serene, but rather like she was fighting an internal war only she could see. Her brow furrowed, and if I didn't know better, I'd say she was concentrating while she slept. Perhaps she was. Concentrating on not dying.

Asher, having disappeared to heavens knew where, was the last to arrive. He shut the door firmly behind him and moved a stack of boxes in front of it. Jude had been given instructions to keep the others outside, but on the off chance something went wrong, we needed a little warning before one of the other practitioners or tram masters stumbled upon what we—*I*—was about to do.

"May I?" All the smugness and condescension was gone from Holdan's voice as he looked at Asher and gestured toward where Gen lay dying.

A brief nod from our lead escort and Holdan was kneeling next to the cot. He cocked an elegant auburn eyebrow at me standing dumbly where I was. "Ms. Morris?"

Feeling the blood rush to my cheeks, I stumbled forward.

"No need to be nervous, my dear. You will do marvelously. I'm certain." The words should have been reassuring, but still I felt uncomfortable with the way they were said. As if I were doing something wrong by agreeing to work with him—even to save someone I'd come to admire so much.

Hale slid his bucket toward the head of the bed, giving me room to kneel opposite the man who, up until that afternoon, I had assumed was full of shit. He might still be, I reminded myself. Nothing had been done yet to prove otherwise.

My mind was telling me this was never going to work. All my years of schooling said it was not possible. Years spent falling asleep with a textbook in my hands—studying for so many hours my mind just shut down. Years of tests and lectures, lab work, and shadowing other practitioners. The grueling months spent in a cadaver lab, dissecting each nerve and blood vessel, muscle and tendon—the smell never really leaving my nose, no matter how many showers

I took. All those things told me this would never work. Medicus told me it would never work.

Then I thought of my mother. My sweet and fierce mother. Her warm brown skin and warmer brown eyes, always believing in the miracles but not daring to say too much lest it seem like a reprimand on my studies. She believed even if my father and I scoffed and laughed at the idea. My gentle mother, who I might not see for a very, very long time. If she could believe in the power of wonder-working, then why couldn't I?

Closing my eyes, I took a deep breath. Warm strong hands settled on my shoulders. "Let's see what you can do, Goldie Girl." The words were soft against my hair.

When I opened my eyes, it wasn't my dear friend's face across from me, but Holdan Listerman. He was the one I was going to need to trust. I took another deep breath and, asserting myself, said, "How do we begin?"

"Center yourself and focus not on the patient but on your inner strength," the man across from me began. "Deep breathing in and out. Calm and unfettered from the stress which wants to break you. Think of nothing, not your worry, not your fear, not your friendship with this woman. Do not let risk play a part. Right now you are only Aurelia Morris. Practitioner. And wonder-worker."

I drew the breaths in as I was instructed, blowing them out with a steady force. I'd taken some meditation classes many years earlier, when the stress of school was really getting to me. I tried to use the breathing and mindfulness techniques now. I closed my eyes to calm my mind.

"Keep them closed for a moment if you like," Holdan instructed me, "but soon you will need to be present here, and that will require a different kind of focus."

I didn't understand and opened my mouth to say as much, but he continued, "Breathe and focus. You are a practitioner of the healing work. Your strength lies not simply in your knowledge, but in your heart and soul. Your dedication. It radiates from you." I ignored the shudder that ran through me at those words. *You do positively radiate, don't you?* One of the first slimy things he'd said to me just a couple of weeks ago. "Call on those traits. Think of every patient who has ever smiled when you've reassured them. Every family member you have treated and healed. Every baby you've delivered pink and healthy into this world and into its loving mother's arms. Every weary soul you have sat with and brought comfort to as they leave this world."

This was more difficult. For the past several weeks, my mind had been focused on all the times I could not help. Lita and Jonaten immediately sprang to mind, as did Tif and her battered body. The elderly man with his list of minor aches and pains. The teenage boy with anxiety. The young mother with seizures. All those patients we tried to help but couldn't. That *I'd* tried to help but couldn't.

"No, Ms. Morris. Do not focus on the lost cases. Focus on the moments when you *did* choose the correct medication. When you *did* mend the shattered bone. When you *did* rid the infection from a vicious wound."

His voice wasn't a harsh reprimand but a gentle coaxing. It was so at odds with what my view of his character that my breathing hitched for a moment. I drew in deeply again and retrained my focus. Thinking of the positives once more, I thought back to my early days of Medicus and the joy I had in even the most minor of achievements. Hugs from tiny patients and tears of gratitude from spouses or parents.

"Yes," he encouraged. "Now keep those thoughts and open your eyes to your current patient."

I did as he asked, and while my heart clenched to see Geneva in the state she was in, a part of me knew I had the ability to help her. I was a Medicus practitioner and I would use my skills to help.

"Good. Now don't lose that focus on yourself, but place your hands on the patient."

"Geneva," I said. "Her name is Geneva."

I expected an exasperated scoff, but to my surprise he only continued, "Yes. Geneva. Place your hands on her."

"Where?"

"Her arms will do for present. In the future, you may find applying your gift directly to the site of injury is best." My memory flashed to the tingling I'd felt when suturing Hale's arm. "But tonight, anywhere will do."

I placed one hand on the crook of her elbow and the other on her wrist. The skin there was dry and hot compared with the clammy sweat on my own palms. I'd long since lost any sense of the others in the room. Asher and Jake had been nervously pacing, but I no longer noticed their movements. Even Roe and Hale, perched on either side of me, faded into the background as I split my focus between my inner gifts and the waning life in front of me.

In and out my breathing continued. My arms were getting the pins and needles sensation, and while I wanted to reposition myself, I didn't dare move until this was done. Holdan was silent for several long minutes, and I thought perhaps I was supposed to be healing her while he watched. I panicked for a moment, sure I was failing.

"Continue to focus, Ms. Morris. Breathe. In and out. In and out."

I retrained my thoughts on the scorching skin under my fingers and the deep well of devotion I had for medicine.

"Do you feel the energy in you?"

I shook my head.

"No?" He was skeptical. "No pulsing in your fingers or perhaps a buzz behind your sternum?"

"Oh, yes. Yes, I feel like my arms are asleep. Is that it?"

"Yes. Grasp that feeling. Hold it tight and do not let it leave without a direction."

"I don't understand."

"Now is the time to utilize all those years of training and reading." Holdan's voice was more direct now, a supervising practitioner telling me to use my head. "You know what Geneva's ailment is, how do you fix it?"

"I don't . . . she needs antibiotics and fluids and—"

"No. Not what she needs from these other practitioners. What does she need from *you*?"

Hale made a grunt of disapproval and shifted toward me, but I gave my head a fraction of a shake. I didn't want to lose this battle now. Not when I could feel the energy in my hands. Was this what miracles felt like?

If it didn't work, he and Asher could deal with Holdan then.

Holdan must have sensed my resolve. "How do you *heal* her, Aurelia?"

My brain whirled through the pathophysiology of her illness. Hale had already repaired the perforation the knife had caused in her intestine, but the damage had been done. She was septic. The bacteria from her gut had infiltrated all the other corners of her body. The cascade of ill effects was fulminate and her organs were shutting down. So what would reverse those effects?

First, the infection needed to be dealt with. The bacteria in her bloodstream needed to be killed off—her body cleansed of their malevolence. I thought of her immune system charging into the fight and attacking the invading bacteria. As I drew this picture in my mind, the tingling in my hands grew, snaking up through my wrists into my elbows and biceps.

Next, the effects of the bacteria and their destructive toxins needed to be managed. Her kidneys—those mysterious things—and her liver needed to ramp up and assist with the body's functions once more. Her blood needed to function properly, and her cardiovascular system needed to regain its control over her circulation. I pictured the notebooks full of pathways done in various colored inks and the drawings I'd doodled to learn how each chemical pathway interacted with the next. My brain struggled to recall some of the more intricate steps, but my gift seemed to know where my memory lapsed and filled in the gaps where needed.

Vaguely I registered Hale's voice. "Her heart rate is steady, but breathing's still shallow."

The tingling had reached my neck, and what had been a mild discomfort and annoyance before was becoming a deep burning pain. Thousands of tiny fire ants marched over my skin and buried their stings deep into the muscle and bone. A thick sweat was pooling along my neck and under my arms. Even my glasses were fogging up.

Holdan, sensing my discomfort, demanded, "Don't let go. Continue to direct the energy."

Through the hazy fog of my lenses, I studied him. He looked just as bad as I felt. His skin had gone a waxy sour color and perspiration dripped from the end of his nose. His hands trembled where they'd been placed in similar positions as mine. Holdan Listerman was pouring his own wonder-working into Geneva as well.

Through the strain, I barely registered Hale's soft awed voice. "It's like she just got a bag of fluids. Heart rate is damn near normal now."

"We can't let this go on." Roe's voice was anguish incarnate. "Look at her."

"We're almost done. Let her finish." Holdan's voice brokered no argument. Then in a gentler but still firm voice, he directed at me once more. "Almost there."

After the effects of the infection and toxins, the only thing left was to heal the necrotic areas to prevent a significant relapse of her illness. I pictured the tissues mending—the platelets and proteins sealing over any and all microscopic gaps in the layers of cells. The leaking of fluids stopping and the skin coming together on the surface.

The fire lancing up my arms became an inferno. It coursed from my elbows to my shoulder, up my scalp and down my back to my pelvic bones. Only my lower legs and feet were spared. Maybe Holdan was wrong, and I'd be able to walk just fine. I couldn't help the hysterical laugh that bubbled out at the thought.

The energy flowed out from my core, and I knew it was working. I pushed harder. "Too much, Ms. Morris!" Listerman's voice was distant. I pushed further, giving my gift over to Geneva.

"Too much. Rein it in!" He was a thousand miles away, and all I knew was the flow of healing rushing from my core to my hands. The burning had reached my feet, and that was a fair trade as long as Geneva would live.

"Aurelia! Stop."

But I didn't listen. I gave and gave. Searching for any tiny crack or crevice. Energy flowed through me—from me—to Geneva.

"Auri!" Was that Roe? He sounded desperate but so very far away. I tried to look at him, but the world tilted.

Something slammed into me. Time stilled. I closed my eyes and felt no more.

35

ROE

The images wouldn't leave my mind. The color returning to Geneva's face. The thick oily sheen of sweat coating Aurelia's. The shock and horror flooding from Holdan Listerman as he commanded her to pull back her healing energy. The violent shaking contorting my best friend's body. Hale slamming into her, tackling her to the ground and severing the connection between the two women. Over and over they played behind my eyelids. I sat on the cracked concrete floor of the building that initially served as Geneva's sick room. Now it served the same for Auri.

The sunrise was glorious—golden and apricot light diffusing into the pale soft blue. I could see it through one of the structure's old windows. The glass was as dirty and crusty as I felt. It was cracked and broken in one corner, but still I could see to the east.

It had been only a few hours since Auri and Listerman had worked their miracle. Was it a miracle? I certainly didn't have anything else to call it. According to Listerman, Aurelia would be fine. She just needed to recoup what energy she had expended. At least he thought this was the case. He did mention he'd never seen a demonstration of this magnitude in an untrained wonder-worker. He himself had learned the principle of magical healing by starting with small minor cuts and scrapes. In fact, he only ever attempted more intense sessions when Nanette was there to pour her energy into him. The way it sounded, it was as if he were merely a tool to be plugged in. Auri, however, was the battery and the machine.

The details were a trifle murky as I hadn't spoken to the miracle man myself. Once the connection between Auri and Gen had been broken, Hale and I were so focused on Aurelia, neither of us noticed when Listerman silently slipped into the night. Asher was also more than a little distracted as his wife and partner sat up wide-eyed and full of questions. Jake slipped out to follow Listerman and retrieve what little information he could about Aurelia. The convulsions that had racked her body were so violent, I thought perhaps I'd lost her. She had been limp and unresponsive when Hale scooped her from the ground after slamming into her. If nothing else, when she woke she was sure to have a few aches from that contact alone.

So now she slept and I dosed on and off beside her cot, catching a few bleary-eyed glimpses of the sunrise.

We must have stayed there for several hours more. By the time Hale came to tell me the others were asking questions, the temperature inside was close to stifling.

"It's probably best to tell them as little as possible," I said.

My brother looked worried as he studied Auri lying so still on the cot. Sweat dripped from her temples and pooled in the hollow of her neck. "I agree. But if the story is simply that she's sick, they'll want to pitch in and help. I'm not so sure that's a good idea."

He walked over and sat on the edge of the cot. "I didn't mean to hit her so hard."

"I don't really think that's the problem, do you?"

"No. But still. . ." He placed a hand on her cheek and wiped the perspiration away with his thumb. The look he was giving her was nothing short of tender. "I didn't know what else to do."

"At least you did something. I just sat there freaking out."

He glanced at me with a sad smile on his face. "She'll pull through this, Roe."

I heaved a deep sigh. "She better so I can strangle her when she wakes. You know, she scared the shit out of me."

He smiled again and turned back to stare down at her once more. "I'm really happy you have each other."

I started to protest, but in typical Hale fashion he cut me off. "I don't mean anything intense. I just mean I'm happy you have a fierce little friend who would do anything for you. A Tiny Badass."

"Oh, I like that. I'm going to add it to the list if you don't mind me stealing it. Tiny Badass." I chuckled. "Are you jealous?" I said lightly, meaning to get under his skin just a little. "It might do you some good to take a break and let someone else worry about me for a change."

He was serious when he responded. "Yes, actually. I am jealous. Of both of you."

"So now you like her? After all this time, she has finally made the grade?"

"I've never not liked her, Roe. I just . . . I've always wanted what's best for you."

"And she wasn't what was best for me before."

"I didn't say that. She's the best friend you could ever have. I just never saw it."

I owed my brother more in this life than I could ever repay, and seeing him unhappy was just as bad for me as it was for him when the roles were reversed. "You know, the three of us can be here for each other. It doesn't need to be all or nothing."

"I'm pretty sure she loathes me. With good reason. I haven't always been the easiest person to be around."

"I'm not so sure about that. There's definitely been a bit of a shift in the past few days. Something tells me you two might like each other a little more than either of you wants to admit."

Whether this was true of not, it seemed he was in no mood to discuss it.

"Do you have her glasses? She'll be pretty bent if she wakes up and can't see anything."

I'd scooped them off the floor in the early hours of the morning and placed them on the window ledge for safekeeping. I pointed them out and informed Hale I needed to stretch my legs.

There wasn't a sense of outright excitement exactly when I ventured out into the bright warm late morning, but at least a bit of cautious relief was in the air. The tram masters and other practitioners, not knowing the extent of Auri's illness, were simply pleased Geneva seemed well. I wasn't fool enough to think there'd be no speculation on her speedy recovery. Helena, Wade, and Phoebe were certain to question why all of the sudden she was up and walking when none of their care had made a difference. My plan was simple. We'd tell them Holdan Listerman was in fact a man of miracles. He alone had prevented Geneva from sliding into the blissful unending sleep of the dead. What choice did they have but to believe it?

I found both of them, Gen and Listerman, sitting together enjoying bowels of warm oatmeal with pecans and canned peaches.

"Look at you!" I smiled warmly and bent over to give Geneva a quick peck on the cheek. "Happy to see you amongst the living! Where's the grumpy old man?"

"Sleeping." Geneva's voice was slightly hoarse and her lips were cracked and dry, but otherwise she looked remarkable healthy. It was beyond astonishing. All thanks to the monster sitting next to her and the Tiny Badass lying unconscious a hundred yards away.

"I suppose Asher does deserve some rest. He looked as if he hadn't slept in a few days." I turned my attention to Holdan Listerman. "I know you gave Jake the basics, but how long will she be like that?" I pointed toward the crumbling stucco structure.

"I had hoped she'd be awake by now." Lowering his voice, he said, "I'm wiped out, and Ms. Morris expended quite a bit more energy than I did. I should have been clearer in my instruction. I take the blame for this."

Geneva looked down. "I can't thank you all enough, but you shouldn't have let her do it."

"What's done is done," Listerman stated. He'd gotten cleaned up. Other than the disgracefully shabby state of his clothing, he was back to the sparkling gentleman of weeks past. Hair combed. Face clean. Smile rapturous.

I sighed and looked at Geneva. "You know none of us could stop her if she thought she could help."

"I realize you couldn't have stopped her, but Asher should have." She didn't smile as she looked toward the carriage her husband slept in.

"Like Listerman here says—what's done is done."

36

HALE

The last time I could remember being that scared was the day I held a knife up to my father. I had been so concerned he was going to hurt Roe, I hadn't thought—just acted. Thankfully, I hadn't needed to use the knife in my hands that afternoon. I'm not sure what would have become of me if I had.

The same sort of terror which had flooded me on that bright autumn afternoon when I was eight years old flooded into me again as I watched Aurelia's body jerking and shaking in the warm spring night. The horror of it short wired my brain, and once again I acted without thinking. Breaking the connection between her beautifully delicate hands and the upper extremity of the woman she was dying for had been the only goal.

Dropping my shoulder, the athlete in me took over as I dove into her, taking us both to the floor. I had enough presence of mind to cradle her head with one arm, preventing it from striking the concrete with the force of our combined weight. Still, the impact was solid and her body no match for my larger frame.

Panic overcame me as I lifted her off the floor. She was unresponsive, and I had no idea if it was from whatever the hell she'd done to save Gen or from me bashing her to the unforgiving ground.

Either way, her limp body made me want to vomit what little I had in my stomach. This clever, compassionate, fierce creature had to be okay. She had to be.

When things settled, Geneva decided to sleep in the tram with Asher and Roe insisted on staying here with Aurelia.

I might have argued with him, or offered to stay with both of them, but after getting her settled, it did appear she might simply be in a deep slumber. It didn't seem as if Roe could do anything for her, much less two of us, and the other practitioners had set up our tent not more than a stone's throw away. I could be in there within a minute if I was needed. I doubted I would be needed.

In truth, I could use a little time to process all I had just witnessed. Sorting out how such a thing was possible, and what to expect for the future knowing the gift Aurelia possessed, was too great a task for one night.

My brother was right. I had been jealous of her and her friendship with him. But as I sat next to Auri's cot, the clarity I needed began to appear. I was jealous of her, but I was more jealous of Roe. He meant everything to me, and he'd go to the ends of the earth for me as well. But now I wanted more. I wanted a friend who would go up against a madman for me. I wanted someone to laugh with and cry with. I wanted the kind of easy relationship they shared. And more than anything, I wanted Aurelia Morris to look up into *my* face with those amazingly gorgeous eyes of hers and smile at *me* with her pretty mouth. Not because she wanted to get along with me for my brother's sake, but because she wanted to for my own.

A deep sighing breath startled me from the selfish thoughts racing through my brain. When I turned my head toward the sound, my heart thudded to see the gorgeous eyes blinking rapidly at me—no thick lenses to obstruct my view.

I couldn't help the wide grin spreading across my face as I took in the fact she was alert. Alive. Amazing. I hung my head and took a deep shaking breath. "You're awake. Damn it. You scared Roe. And me. You scared me."

"Sorry." She groaned. "I didn't mean to."

"How are you feeling?"

"Tired. Really, really tired. But I think I can sit up."

I stood, knees popping from being in the same position for so long, and helped her carefully into a sitting position. Once there, I swung her legs over the side of the cot. As I did so, her hair fell over one shoulder. It was a riot of unkempt curls and matted with dust. It didn't matter. Roe was right. She was a tiny goddess. I captured one of the curls and ran my fingers over it, earning a crooked questioning smile in response.

"I was kind of a stone-cold asshole last night. I might have tackled you. Sorry." My voice was low and hoarse.

Her eyes held mine as I continued rubbing the hair between my fingers, and her voice was a tinge huskier as she replied, "I think I'll survive."

The next thing I knew, I was leaning into her. I stopped a breath away from her lovely full lips, giving her time to move back if she chose to. "Do you smell lightning?" I whispered.

She shook her head a fraction of an inch, a question in her eyes.

"Then hopefully nothing bad will come from this." My lips brushed against hers for the briefest of touches. I pulled back to look at her again. She was the most wonderful creature I had ever seen. I didn't know how or why it had taken me so long to realize it.

One side of her mouth curved upward as she placed a palm on my stubble-covered cheek, and I leaned my forehead against hers. As much as I wanted to kiss her again, I was wise enough to know this wasn't the time.

We were going to be stuck in Devil's Meadows for years to come. I could stand to be patient.

37

AURELIA

Climbing down from the still-moving wagon, I couldn't believe my eyes.

She was standing in the center of the road, arms outstretched, face lifted toward the pale robin's-egg sky.

Night was hours away and even though it was still only mid-spring, the temperature was scorching. How Nanette managed to look so comfortable—as if it were a cool misty autumn morning—was beyond me.

We must have warranted a bit of extra effort as far as she was concerned. The glitter had made a repeat appearance, kohl lined her eyes, and her long lush hair flowed past her shoulders in perfect waves. If I didn't know her to be the snake she was, I might have gladly gone with her, just to experience that sort of grace and beauty up close. But I *did know* her and there would be no sacrifice that day.

Luc's tram—the first in the line—stopped perhaps twenty-five yards before reaching the bit of road she commanded. Her own rig—the Wonder Wagon—was parked cockeyed off the road beyond her statue-like form. Darner was perched happily in the driver's seat, apparently no worse for wear. His glare was menacing, but it was better than the creepy giggling he seemed fond of.

The clambering of wheels quieted as Hera, and finally Minton, reined in their horses.

Thanks to Holdan, we'd known roughly where Nanette would be waiting, but it still came as somewhat of a shock to see her there. The sheer gall it took to stand sentinel and presume to think she could impede our progress made me angrier than I would have guessed. The pain I still saw in Roe's eyes and the memory of the burns across Holdan's chest certainly didn't help improve my goodwill either.

Unlike Nanette, I was not the picture of calm tranquil beauty. My hair was tied in a filthy tangled bun atop my head. Dirt coated my skin, and my glasses were scratched and smudged. Roe's oversized shirt draped over my tank top and hung nearly to my knees. In a reflection of how I felt, it was sweat stained, torn, battered, and tattered.

The Belstrohms came to stand with me, identical looks of disgust clouding their faces. Holdan, as planned, remained tucked away and out of sight. Nanette was sure to know he was with us. It was his duty after all to present me to her. We had all agreed, though, he should stay hidden for as long as was possible.

"Do you think this will work?" I asked the brothers.

"I sure as hell hope so," Hale responded.

Roe, ever the optimist of the two, was more confident. "It'll work."

Our escorts flanked the forward carriage—two on either side.

It had been three days since Geneva had hovered so close to death. It was remarkable, but she'd never looked healthier than she did staring down the other woman. None of the four raised their rifles, but their faces promised swift and violent action should the need arise.

Nanette hadn't yet looked at them—at any of us—for all that it mattered. She held her head back, studying who knew what in the cloudless sky.

Asher appeared content to wait.

Not changing her stance, finally she spoke. "Where is the coward, Hollis?"

We'd of course expected this. Holdan Listerman—Hollis to this conniving witch—had told us to expect it. She would assume he would crawl back to keep some long ago bargain. She'd expect him to either return to her service or trade me for his won freedom. The thought of him doing so willingly made me shiver. Even after what he'd done for Gen, I wasn't completely convinced we could trust him, and to be fair, I'm not sure he trusted himself.

"I'm afraid I don't know," Asher lied smoothly. In the time between Geneva's healing and our stop here in the road, the confidence and authority had returned to him. Save for the quiet moments when I caught him looking at his wife when he thought no one was watching, it was almost as if it had never been gone at all. I didn't like to think what would have happened if Gen hadn't recovered—if Holdan and I had failed. "We've got none in our group by that name."

"Hmmm. . ." Slowly she lowered her chin, arms still elevated at her sides and dark eyes flashing. She studied Asher. "So you left him at the side of the road like the rubbish he is, then?"

"What makes you think we've encountered him at all?" A question for a question.

"Don't think me a fool," she warned with ice in her voice as well as her eyes. For such an intensely beautiful woman, she looked painfully grotesque.

Asher, heavens love him, shrugged and casually responded, "Wouldn't dream of it."

"I felt the energy three nights ago. A surge unlike I've felt in some time. Very powerful. And unless the little practitioner suddenly learned some decidedly interesting tricks, I'd say Hollis was involved."

This too was expected. Holdan had informed us those with similar gifts would feel the power of the miracles. It was, in fact, how he and Nanette had found me in the first place—the small wonders I'd unwittingly worked first on Hale and then reaffirmed with Jonaten. When he'd mentioned it as we walked away from the ramshackle building surrounded by wild burros, I'd almost fallen to my knees. I had felt something tingly at Jonaten's bedside. I wasn't fool enough to believe I had cured him, but perhaps I'd done enough to make him a bit more comfortable, and if I were truly blessed, maybe he would hold out long enough—be well enough—to travel to Devil's Meadows. Was there a chance I could finish what I'd started and actually heal him? It was a small hope, but one I carried nestled close to my heart just the same.

Asher chose not to comment on the energy burst Nanette had felt. Instead, he smoothly drawled, "As I said, no one by that name travels with us. Now, if you don't mind, we need to be traveling on. I hate losing the daylight."

Nanette sneered. "You will not keep me from what is mine."

What is mine? A chill traveled down my spine at the implication of those words. She truly thought she could own someone based purely on the strength of her power.

Ozone filled my nose.

Hale must have sensed my reaction. He stepped closer and wrapped my hand in his, lacing our fingers together.

Over the course of the previous days, he hadn't mentioned what had happened between us when I woke. A part of me believed maybe it had been a dream or the imaginings of my befuddled mind as I tried to claw back from the blackness that had claimed me during the healing. Still, he was more apt to smile and seemed not as annoyed to have me around, so . . . baby steps.

The gentle pressure on my palm reassured me. Whatever lay ahead, I wasn't alone. I would always have Roe, my best friend—the other half of my soul. Maybe now I could have Hale too. In a different way.

The crackle in the air grew. It was more intense than the previous episodes. I wondered for the first time if Holdan could sense it as well. I'd need to remember to ask when we got out of this.

"Look lady," Asher said. "I don't give a damn about what you want. We're moving. I'd rather you step aside, but if need be, we can always go over rather than around."

Even from the distance separating us, I could hear the tittering giggles of Darner. They drifted from his perch through the calm desert air like the call of the quails we'd seen everywhere. Heavens, the sound was disturbing. Maybe he couldn't help it? The driver's chuckles were answered by the faintest of hissing from the tram to my right. My eyes slid sideways of their own volition—willing Holdan to keep quiet.

The air around us moved and shifted, but I seemed to be the only one to notice. I'd heard stories of the sea pulling back minutes before a tsunami hit, and although I'd never experienced it, I could guess this was similar.

The air was dragged from my lungs as Nanette lifted her arms higher over her head. Her hands were bathed in a subtle shimmery shifting light—just barely visible in the already brilliant desert sun. At the same time—and almost in unison—Asher and Geneva, along with Jake and Jude, shouldered their weapons.

The pull of the air intensified. No. It wasn't the air. It was the pull of the energy around me. I was sure I knew what was coming, and although we were aware and had planned for what Holdan told us might happen, my entire body trembled.

"If you aren't willing to hand him over, I'll gladly settle for your talented little practitioner." A slight smile curved her lips. This was what she'd wanted all along. We were playing directly into her hands. "What a wonderful partnership we could make. I doubt she would underestimate me as all the men seem to." The smile turned wicked as she looked at Roe. "Maybe not all of the men. I'm fairly certain Mr. Belstrohm has a sense of me."

"That you're a psychotic bitch? Yeah. I've sensed that," Roe responded.

It happened in a flash. A flick of her wrist and a whip crack of energy shot upstream against the pull. Roe's scream was guttural as the bright red slash appeared across his right cheek and trailed down along his neck to his collar. Another flick and a matching slash adorned the left. He fell to his knees panting.

Hale's cry of rage was lost in the series of gunshots unleashed a split second later. I dropped in front of Roe, my back to our escorts as well as the madwoman beyond them. Cool metal dug into my lower back, but I didn't dare move to adjust what I held in my waistband.

I didn't know if Nanette had been hit, but judging by the continued flow of energy around me, I presumed the answer was no.

Roe was shaking. His breaths rapid. A fine sheen of sweat coated the handsome face I knew as well as my own. Tears burned behind my eyes as I took in the burns bubbling to blisters on both of his cheeks. We knew this might happen. Had planned for it, but still. . .

My hands tingled as I cupped his face gently. Ever so gently.

"Auri. . ." A moan escaped him. "It can wait."

He was right. I needed to be aware. Nodding, I sent one final push of power through my hands and helped him stand.

Nanette was walking an invisible line across the stretch of old asphalt. Obviously the bullets had been as futile as Holdan had told us they would be. Back and forth she paced. Back and forth. "I have a certain rule I tend to live by," she mused. "Ask. Tell. Force. I've already asked. Rather politely I feel. Now I am telling you. Hand over one or the other."

"Not going to happen." Asher and the other escorts had fanned out but were closing ranks tighter to the trams. I wasn't sure what good it would possibly do against the type of weapon Nanette seemed to wield.

"You really do not want me to force you."

Again Darner tittered. If he kept that up, one of us would slit his throat just to end the sound.

The other practitioners were tucked safely in the fiberglass hull of the third wagon. This wasn't their fight. Even though they likely suspected what had actually happened to get Geneva back on her feet, all three had been savvy enough not to voice those suspicions. The goal was to keep our friends both as safe and as ignorant as was possible until we went our separate ways.

I really *really* wanted to climb into the tram with them. But again, that wasn't the plan.

"If you must, have it your way." Nanette raised her hands again, and this time when the whip cracks sounded, both Hale and Jake cried out. Each now bore the same type of linear burn as Roe. Hale had been hit across his right hand and forearm. I couldn't see Jake.

Still the others stood their ground. Another burst of energy and Jude grunted in pain. Within a blink, another wave surged our way. The strikes were invisible save the movement of Nanette's hands and the resulting burns. I could sense the distortions of energy, but the others could not. Hale was moving and dodged a blow as he dove and rolled, barely staying on the road.

Several more lashes had the others moving in a variety of directions. They seemed to realize erratic patterns were their only hope. No sound came from the tram in the rear where Helena, Phoebe, and Wade waited. From the carriage to my right I could hear the hushed voice of Holdan. "Just another minute. Wait, my petite. Wait."

Come on, I thought. *Come on.*

Roe had taken one more lash of energy—the burn this time crossing his hip and left leg. His pants were flayed open, revealing the bubbling skin beneath.

I edged in front of him, not caring that Holdan had instructed me otherwise. It had to be nearly time. We needed to act soon.

Come on, Holdan. *Come on.*

Wave after wave. Lash after lash. The assault went on for what felt like eternity but in reality was likely no more than a minute. With every second, however, my friends were punished. Roe and Hale each suffered another blow, and while the escorts returned the attack with gunfire, they couldn't move fast enough to evade the piercing whips of energy. There simply was no way to keep track of who suffered the most.

Only I was spared. Somehow, even though I stood in front of my best friend and made no effort to move, she didn't hit me. Did Nanette think sparing me would win my allegiance? If so, she was immensely delusional.

Holdan still didn't act, but I could wait no longer. On adrenaline-fueled legs, I strode forward, hands out to the side in a mimicry of Nanette's posture when we arrived. She needed to see my surrender. My defeat. She needed to *believe.*

Roe cried out again. His voice mingled with Hale's as the older brother screamed my name. If Holdan didn't understand what was happening and remained hidden, this might be the last time either of the brothers saw me alive.

Nanette noticed me when I was level with the second tram's horses. They were jittery and dancing but seemed to be unmarred by the whip lashes. Luc and Hera huddled together behind the fiberglass hull of the lead tram, safe from the line of attack. The battery on my friends quieted.

Nanette was breathing heavily. Her magic took a physical toll then too. Good.

"Enough," I stammered. Closing the distance between us. Step by frightening step. "Enough."

"He really is a coward then. Sending a little lamb out here to the wolf while he hides in among the baggage." Keep moving. Just a bit closer. Still I didn't hear Holdan's feet on the pavement. He should have jumped from the tram by now.

Raising her voice, she called, "You're pathetic, Hollis."

Was she breathless?

"That's not his name." I made it to the front of the first fiberglass carriage. My friends and protectors were all in some form of agony. Asher seemed to have taken the worst of it, no doubt a result of trying to shield Geneva as much as possible even though she'd be angry at him later for it. He was on his knees, red lashes crisscrossing his rugged face. Bright red bands were visible on both of his hands and across his chest and neck. A band even raced across his scalp, the hair missing where the burn had destroyed his skin.

Gen was at his side, hand on his shoulder, murmuring reassuring words. I didn't stop to listen.

Ten feet separated us now. I kept moving.

Heart in my throat, pulse pounding, I closed the distance. Nine feet. Seven. Five.

I stopped and, with every bit of willpower I possessed, raised my eyes to look at her.

The kohl had smudged and mingled with the perspiration coating her face. Dark black rivulets stained her cheeks as she cocked her head, studying me.

"Enough," I repeated.

As if she could taste my terror, she licked her lips. "First lesson pet—it's enough *when I say it's enough.*"

As if to prove her point, she flicked her wrist once more and Jude grunted with the impact.

"The second lesson is this—unless you want to experience exactly what your friends are feeling now, you'll do everything I say. When I say. And exactly as I say. Do you understand?"

I nodded.

Where was Holdan? I couldn't do this alone. Suddenly I was quite sure he'd played me for the kind of naïve fool I was. I had trusted him and now here I stood as Nanette said—a lamb willingly placing her neck between the wolf's jaws.

The stupid mirror I had tucked in my belt was probably a useless piece of junk too. Roe had remembered seeing it close to Nanette in the wagon, but that didn't mean it was what Holdan had claimed it to be. Maybe she only kept it near her because she was vain. It made perfect sense; if it was so powerful, wouldn't the magician before me have noticed it missing by now? Wouldn't she have guessed Holdan had taken it? My only consolation was what I knew Roe and Hale would do to him for tricking us all so thoroughly. He would be a dead man before the day was done, but little good it would do me when I was carted away in the nightmare wagon.

My eyes drifted to the large red and gold monstrosity as I thought about what was to come. My heart thumped as I caught sight of Darner slumped over in his seat and then movement from the back of the contraption.

Keeping my hands out from my body, I watched as Holdan sprinted from his hiding spot. He must have snuck around while my attention had been focused on Nanette. And hers on me. Perhaps I wasn't the fool in this scenario after all.

I wasn't sure if it was the expression on my face or the sound of his heavy footfalls that alerted her, but Nanette turned before Holdan could slam into her. Either way, it didn't matter.

She flicked her wrist, and Holdan spun with the impact of the energy slashing into him once again. He knew it was coming, had planned on it in fact, but still the look of pain and burning hatred on his face was staggering.

I was in motion a fraction of a second later, reaching my right hand behind my back to the mirror hidden there while grasping for her wrist with my left.

She flicked her wrist as I spun her around with my free hand, the energy whip missing its intended target and hitting the blackened murky mirror instead. The impact reverberated through my wrist into my shoulder. The glass and silver object went skittering down the asphalt but not before it reflected the whip crack of energy back from where it had originated—directly across Nanette's throat.

If she tried to scream, I didn't hear it. The only noise came from the desert wind tinkling the bells on the side of the wagon and the wheezing choke of Nanette's breath trapped in her throat.

Her face turned first red then purple and finally the deep dusky indigo of a fresh bruise.

It was so quick, at first I didn't realize what was happening, but then she was clawing and grabbing her throat. She was being strangled by the very energy she had unleashed on my friends. Rather than a burn, however, it formed an arcane rope, constricting and squeezing her airway shut.

I didn't know how to remove the invisible noose around her neck, and if Holdan did, he certainly wasn't offering up the information.

Footsteps pounding behind me, I knelt next to the woman as she thrashed and flailed on the ground.

"What do we do?" I asked Hale as he dropped next to me.

"I have no idea."

"Nothing." Roe spat the word out from where he stood, arms crossed, staring down on her as she slowly suffocated. "We do nothing."

"We have to do something," I cried.

"Do we?" Holdan asked. "I'm not sure that's true."

When he saw the look on my face, he shrugged. "I don't know that kind of miracle work. The mirror amplified and reflected her own magic back on her. Could you not feel the wave of energy?"

I could. It had flung the mirror from my hand, but not before I'd felt how different it was from my own. Dark and thick and oily. I didn't know what to do with that type of thaumaturgy.

"Just as she never saw fit to teach me to heal myself, she never taught me how her well of dark wonders worked. She would only use mine to amplify and mold it. Not the other way around," Holdan explained.

Nanette stopped thrashing, but her depthless eyes were full of a dark pleading as she looked up at me. So I did the only thing I could in the moment. I pried her fingers from her throat and held her hands while she died.

38

HALE

The little troll of a man Darner wasn't dead, and we weren't going to change that. After allowing Listerman inside to collect whatever he wanted from the wagon, we left him to sleep off his concussion on the settee inside.

The Tiny Badass refused to rest until all of our burns were healed. She worked first on Listerman so he could help with the escorts. Then I insisted she look at Roe before she graced me with her hocus-pocus. Given the situation, it became obvious we weren't going to hide it from Wade, Phoebe, and Helena, so they assisted with clean cooling compresses and aloe paste until Auri and Listerman could do a more thorough job.

We buried the woman off the side of the road and, not wanting to sleep at the sight of such an encounter, made it another handful of miles before we camped for the night. None of us slept worth a damn.

Two days later, we crested a gentle incline, and the ruins of a massive city came into view. It was much larger than Renfield, but Geneva reminded us as we gawked that the population didn't match the sprawling enormity of the buildings.

"It's so open." My brother was referring to the valley itself. Devil's Meadows sat in the massive expanse between two large mountain ranges. It was easily fifty miles across, yet we could see not only the road before us and the cityscape in the center, but all the way across to the other side where the mountains kissed the desert again. The sky was the same pale washed-out barely-blue it had been for days. Not a cloud marred it.

The temperature was nearing the century mark, and the asphalt was hot and uncomfortable under my feet.

Aurelia sighed and crossed her arms, tilting her head and studying the sight before us. "I've never seen so many shades of brown and tan." She looked at Geneva, smirked, and announced, "I believe I'm going to love it here."

Interested in reading more about Aurelia, Roe and Hale?

Look for *Breath and Starshine*. Coming Spring of 2023.

FROM THE AUTHOR

Well here we are. It's hard for me to believe another story has hatched from my brain and made it out into the world. For anyone who knows me well, bits and pieces of this novel might feel more real than others. As a pediatrician, I can't tell you the number of times I wished for some kernel of magic, a wand or spell, anything really, to wave at a patient and make them all better. Unfortunately, medicine doesn't work like that. Many of my friends would also attest if it did, there might be a little less suffering in the world.

Writing stories lets me pretend—for just a minute—that magic does exist. In reality, the true magic comes when the story is read. So for everyone who made it to the end, thank you. I would also like to thank everyone who read *A Simple Tale of Water and Weeping* and told me how much they loved it. Just as importantly, I want to thank those who read it, didn't love it, but kept that to themselves! You all gave me the courage to put Blood and Wonder down in ink.

Once again I would like to thank Karen Robinson for her amazing talent and ability to help me fine-tune my words into something I'm not embarrassed to publish. Your talent with language knows no bounds.

For my sweet Addie, thank you for being you. I am amazed daily by your hard work, dedication, and creative love for life. Don't ever settle for less than happiness.

Thank you to my developmental editor and the first person to always read my words, Lily Larsen. You always push my characters in the right direction and keep my stories on track. You are also a brilliant and wonderful daughter.

Thank you to my mom, Sharon. Your years of love and encouragement have made me the person I am today.

As always, the person who I need to acknowledge the most is my amazing husband Brian. For every time I went a little mad, lost my cool, or threatened to pitch the computer out the window, you were always there to talk me down and help me figure out what needed to be done. The physical production of this book is just as much an accomplishment for you as it is for me. I love you more than words can express.

If you have ever driven through the desert in the western US—say from Reno to Las Vegas—chunks of the scenery here may seem familiar. It is a long and incredibly brutal drive, dotted every so often with run down places barely big enough to be called towns. During one of my many trips along this desolate highway, I started to wonder what it would be like to have to walk the distance on foot. And just like that, the setting for Blood and Wonder was born. While I used a ton of liberty with the landmarks, there is one little spot, in a small town not too far from Reno that I simply had to include. So for you Dad, I hope you appreciate my nod to your epic track and field days. I miss you.

Also by Kami King Larsen

A Simple Tale of Water and Weeping

Let's Connect!

Find me on Instagram
For all things bookish @klarsenmd_booksandbits
For author updates @authorkamikinglarsen

On Amazon: amazon.com/author/kami_books

And on Facebook @KamiKingLarsenBooks

274

ABOUT THE AUTHOR

Kami King Larsen is a native of the desert southwest and studied biology before attending medical school. Although she is a practicing pediatrician by training, she is a bibliophile and lover of great stories and all things whimsical by birth. Kami lives in Nevada with her husband, two daughters, and two dogs.